E.J. GORSE

Gastronauts

First edition

To James and Evelyn, for everything.

Contents

I

Part One

Matthew 5:6: Blessed are those who hunger and thirst for righteousness, for they shall be satisfied.

1

Any Old Borscht In A Storm

The woman with the gray dog appeared at eight-fifteen as she always did, and Kerwin Merle stood at the window pretending his entire day did not hinge upon the sight of her.

From up here she was a small, neat figure moving along the wet ground, her coat a dull, serviceable gray that might once have aspired to be blue and her hair, twisted into a bun at the back of her head, matched it closely enough that on misty mornings she seemed to be made of the same stuff as the sky. The dog was gray too, some sort of elderly terrier that moved in short, careful bursts, pausing at every lamppost while she waited with the leash slack in her hand; if Kerwin concentrated, he could time his breathing to those pauses, inhale for the shuffle forward, exhale for the halt, until his chest rose and fell in the same small, patient rhythm as the animal's.

He watched her round the corner by the bus stop and enter the narrow strip of street that constituted his view of the world. She passed the laundromat with its fogged windows, skirted the shallow dip where rainwater collected in a long, shining tongue and continued toward the post office at the far end.

She did not pause to look in any of the windows.

She did not look up.

His fingers tightened around the mug he held, registering belatedly that the drink inside had cooled to lukewarm. He could have put it down but he did not; there was something fortifying about the small fiction that he was merely a man having his morning drink, not a man who knew, to the minute, the comings and goings of people who had never once seen his face.

On weekdays, she passed at eight-fifteen precisely, on Saturdays, she permitted herself a grudging nine-oh-three, and on Sundays, she did not appear at all. On Sundays, the street belonged to churchgoers in their good coats and the occasional hungover student making a penitent journey to the corner shop and the woman with the gray dog vanished from his portion of the world as completely as if she had never existed.

He had not chosen to memorize her schedule. The one time he had tried to ignore it, to stay in his chair, his eyes on the flickering screen while the anchors silently mouthed on about catastrophes and weather, his heart had begun to thud, a low, unpleasant rhythm coinciding almost exactly with the click of the clock to eight-fifteen. By eight-seventeen he had been at the window anyway, lips pressed into a thin, white line, in time only to see the last sway of her coat as she turned out of sight.

He did not know her name. He knew nothing of her life beyond these brief appearances, whether she had a husband or children, whether she worked or had retired, whether she was happy or merely enduring; he knew only the shape of her moving down the street at quarter past eight, the gray coat she wore in every season, and the patient way she looked after her dog. She did not know he existed and he preferred it this way; there was a kind of peace in watching without being watched and in knowing someone's schedule more intimately than they could ever know yours.

Today, Kerwin did not test himself. He watched her all the way along the street, noted the way the dog's paws made no sound he could hear even though he leaned a little closer to the glass as if proximity might supply it instead, and when she and the dog reached the end and turned the corner, vanishing as neatly as if a curtain had dropped, he exhaled a breath and unclenched each pair of his muscles in turn.

His drink had gone cold. He gulped the last of it anyway and turned back to his sitting room.

* * *

The apartment was cold, as it always was. Something to do with the windows, his mother had said; they had warped in their frames over the decades and admitted drafts that no amount of weather stripping or heavy curtaining could keep at bay. She had tried everything in her time, stuffing fabric snakes along the sills and taping plastic sheeting over the worst of the gaps, but the cold had come in anyway, settling into the walls and floors and Kerwin had long since stopped fighting it. He wore an extra sweater when the temperature dropped and otherwise tried not to think about it; there were, he knew, worse things than cold.

He rinsed his mug in the narrow kitchen and left it in the basin beside the ring of limescale he had also stopped trying to scrub away. The window above the sink showed a line of jumbled dumpsters; a delivery van idled at the far end, the low rumble of its engine vibrating faintly through the thin glass while a man in a reflective vest wrestled a crate of something onto a dolly. Someone had left a mattress propped against the opposite wall some time in the night; its pattern of faint blue flowers was already darkening along the bottom where it wicked up rotten puddle water and above it all, a thin strip of sky showed between the rooftops.

The sill beneath it was bare, though it had not always been so. His mother had kept herbs there once, basil and thyme and something with small purple flowers whose name he had long since forgotten but he remembered the smell of them; the way she would pinch off leaves while she cooked, adding them to whatever was simmering on the stove. He could not remember when they had died, whether she had stopped watering them or whether they had simply failed, one by one while no one was paying attention. What he remembered was the morning he had finally thrown the pots away, the leaves there thin and powdery, the roots like pale threads. He had not replaced them.

Below him, the convenience store was open, he knew, announced by the dull, familiar thud of something heavy meeting tile, a crate of canned drinks, perhaps, or the obstinate back-room door driven into its frame with the side of a hip. He could hear the two-note chime of the door and beneath it the low murmur of voices, the beep of the register, small, ordinary sounds;

evidence of a life happening ten feet beneath him. Amir's voice rose briefly, warm and easy, saying something that made a customer laugh, and Kerwin found himself listening without meaning to, his hands gone still at his sides.

The shop had belonged to his parents once. His father had stood behind the counter and his mother had restocked the shelves, and the apartment above had been home rather than merely the place where Kerwin lived. He remembered the smell of newsprint and penny candy, the brass bell that had hung above the door before the electronic chime replaced it, the way his father's reading glasses had always slid down his nose when he bent over the account books in the back room. All of that was gone now, sold off…after, and in its place was Amir, a man Kerwin had watched through the window perhaps a thousand times but never spoken to.

He knew things about Amir anyway, like the fact that Amir arrived at seven each morning and unlocked the door at half-past; he took Wednesdays off because on Wednesdays the shop stayed dark and silent and Kerwin found himself listening for sounds that did not come, the absence of them louder somehow than the sounds themselves. He knew that Amir locked up at nine-fifteen each night, the scrape of the bolt and the rattle of the security gate marking the end of another day and that his footsteps retreated afterwards into a silence that pressed against the walls.

There had been a lawyer when the shop was sold from his parents' estate to Amir, there had been documents and signatures and all the bureaucratic machinery of transfer and Kerwin remembered signing things, the pen in his hand and the scratch of his name on the line, but he could not recall anymore whether he and Amir had ever occupied the same room. What he remembered was the feeling of something ending that had already ended long before; the paperwork merely catching up to a truth that had been evident for years.

His coat hung on the hook beside the front door. He put it on, checked his pocket for the bus pass he already knew was there, and went out the back way.

The stairs at the rear of the building were narrow and dim, the walls close enough to brush with his shoulders if he did not take care. They smelled of damp and something faintly chemical, cleaning products perhaps, left over from the days when his mother had scrubbed them every Saturday morning. She had taken a strange pride in those stairs, though no one but themselves ever saw them; she had scrubbed them anyway, once a week without fail, their cleanliness something she could control when so much else was not.

No one scrubbed them now. The banister was loose, had been for years, and Kerwin descended without touching it, his hand hovering just above the wood out of long habit.

At the bottom were two doors. The one on the left led into the stockroom behind the counter where his father had once done the accounts and Kerwin did not look at it. He had not looked at it in years, training his eyes to slide past it as if it were not there at all, as if the wall were smooth and unbroken and the door had never existed. There was no reason to look; there was nothing behind it that belonged to him anymore.

He turned to the right instead, to the door that led outside, and stepped into the alley. The morning air was thick with the promise of rain, and he pulled his coat tighter as he walked around to the front of the building. He could hear Amir's voice through the shop window as he passed, warm and welcoming, greeting another customer, and he kept his eyes fixed ahead and did not slow his pace.

The bus stop was at the corner, a three-minute walk from the apartment. The street had begun to fill with the usual morning traffic, a woman pushing a stroller with a squeaking wheel, a man in a suit walking fast with his phone pressed to his ear, two girls in school uniform sharing a cigarette and laughing at something Kerwin could not hear and none of them looked at him as he passed.

He did not expect them to.

He had long since grown accustomed to moving through the world without being seen, a kind of negative space that people's eyes slid around without registering, and he had ceased to find it troubling. There were worse things than invisibility, and there were plenty worse things than being left alone.

At the bus stop he took his place at the edge of the scrum of people waiting, close enough to board when the bus arrived but far enough from the others to maintain the distance he preferred. A woman with a face like a pencil sharpener stood nearest the curb, and beside her an old man leaned on a cane, and a teenage boy nodded along to whatever was playing through his headphones, and Kerwin stood apart from all of them, watching the street.

Across the road, between the parked cars, he could just make out the woman with the gray dog. She had reached the entrance to the park and paused there while the dog investigated something in the gutter, her posture as patient as usual, her face still turned away. He watched her for a moment longer than was necessary, though he could not have said why, and then the bus rounded the corner and he looked away.

The doors opened. Kerwin got on.

The bus was half-full when he boarded, which meant the seat he preferred (third row from the back, left side, against the window) was available. He took it without allowing himself to feel relief; relief implied that the alternative would have mattered and he had long since trained himself not to care about things that could not be helped. He settled against the cold glass and watched the street slide past as the bus pulled away from the curb.

The other passengers arranged themselves in the usual configuration; three rows back, the man with the newspaper sat hunched over the sports section, his face obscured by the angle of his head and the gray wing of newsprint. Kerwin had ridden this route perhaps a thousand times and had never once seen the man's face straight on; he knew only the shape of his shoulders, the way his fingers creased the paper when he turned the page, and the coffee stain on the cuff of his jacket that had been there for as long as Kerwin could remember. In the seat across the aisle, a woman worked at a crossword puzzle, her pen moving in short, deliberate strokes. She did it in *pen*. He had noticed this months ago and could not say why the detail had lodged itself in his mind, only that it had, the way small things did when there was little else to fill the hours.

The driver's eyes flickered to the rearview mirror and then away again, not meeting Kerwin's gaze. None of them ever did. It was not hostility, exactly, or not only hostility; it was something more instinctive than that, a wariness that operated below the level of conscious thought. People moved around him the way they might move around a dog of uncertain temperament, not with fear, precisely, but with a kind of careful blankness, an unwillingness to engage. He had grown used to it, so used to it, in fact that he no longer remembered whether there had been a time before, when strangers had met his eyes and smiled, when the seat beside him had filled as readily as any other. If such a time had existed, it was lost to him now, worn smooth by repetition until only the present remained.

The bus filled as it moved through the town center: an elderly woman with a wheeled shopping cart, a young mother with a toddler on her hip, a man in paint-spattered work clothes who smelled of turpentine and sweet-sweat. They filed down the aisle and chose their seats, and the seat beside Kerwin remained as empty as it always did. Even when passengers were left standing, gripping the overhead rail and swaying with the motion of the bus, the seat beside him stayed vacant, as though surrounded by some invisible barrier that others could sense but not see and he had decided, after some consideration, not to take it personally. Perhaps he had a face that discouraged company. Perhaps he smelled of the apartment, of damp and old cooking oil and the particular staleness of rooms that were never properly aired; perhaps it was nothing to do with him at all, and people simply preferred, when given the choice, to stand.

He watched the storefronts pass, the dollar store with its faded awning, the check-cashing place, the laundromat, the Baptist church with the marquee that always bore the same message in faded signage (ARE YOU HUNGRY FOR THE TRUTH??) and the reflections of the people instead of their faces, the way the glass turned everyone into pale ghosts sliding over the moving backdrop of the street. His own reflection hovered there too, faint and insubstantial, superimposed over shopfronts and traffic lights; a narrow, colorless man with a mouth that seemed, even in the blur, to default to a line.

The city changed by degrees; the sidewalks widened, the traffic slackened and the shops thinned out, replaced by gas stations and budget auto mechanics, by sporadic low brick buildings with over-flat roofing. A supermarket went past, then a row of manufactured homes with neat shrubbery and plastic toys abandoned on the grass. He had been riding this route for years and could, if pressed, have listed the sequence of landmarks as easily as he could recite the woman-with-the-dog's schedule, but he did not think of them as places, exactly. They were simply the frames in a filmstrip that always played in the same order between Here and There.

Kerwin let it wash over him, image after image, and waited for the journey to end.

* * *

The Evergreen Senior Center sat at the end of a street lined with triple-deckers, their aluminum siding gone dull with age and their porches sagging under the weight of plastic furniture and empty planters. It had been given a youthful name by gross misdirection as nothing about it suggested greenness much less anything that would last; someone had once gone to considerable effort to make the sign out front look welcoming but the paint had started to peel now, the cheerful script flaking away in pale curls and the flowerbeds beneath it were mostly soil and cigarette ends. Large windows stared out at the narrow parking lot, their sills lined with plastic plants and laminated notices about visiting hours and a single, thin tree stood by the entrance, its branches bare, its trunk encircled by a concrete ring that suggested someone had once intended to plant flowers there too and had then, at some point, thought better of it.

The building itself was a squat brick rectangle that might once have been a school or a small factory; now it served the county's elderly poor, those who had outlived their savings and their families' patience, and it smelled, when Kerwin pushed through the front doors, of overheated air and industrial disinfectant poured over old piss. He paused just inside, letting the door close behind him. The bus, the street, the woman with the gray dog, they all belonged to the outside; in here, there was only the distant beeping of some unseen machine and the soft, shuffling sounds of people moving very slowly toward whatever was left to be done for and to them.

He signed in at the front desk without speaking, the pen familiar in his hand, his name appearing on the ledger in the same cramped script it always did. The woman behind the desk (Marlene, her name tag read, though he had never addressed her by it) glanced at him and then away, her expression flickering between recognition and discomfort before settling into the blank professional pleasantness that was, seemingly, her default.

The dining room was through a set of double doors propped open with a rubber wedge that led into a long room with close ceilings, filled with square tables that had been pushed together in clusters and covered with plastic tablecloths dyed an alarming shade of yellow. The same fluorescent tubes presided here, buzzing faintly and their light reflected in the stainless-steel carts parked near the battered kitchen door.

He took a tray from the stack and joined the short line of residents shuffling along the rail. Snatches of conversation rose and fell around him, a running commentary on the inadequacies of the food, the temperature of the room, and the state of someone's grandchildren. The residents spoke to him the expected amount which was, of course, not at all.

Today's offering was Salisbury steak, though the menu's description bore little resemblance to the grayish patty on his plate, a dark, oblong lump lying in a pool of glossy brown gravy, accompanied by a scoop of mashed potatoes that held its shape like plaster and green beans that had been boiled to a uniform olive drab. At the end of the line, beyond the bread basket and the little packets of butter, a volunteer was ladling something bright into small bowls.

"Borscht," she announced, with determined cheerfulness. She was new, she must be, and young by this room's standards, which made her somewhere in her thirties, with her hair piled up in a loose knot and a badge that said *HELLO, I'M KATY* in friendly letters. "It's a cold beet soup. Very refreshing."

The borscht, in startling contrast to the beige and brown of the rest of the meal was an alarming magenta. The residents ahead of him eyed it with deep suspicion.

"I don't want that," one woman said, her mouth pinched. "It looks like something from a science lab."

"Just the usual for me," muttered a man with a hearing aid, nudging his tray past the volunteer as if the bowl might leap onto it of its own accord.

Katy's smile faltered a tiny bit each time. Still, when Kerwin's turn came, she lifted the ladle with undimmed enthusiasm.

"Would you like to try the borscht, sir?" she asked.

He looked at the bowl, at the improbable, horrible color of it brightened by the fluorescence and shrugged. "Alright."

Her smile brightened back to full wattage.

The borscht slopped into the bowl, a thick, velvety liquid that stained the white plastic spoon a faint pink as it settled. He added a slice of bread, a packet of butter, and moved away from the counter.

He took his usual table near the far wall, where he could see the room without being immediately visible to it while around him, the residents arranged themselves in small clusters, some by habit, some by whatever alliances had formed over the months. They lowered themselves into chairs with small, involuntary groaning noises and began to eat. The sound of cutlery on crockery, the murmur of complaints and appreciations ("Too salty!" "I can't eat *this*") crested and fell around him like a low tide and he sat at its edge, eating without tasting, invisible among them.

A ghost at the feast. The phrase surfaced in his mind and he did not push it away, it seemed accurate enough.

Two dollars and fifteen cents, paid at the door, bought this much: a hot meal four times a week, a reason to leave the apartment and a place to sit among other people even if he did not speak to them and they did not speak to him. It was not a social life, he harbored no illusions on that count, but it was something, and something, he had learned, was preferable to *nothing*, if only just.

He finished the Salisbury steak and the potatoes, ate the borscht in slow spoonfuls and left the green beans in a neat pile at the edge of the plate. Around him, the residents began the slow process of dispersal, gathering their walkers and their canes, shuffling toward the elevators or the day room or the small courtyard where the smokers congregated in defiance of the fading signs. Kerwin carried his tray to the dish return and set it on the conveyor belt, watching it disappear through the rubber flaps into the kitchen beyond; a door swung open briefly as someone pushed through with a load of plates, releasing a fresh gust of steam and the tinny clang of pots.

On his way out, he passed the reception desk again. Marlene was still there, still typing, a half-finished mug of coffee cooling beside her elbow. She looked up as his shadow crossed her paperwork.

"Will we be seeing you again soon, Mr. Merle?" she asked it every week, as if there were any real doubt.

He nodded. What more could he have said?

He stepped back through the automatic doors into the chill of the outside air, blinking against the change in light and letting the smell of the place dissipate from his clothes and his lungs. Behind him, the Evergreen continued in its drudgery; ahead, the bus stop waited where he had left it, and beyond that, the route home unfolded itself in his head, out and back, out and back, along the same tracks, seeing the same faces, never speaking.

On the bus back, the day felt thinner; Kerwin took the same seat he had taken on the way out and let the journey gather him up. The man with the newspaper was gone now, disembarked at some earlier stop and returned safely to whatever life awaited him at the end of the line, but the crossword woman remained. She had shifted to sit nearer the front, book still open, pen still moving in small, decisive strokes. Her brow furrowed as she worked at some private difficulty in the grid and she did not glance up when he boarded; he doubted she would have noticed if he had vanished entirely between one Tuesday and the next.

By the time the bus rolled into his part of town again, the light had shifted from flat to gunmetal and a few tentative drops of rain stippled the window, then stopped just as the bell pinged for his stop. Someone else's finger on the button had prompted it but it made no difference; he rose, feeling the usual small protest from his knees and the faint, familiar looseness in his chest that meant he was nearly home.

The convenience store was lit up against the early dark, its windows bright with fluorescent light, its OPEN sign glowing red in the gloom. Kerwin approached it along the sidewalk with his hands in his pockets and his eyes fixed on some middle distance that allowed him to see without looking at anything in particular, not the aisles in their neat, glowing lanes of color, nor the bottles of soda shining an artificial jewel-blue.

Through the window, Amir was behind the counter, ringing up a customer, his dark hair thinning a little on top and his shirt sleeves rolled to the elbow, exposing thick fingers moving with their usual efficient economy. He passed a packet of cigarettes over the counter, the customer slid coins in return, and they exchanged a few words that did not reach Kerwin's side of the glass.

On the stretch of wall between the door and the window, the teenager from the bus stop had taken up his usual position. He leaned against the brick with one foot up, the sole of his sneaker pressed flat to the wall, and a cigarette burning between his thumb and forefinger held like someone in an old movie, the smoke curling up past his face in thin, wispy threads.

As Kerwin approached, the boy's eyes slid toward him, slow and flat and uncurious and Kerwin did not look back. He walked past the window, the door, the teenager with his cigarette and dull stare and kept his gaze fixed on the far end of the street where a narrow gap led to the alley and the back stairs. He could feel the warm rectangle of the shop window at the edge of his vision and he knew with some strange certainty that if he turned his head even a fraction he would see Amir looking up and with it, the possibility of a nod, a wave or some small acknowledgment that would, in turn, demand a response he could not (would not) give.

He let himself in with his key, shut out the street and the light and the possibility of conversation and started up the back stairs.

Evening came gradually to the apartment; the light that made it through the front windows turned from gray to yellow to a kind of exhausted brown and there was enough of it that he was able to carry out his usual routine without switching on the corner lamps. Reheated dregs from the coffee pot in hand, he carried the mug to his chair and sat down without removing his coat before turning on the television for noise.

The news was still on, different newscasters from that morning sitting in slightly different chairs, their faces arranged into expressions of practiced concern that prime time required. He left the volume low enough that he could hardly hear the details, only the rise and fall of voices and the occasional swell of music when the program went to commercial.

There had been a house fire in Brockton; no injuries, a ribbon-cutting at the new community center and the high school basketball team had won a game. Kerwin watched the sequence until their voices blended into a kind of white noise that filled the room without requiring anything of him.

Through the window, the street had gone dark and so the streetlights were on, casting their pools of yellow light onto the wet pavement. As he watched both the television and the window, the woman with the gray dog appeared at the far corner, making her evening walk. She moved along the street in the same patient rhythm as always, the dog stopping to sniff at the same lampposts, and Kerwin found himself timing his breath to her passage the way he had that morning. She passed beneath his window without looking up, and he watched until she turned the corner and disappeared and then he looked back at the television where the weather report had begun.

The meteorologist was a young woman with too many bright teeth and a plastic expression. A storm was coming, she said, and it was going to be a big one. She gestured at the swirl of green and yellow and red that was moving up the coast on the map behind her and she used words like *significant* and *historic* and *potentially dangerous*. People should prepare, she said; they should stock up on water and batteries and non-perishable food, they should stay off the roads if possible and, if they had any heart, they should check on elderly neighbors.

He sipped his drink and watched the animated arrows sweep across the map. Somewhere, everywhere, people were buying batteries and candles and bringing in their garden furniture, they were checking flashlights fished out of the back of the closet. He could picture it from old experience, their quiet, productive anxiety, their sense of collectively bracing for impact.

He did not prepare. He had food enough for a few days, some canned soup and crackers and if he ran out, he would simply not eat until the storm passed. He thought about what he had to protect and came up with nothing; the apartment would be fine or it wouldn't, the power would stay on or it wouldn't.

There was nothing, he thought, in this apartment that a storm could take from him that life had not already been busy removing for years. The worst that might happen was a power cut and a few hours of darkness, and he had lived through worse kinds of dark than *that.*

A commercial, overly loud and much too bright came on, advertising something he surely did not need and so he turned off the television. Immediately, the silence rushed back in, filling the room like water; there was a peculiar stillness then, a queer sense of being levitated inside a great bubble wherein the world outside was rearranging itself into storm, and the world inside was exactly as it had been that morning, and the morning before that, and the week before that.

He should go to bed. He was simply being foolish now; there was nothing else to do and certainly no reason to stay awake. He carried his mug to the kitchen and poured the cold coffee down the drain, and he hung his coat on the hook beside the door before walking down the hallway to his bedroom without turning on the lights.

Kerwin lay in bed and stared at the ceiling he could not see, and he listened to the wind beginning to pick up outside, rattling the windows in their frames and he thought about nothing at all.

The storm was coming. Something was about to change.

He did not know this yet. He only knew the flatness, the nothing, the long habit of his days and as he closed his eyes and waited for sleep he repeated what he knew, then, which was:

Nothing was coming for him. Not the storm, not the world, not anything.

2

Storm Door

On Thursday, the Daily Bread van pulled up at half past four, same as it always did. The light had settled into that particular mid-afternoon gray that made the apartment feel lower in the street than it was, and Kerwin had reached the point in the day where he could no longer pretend he might do anything other than eat and then wait for it to be late enough to sleep. He set his book face-down on the arm of the chair, careful not to lose his place even though he could recite the paragraph he'd just read from memory and went to the door.

He opened it the cautious width of the chain first (a habit his mother had taught him and which had survived her by sheer force of muscle memory) and saw the familiar navy polo shirt and laminated ID badge of the Daily Bread driver. The man stood there holding the insulated carrier in one hand and the clipboard in the other, an appropriately blank expression on his face. Kerwin couldn't have said, with any confidence, whether this particular driver had been coming for three months or three years; the Daily Bread uniform effaced individuality as thoroughly as their irregular rota of minimum-waged help.

"Afternoon, Mr. Merle," the man said. He was heavyset with a face that looked permanently windburned and his voice carried the faint trace of an accent Kerwin had never bothered to pin down.

"Afternoon." Kerwin unhooked the chain and opened the door far enough to accept the carrier. It was cool against his palms. The clipboard came next, thrust with the same automatic motion the man surely used with every customer.

He signed in the box marked *recipient*, in small, looping script on the line and handed the board back.

"See you," the driver said, already pivoting away, his weight shifting toward the next address on his list.

Kerwin made a noncommittal noise and closed the door. He slid the chain back into place and carried the carrier through to the kitchen.

On the narrow counter, he unzipped it with the same care another man might have used on a woman's dress and unpacked it with the same series of movements he had performed weekly for the past six years. Someone had written his surname on the corner in thick black marker, and he allowed himself a moment of grim fantasy in the thought that his meals might be of interest to anyone else. He peeled the lid back and regarded the meal.

When he had first qualified for Daily Bread, which, apparently, was met by some combination of age, income, and what the woman on the phone had diplomatically called "mobility concerns," he had expected the food to offend him. It did not.

The meal was shepherd's pie, or what Daily Bread called shepherd's pie, which was a layer of gray beef napped in its own grease beneath a crust of instant potato, the whole thing congealed slightly at the edges where it had cooled during transit. There were peas as well, bright green and obviously frozen and a small plastic cup of gravy that had separated into something translucent on top and something thick and sludgy underneath.

He stirred the gravy and poured it over the pie and told himself it didn't matter what it tasted like because taste was not the point; the point, he reminded himself, gesturing with the fork in his hand, was not having to go anywhere or speak to anyone or navigate the world beyond these walls. The point was this (and here, he stabbed at the air above the sagging counters) a meal, delivered to his door, three times a week, so that he might continue to exist without having to participate in his own existence.

He slid the tray onto a plate because eating straight from the foil made him feel like a criminal, again, and he was not prepared to revisit that *ever*. The microwave beeped in its corner as he set the time and he watched the tray revolve behind the greasy plastic door, the food sweating and then steaming as the minutes ticked down.

While he waited, he flicked on the small black and white television that sat at the end of the countertop. The sound came in too loud as it always did, the booming voice of a newscaster in a suit mid-sentence about something catastrophic filled the small space in an instant and so he turned it down until his mouth moved in perfect silence. A graphic bloomed over the man's shoulder: a swirl of cloud rolling in over a cartoon map, arrows pointing inwards, words marching along the bottom of the screen. SEVERE WEATHER WARNING. STORM EXPECTED FRIDAY AFTERNOON. RESIDENTS URGED TO PREPARE.

He watched the arrows advance on the stylized version of his county and felt nothing in particular. The microwave beeped again.

He ate standing at the counter, as he sometimes did while looking out the window at the alley below. The dumpsters were their usual full; someone had added a broken office chair to the pile since yesterday, its torn seat flapping in the gaining winds. The sky beyond the rooftops was close, and the air that seeped through the gaps in the window frame had a weight to it that suggested rain.

Kerwin scraped the last of the shepherd's pie from the corners of the tray and dropped it into the garbage before rinsing his knife and fork and placing them in the rack beside the sink to dry beside yesterday's, a small, tilting cairn marking the passage of the week. The apartment would be the same whether it stormed or didn't and so would he, and so would the hours between now and whenever the storm ended. He would sit in his chair. He would watch the window. He would go to sleep and wake up and do it again, and the storm would be a nothing more than a sound, (loud yes, and then not so) outside of the glass.

Here, in this room, the only concession to the coming storm was the awareness that if the power went out, the food would be cold, which was really no concession at all.

He dried his hands on the dish towel, turned the television down to a murmur, and drifted, as he always did, back toward the front window where the street was easing itself into evening. Headlights slid along the wet tarmac; the first umbrellas of the season bobbed past in ones and twos and outside the shop, the teenager in the ill-fitting jacket was in his usual place, shoulder to the brick, cigarette cupped in his hand against the wind. Every now and then Amir appeared in the doorway, the two of them exchanging a few words Kerwin could not hear before the boy ground the cigarette out and wandered off, only to reappear the next night and the one after that.

He watched all of it, as usual, the small movements of other people's lives, the sky lowering by imperceptible degrees and felt the familiar, heavy sameness settle in. The forecast could flash as many warnings as it liked, but tonight would be like every other Thursday; he would wait for it to be late enough to justify bed, lie awake longer than he meant to, and wake up on Friday to find that nothing important had changed. It was, he thought, a kind of storm in itself, albeit one of all sound and no impact.

***

By Friday, the forecast had stopped being hypothetical and started throwing itself against the glass. Kerwin woke to the sound of rain drumming the roof in thick sheets and of wind fingering the gaps around the window frames with the restless persistence of a prowler trying the locks. For a moment, half caught between sleep and waking, he thought it was the white noise of the television left on overnight but then a gust rattled the pane above his bed hard enough to make the headboard tremble, and he opened his eyes to the dull, close light of a livid sky instead.

The bedroom felt smaller with the weather pressed up against it. He lay there for a while, listening to the storm work its way into the bones of the building, and considered the day ahead wherein the conclusion was the same as always; there was nothing on his calendar but survival and so he got up because lying down any longer made his hips ache.

He pulled on a second sweater over the one he had slept in and went to the kitchen, the floorboards colder than usual under his bare feet, leeching heat from him with each step. It was cold enough that he could see his breath if he exhaled slowly, which he did once, experimentally, like a child, and then felt foolish for having done so. There, the light through the window blurred the view to an impression of cans and brick and the occasional car headlight sliding past the mouth of the alley like a fish in a murky tank. He filled the coffee pot and set it on to heat, the small domestic noise of it lost almost immediately under the larger noise from outside.

On the countertop, the little television sat where he'd left it, mute and dark, its black-and-white screen reflecting a pale, distorted version of his face with its too-sharp cheekbones, mouth set a little too firmly to invite approach and eyes that blinked out from their deeps in a way that suggested disapproval even when he felt nothing at all. He turned it on more to prove to himself that the power was still working than out of any particular desire to hear what the world had to say. The set hummed, flickered, and then produced a picture of the same newscaster from the night before (or someone indistinguishable in the uniform suit) standing in front of a map that had sprouted more colors and arrows since yesterday.

"...already causing significant disruption in the west," the man was saying, voice pitched somewhere between professionalism and the faint, secret thrill of someone who had been given something dramatic to narrate. "...flood warnings in effect across—"

Kerwin turned the volume down until the words blurred into noise and watched instead as the animated storm spiraled resolutely toward his portion of the country, flicking quickly on to footage of flooded underpasses, cars abandoned in rising water and reporters in bright anoraks struggling to hold their microphones steady against the wind. The crawl at the bottom of the screen said what he already knew: SEVERE WEATHER WARNING IN EFFECT. ROADS CLOSED. RESIDENTS URGED TO STAY INDOORS. He glanced, reflexively, at the ceiling as if the newscaster might be looking down at him to see that he, too was doing his part and felt twin stripes of heat smart his cheekbones when there was nothing there but the usual water stains.

The pot clicked off. He made his drink and took it to the front window, standing to one side of the frame where the draft was less aggressive than the other. The street had been simplified by the weather, its details had washed out until only the basic shapes of things remained: cars loomed up out of the gray, tires sending sheets of water fanning out from their sides. Foolhardy pedestrians hunched their shoulders and hurried along with their backs to the wind, umbrellas listing at dangerous angles.

He scanned the natural markers of his morning (bus stop, lamppost, shop door) more out of habit than hope and when the woman with the gray dog did not appear at eight-fifteen he reminded himself that he had not expected her to; even in his private cataloging of routines, there were allowances for storms. The dog's joints would not tolerate this kind of weather, and neither, he suspected, would hers. Still, something in his chest loosened a fraction when the clock ticked past their usual time and the sidewalk below remained blank as if it was easier, somehow, to absorb the disruption when the cause was visible.

The hours between morning and late afternoon collapsed into themselves and so he moved through them in slow, small ways; washing a mug here, putting a book back on the shelf there, heating a can of soup at lunchtime because Thursdays' shepherd's pie had left him thick-tongued and vaguely queasy. The storm outside went about its business gusting and hammering and occasionally throwing something heavier against the building with a thump that suggested a can lid or an unsecured sign and each time, in what passed for a game in his small life, he paused and waited for the follow-up sound of breaking glass. It never came.

The light had failed by four, swallowed by the storm into a kind of permanent dusk that made it impossible to tell what time it was without consulting a clock. The street below had become a small river with brown water flowing over the sidewalks and eddying around the steps of the buildings opposite, and the rain showed no sign of stopping. Through the window of the convenience store, Kerwin could see Amir moving behind the counter, the fluorescent lights bright against the gloom, but no customers came or went. The OPEN sign glowed its futile red and the door stayed stubbornly closed.

Half past four came and went. No van, no knock.

Kerwin told himself it didn't matter. He had food, although not much, but surely enough—he could survive a day or two without Daily Bread, even longer if he had to. It was not as though he had ever depended on them for anything other than the convenience of not having to leave the apartment and the luxury of meals that arrived at his door without requiring him to navigate the world outside.

By quarter to five, he had given up. He was in the kitchen, taking inventory of his meager supply (one can of tomato soup and half a packet of crackers gone slightly soft in their sleeve) when the knock came.

It was wrong. He knew it immediately, before he had even registered what he was hearing. The Daily Bread driver knocked twice, *always* twice, two firm raps and then a pause before stepping back to not crowd the door frame. This knock was fast and hard and irregular and it embarrassed him to admit, even in the privacy of his own thoughts, that the variance frightened him, conjuring all sorts of shadowy figures that might wish to become the stuff of very small, very boring legend by doing in the recluse under the cover of a nasty storm.

Kerwin went to the door. He did not hurry, as hurrying was not something he did anymore but he did not dawdle either. He undid the chain his mother had installed decades ago, opened the door the cautious width she had taught him, and looked out.

The woman on the other side was not in a navy polo shirt.

She was young, mid-twenties, he guessed, though it was hard to tell with her face screwed up against the rain still driving in through the stairwell behind her and she stood with one hand braced on the doorframe, the other gripping the handle of a familiar insulated carrier. The storm clearly had done its level best to dismantle her; her hair, whatever its original arrangement, was plastered to her skull in dark curls and ropes, rainwater running off the ends of it to drip onto the mat. Her coat clung damply to her arms and shoulders, dark patches spreading down the sleeves where the water had soaked through and her jeans were visibly wet to mid-calf; the scuffed sneakers on her feet had given up pretending to repel anything and squelched faintly when she shifted her weight.

"Mr. Merle?" She had to raise her voice over the wind. "I'm so sorry, I know I'm late, the roads are — you wouldn't believe — I've been stuck for an hour trying to get through." She stopped, pushed a strand of wet hair out of her eyes with her free hand. "I'm Eleanor. I'm new."

He stared at her for a moment, mind catching on the details and failing to rearrange them into anything that fit his expectations. He looked at the carrier, at the laminated logo on its side, at the clipboard tucked under her elbow, and then back at her face.

" I should have called, but my phone died, and then the traffic, and I thought I could make it but—" She held out the carrier like an apology. "It might be a bit...well. The food, I mean. I'm sorry. I can call and have them send another one when the roads clear, or—"

"You're not—" He stopped himself before the sentence could complete itself into an accusation.

"No," she agreed, as if he had finished the thought aloud. "I'm not Danny. Or Steve, whichever one you usually get. They've shuffled everyone around because of the storm. The county released some emergency funding to make sure the most—" She stopped, and her eyes flicked over him in a quick assessment that she probably thought was subtle; his face, his posture, the way he was standing in the doorway with both legs apparently functional and all his faculties intact. "To make sure everyone on the list gets fed," she finished, a little too brightly. "Even in weather like this."

He felt his face heat. The most vulnerable, she had been about to say. The most in need. He knew what he looked like, not old enough, not frail enough, nothing visibly wrong with him that would explain why he required meals delivered to his door so regularly. She was wondering, he could see, what particular variety of damaged he was...perhaps she thought him a hoarder with rooms full of newspapers and cat skeletons, or someone who talked to the walls, or kept his toenail clippings in labeled jars, or stood at the window for hours on end watching the neighbors and making notes.

That last one was uncomfortably close to the truth.

"Anyway," she said, filling the silence he had left, "I'm new, like I said. Eleanor. And I'm very sorry about the food." She tipped the carrier a fraction, as if to prove her point, and winced as the movement sent another cascade of cold water down her sleeve.

Kerwin's first instinct was to look at the carrier, as if the mere act of staring at it would allow him to see bacteria blooming through the plastic. His second (the loudest, and therefore the one he distrusted most) was to stand aside and let her in, not because of the food but because she was shaking, very slightly, with cold and her hands, where they gripped the carrier, were white-knuckled and raw-looking and the thought of closing the door on that felt, in some deep, primitive way, like an act of violence.

He should have told her to leave it and go, knowing that she could wait in the stairwell, or in the shop downstairs — Amir was there, with his generator and heat and light and the ability to make conversation, all the things Kerwin did not have and did not want. She was not his problem. She was not his responsibility. He did not know her, and he did not want to know her, and the thought of having a stranger in his apartment, in his space, touching his things and breathing his air, made something in his chest tighten unpleasantly.

He did none of those things.

"You're late," he said. It was not what he had meant to say. It was, however, the truth, and his mother had raised him on the understanding that truth had value even when it sounded foolish to say aloud.

She blinked at him, rainwater dripping from the end of one damp hank of hair onto the collar of her coat. Then she huffed out another of those not-quite-laughs.

"You're not wrong, but I *said* I was sorry, sir. The storm..." Her teeth clicked together on the last word; she was colder than she was letting on.

Kerwin looked past her, down the dim stairwell while the forecast replayed itself in his head— *avoid unnecessary journeys.* He considered, briefly, whether the return trip this woman would have to make fell into that category.

"You'd better come in," he heard himself say, already undoing the chain.

She did not move when he said it. For a heartbeat he thought perhaps she hadn't heard him over the wind, that he might be given the mercy of pretending the invitation hadn't been issued but then she stepped forward, already angling her shoulder to slip past him, already stepping out of her sodden shoes, already looking around for somewhere to set down the carrier, already shivering and dripping and existing in his space as though she had every right to be there. As though this were a perfectly normal thing, a stranger walking into his apartment and making herself at home.

Water dripped steadily from the hem of her coat, pattering onto the hall floor in a widening constellation of dark spots.

"Thank you," she said, her teeth chattering slightly. "God, I'm sorry, I know this is—I'm not usually—it's just the roads are completely flooded, and the van is ancient, and I tried to go back but the underpass is underwater, and I couldn't..." She stopped, took a breath, tried again. "I'm going to have to wait here until it lets up a bit."

She rubbed her hands up and down her arms as she said it, warming herself against his reluctance. Something in his chest gave a short, painful flutter, like a trapped bird testing its bars.

"I'm sorry. I won't be any trouble, I promise."

She hadn't asked. That was the thing that struck him. She hadn't asked if she could stay, she had simply told him that she was staying, as though the decision had already been made and his permission was a formality she couldn't be bothered with.

He found this unbelievably rude.

Without waiting for instruction, she set the carrier on the floor with a soft thud and reached for the buttons on her coat. Her fingers were clumsy with cold; it took her two attempts to work the first one free. She muttered something under her breath and began peeling the coat away from her shoulders; as she shrugged it off, a spray of water shook loose, darkening the carpet in a rough arc.

"There," he said, too quickly, rougher than he intended. "By the door."

The single hook beside the frame held his own heavy black coat used for church once upon a time and for the bus now. He had hung it there that morning out of habit even though he had had no intention of going anywhere and the sight of it, doubled now with hers, gave him a brief, distressing sense of having been joined in a way he had not agreed to.

She followed his gesture as if he had spoken like a normal person, took three quick steps on her squeaking sneakers, and, without a flicker of hesitation, lifted his coat down, draped it over her arm, and claimed the hook for her own.

"You don't want this getting splashed," she said. "Here—where do you keep it?"

He ought to tell her to give it back so that he might hang it where it belonged himself, to restore at least that small piece of order he understood. Instead, he heard himself say, "Hall closet," and found his hand rising, traitorously, to indicate the narrow door just before the bathroom.

She opened it without ceremony, revealing the jumble of shoes and carrier bags and the crumpled skeleton of his mother's Sunday hat. She slid his coat onto the rail as if she had hung it there a hundred times before, then shut the door on all of it.

"There," she said, turning back to him with a briskness that reminded him unpleasantly of institution nurses.

"The bathroom's just down the hall," he heard himself say. "There are towels in the cupboard above the toilet."

She nodded, still shivering, and went further in the direction he had indicated. He listened to her footsteps recede, the wet slap of her socks on his floor, the creak of the bathroom door, the click of the light switch, the rattle of the cupboard where his mother's towels still sat in neat, folded stacks. He stood in his own hallway holding her ruined carrier and tried to make sense of what had just happened.

There was a woman in his bathroom, a *stranger*, who was currently using his towels, standing on his bathmat and *existing!* in the space that had been his alone for longer than he cared to count. He could hear her moving around in there, could hear the tap running, the rustle of fabric and the small sounds of an unbelievably rude person making themselves comfortable in a place they had no right to be.

The carrier in his hands was heavy and wet. He took it to the kitchen and set it on the counter without opening it and could smell that the food inside was almost certainly spoiled.

From down the hall, he heard the bathroom door open.

She emerged with her hair wrapped in one of the blue towels his mother had bought years ago. She had taken off her shoes and her socks and padded down the hallway toward him in bare feet, leaving damp footprints on the carpet.

"Thank you," she said again. "I mean it. I know this is incredibly weird and I'm really sorry." She looked around the bare walls, the old furniture, the nothing of the apartment and if she had any opinion about what she saw, she kept it to herself. "I'll stay out of your way. You won't even know I'm here."

That seemed extremely unlikely, Kerwin thought, but he didn't say so.

"I should—" He gestured vaguely at the kitchen, at the carrier on the counter. "The food. I should see if any of it's salvageable."

"Right, yes, of course." She followed him into the kitchen uninvited and stood watching as he unzipped the carrier and began to examine its contents. The meals inside, two plastic trays in foil containers, were lukewarm to the touch, which meant they had been slowly warming for hours.

"Inedible," he said.

"I really am sorry."

He looked at her. She was still shivering slightly, despite the towel, and there were dark circles under her eyes, and something about the set of her shoulders suggested that she had been having a very long day even before the storm and the flooded roads and the problem with the food.

"It's not your fault," he said, which wasn't entirely true but seemed like the thing to say.

"It is, though. I should have checked it before I left. I should have called when I realized. I should have—" She stopped, shook her head, and he saw something flicker across her face that made him think briefly, wildly, that if he were any less agitated, he might want to chew that look down to its bone. "Anyway. I'm sorry."

She wrapped her arms around herself. Her hair, drying now in uneven chunks, was very dark and cut in a way that suggested either odd intention or neglect with choppy bangs that fell across her forehead and the rest hanging around a face that might, on a better day, have been called pretty. There was a scattering of freckles across her nose that the rain had not washed away, and when she caught him looking and smiled, a crooked, slightly gap-toothed offering that seemed to happen to her face rather than be performed by it, he felt his own face heat and looked away. Her eyes, dark and deep-set took in his cramped kitchen with a quick, restless flick that suggested a brain that did not often get the luxury of turning itself off.

He looked back down at the trays. The plastic film had fogged on the inside and Kerwin pressed one finger lightly against the top, watching the moisture smear as he found himself saying, "I'll make coffee" before he had consciously decided to offer anything at all.

"That would be—yes. Thank you." She followed him as far as the kitchen doorway and stood there while he went to the coffee pot, still half-full from that morning, the liquid inside long since gone cold and slightly bitter. He considered, briefly, making a fresh pot but then he thought about the way she had walked into his apartment without asking, the way she had taken his coat down from its hook and hung her own in its place, the way she was standing there now with her arms wrapped around herself, watching him move through his own kitchen as though she had every right to observe him, and he thought, *no*. Reheated will do.

He poured the cold coffee into a mug and set it in the microwave, and while it turned he stood with his back to her and tried to breathe through the crawling sensation that had started at the base of his skull and was working its way down his spine. It was not fear, exactly, though it was adjacent to fear; it was the particular discomfort of having another body in his space and another set of eyes cataloging the details of his life. He had spent years perfecting his solitude, honing it into something functional if not comfortable, and now here was this woman—this stranger—standing in his kitchen doorway with her wet hair and her borrowed towel and her relentless, exhausting *presence*, and he wanted nothing more than to unzip his skin and step out of it and leave it there for her to deal with while he went somewhere quiet and *alone*.

The microwave beeped. He took out the mug, the ceramic hot against his palms, and turned and handed it to her without ceremony.

"Oh," she said, and her whole face changed. She wrapped both hands around the mug, cradling it like something precious, and the gesture irritated him in a way he could not quite articulate; it seemed excessive, theatrical, the kind of performance of gratitude that was meant to make *him* feel something rather than simply acknowledge the receipt of a cup of reheated coffee. "Thank you. Really. This is—you didn't have to—"

"It's just coffee."

"I know, but—" She took a sip and closed her eyes, and the small sound she made was so genuine, so unguarded, that he felt his face heat with something close to shame. He had not felt shame in years, not really; shame required an audience and he had systematically eliminated all of his. If he wanted to eat cold soup straight from the can at three in the morning, he did. If he wanted to masturbate in the middle of his kitchen with his pants around his ankles when the odd mood struck him, he did, and felt nothing afterward but the faint biological satisfaction of a body that had discharged its needs. If he wanted to sit in the dark for hours without turning on a light or talk to himself in his mother's voice, or weep at the kitchen table for no reason he could name—well. There was no one to see, no one to judge, and most importantly, no one to make it mean anything.

"God, that's good. I've been cold for hours. I thought I was never going to be warm again—Are…are you alright?" she asked, and he realized he had been standing there in silence for too long, his face doing something he could not control.

"Fine," he said. "The coffee. Is it—"

"It's perfect." She smiled at him again, that crooked, gap-toothed thing, and he looked away before it could do any more damage.

She drank the coffee in small, deliberate sips, as though rationing it, and he busied himself with nothing, with wiping down the counter that did not need wiping, adjusting the position of the dish rack, all of it the small theater of a host who had forgotten how to be one. The silence between them was not quite comfortable, but it was not unbearable either; it had the quality of two people who had found themselves in a lifeboat together and had not yet decided whether to make conversation or simply wait for rescue.

Through the window, the storm showed no sign of relenting. If anything, it appeared to have intensified, the wind was driving the rain almost horizontal now, and every few minutes a gust would hit the building hard enough to make the glass shudder in its frame. He watched a plastic bag cartwheel past the mouth of the alley and disappear into the dark, and he thought about the roads, the flooding, the forecast that had promised this would last through tomorrow at least.

Eleanor had moved from the doorway to the counter, leaning against it with her hip in a way that suggested she was settling in. She had finished the coffee and was cradling the empty mug in her hands, turning it slowly, her thumbnail tracing the chip in the rim that had been there since before his mother died.

"So," she said. "This is cozy."

His hands tightened at his sides.

"The food," she said, finally. "Should we...?"

"It's been at room temperature for hours."

"I know, but—"

"The bacteria will have started multiplying the moment the cool pack failed. Staph, salmonella, listeria—any of them can reach dangerous levels in two hours. It's been longer than that."

She blinked at him. "You sound like a health inspector."

"I read." He did not say that he had read about food safety specifically because the Daily Bread meals were the only thing standing between him and having to leave the apartment to buy groceries, and that he had wanted to know exactly how much risk he was taking by entrusting his survival to a stranger in a navy polo shirt. It seemed like too much to explain.

"Okay," she said, drawing the word out in a way that suggested she was humoring him. "So we wait. See if the storm lets up. Maybe the roads will clear and I can—" She stopped, looking past him to the window above the sink and sighed. "Or maybe not."

"The forecast said it would last through tomorrow."

"Of course it did." She rubbed a hand over her face. "Okay…so we wait. You said you had other food?"

Kerwin shrugged. "Enough."

"Then we're fine," Eleanor said, with a decisiveness that seemed more for her own benefit than his. "In the morning the roads will be clear and I'll get out of your hair and you can go back to—" She gestured vaguely at the apartment, at the dim hallway and the silent rooms beyond.

She took her mug with both hands and held it close to her face, letting the steam rise up around her. In the stark light of the kitchen, wearing his mother's towel and someone else's oversized denim jacket that she must have had on under her coat, he realized, because it was only damp, not soaked, she looked like a stray that had wandered in out of the rain and was not entirely certain whether it would be allowed to stay.

"Thank you," she said. "For the coffee, for letting me in…for not being a serial killer, so far as I can tell."

"The night is young."

She laughed, a real one this time, surprised out of her, and he felt that small tectonic shift again that he did not know how to name and did not want to examine too closely.

"Come on," he said, and led her through to the sitting room.

She settled into the corner of the sagging couch with her drink while he took his usual chair by the window, and for a while neither of them spoke; he picked up his book from where he had left it on the arm of the chair and opened it without finding his place. The storm filled the silence for them and every now and then Eleanor would look up, startled, before forcing her attention back to her mug.

He watched her without watching her, the way he had learned to watch the woman with the gray dog, the teenager outside the shop, all the small figures that moved through his field of vision without ever quite entering his life. She had drawn her legs up beneath her and was sitting with her back against the arm of the couch, her body angled toward the window as if she could not quite believe what was happening outside. The towel had slipped from her hair, which was drying now into something approaching its natural state, dark and disheveled, the bangs falling into her eyes in a way she kept pushing back with an impatient hand.

She was not beautiful, not close to it, but there was something in her face that kept drawing his attention back to it; the way her eyebrows pulled together when she was thinking, or the particular quality of her stillness when she was not speaking. Or maybe he was inventing that. Maybe there was nothing remarkable about her at all and he was simply starved for novelty, his brain seizing on the first new face it had encountered in months and assigning it significance it did not deserve; maybe she was as plain as a parking meter and the only reason he kept looking was because looking was all he knew how to do anymore. He had spent so long watching people from windows, cataloging strangers from bus seats that he had lost the ability to distinguish between genuine interest and the mere habit of observation.

She caught him staring and raised an eyebrow and he looked away, heat creeping up the back of his neck.

The evening stretched ahead of them, shapeless. On the kitchen counter, the carrier sat where he had left it, the meals inside growing less safe by the hour. He should throw them away. He knew he should throw them away. But something stopped him (some voice that sounded like his mother saying *waste not* and *you never know, Kerwin)* and so he left them there, a problem deferred, and turned a page of his book without reading it.

"This is weird," Eleanor said, breaking the silence so suddenly that he started. "Just so you know. I'm aware that this is weird."

"Yes."

"I don't usually barge into strangers' apartments and—" She made a gesture that encompassed the couch, the coffee, the borrowed towel, the whole improbable situation. "Do…this."

"I assumed."

"I'm just saying. In case you were wondering what kind of person does this. The answer is, not me, and not usually. This is—" She stopped, shook her head, and something in her face flickered that might have been embarrassment or might have been something else. "Anyway. Thank you.

Again."

He nodded and looked back at his book, and she looked back at the window, and outside the storm continued to thrust itself against the glass.

At some point, he knew, they would have to address the question of dinner; they would have to decide whether to open his cupboards or risk the carrier on the counter, but that was a problem for later. For now, there was only the storm, the stranger, and the long strange night ahead of them.

He had not had anyone in this apartment since his mother died and, more importantly, he had not *wanted* anyone inside. The thought of another person in his space, touching his thing and breathing his air had always filled him with a kind of low-grade dread that he had learned to manage by simply never allowing it to happen.

And yet here she was; Eleanor.

Her coat still hung by the door. He could hear it from here, the slow, steady drip of water hitting the floor, each drop a small percussion against the silence. He watched the puddle spread, darkening the carpet in a widening stain, soaking slowly into the fibers, and he realized, with a dull, incredulous certainty, that the storm had finally found a way in.

3

Provisions, Or Lack Thereof

By the time the streetlights came on, there was a faint throb behind his eyes, and then a looseness in his knees when he stood followed by the hollow under his ribs answering the storm with its own low roll. He had been telling himself it was restlessness or the strange tension of having another body in the apartment; his stomach, indifferent to the story he was constructing, made a sound that ended the discussion.

He pressed his hand against his shirt in reflex and across the room, Eleanor's head came up.

She had claimed the sagging corner of his sofa hours ago, her legs drawn up beneath her, her not-uniform dried stiff in patches where it had been wettest. The television and the radio were switched off, though he had offered both; she had declined with a wave of her hand, a gesture that could have meant *I don't mind* or simply *let's not,* and so they had sat in the muffled percussion of the rain, two people who had exhausted the obvious topics and had not yet found their way to the less obvious ones. He had his book open, but his eyes had slid over the same paragraph three times without catching; the room had shrunk to the triangle of lamplight, the dark window, and the knowledge, present as another piece of furniture, that there was food in the kitchen and he had chosen not to eat it.

Now she was looking at him from her corner, one eyebrow raised, and he felt his face grow warm.

"Was that you or the plumbing?" she asked quietly.

He shut the book on a finger and considered lying. "Me," he said instead.

"When did you last eat?"

"This morning," he said slowly, after a beat. "Toast."

"Toast." She repeated it without inflection. "I had a granola bar around eleven…" She shifted, resettled, tucked a strand of hair behind her ear. "So we're both running on nothing, basically." The towel his mother had bought years ago was draped around her shoulders like a shawl and she sat with her elbows tucked in tight, her whole body drawn inward against the cold.

The Daily Bread trays sat on the counter where he had left them. He was aware of them in the way one is aware of a bill that has gone unpaid, or a letter that ought to have been answered; peripherally, persistently, with a low thread of unease that never quite rose to the level of action. He did not look at them directly. When his gaze moved in that direction it slid past, found some other object to settle on (the battered cupboards, the dish towel, the small crack in the grout above the sink) and he understood, without having to check, that Eleanor was doing the same.

He closed the book completely, marking his place cleanly with the ribbon. Pretending to read in front of someone who knew he was not reading was approaching unbearable.

"There are things in the cupboard," said Kerwin as he got to his feet, aware of the faint lightness in his head. It occurred to him that if he had been alone, he would have waited and watched the time crawl past the point of sense and then gone to bed rather than make the effort; the presence of another person made his self-neglect feel like performance instead of habit. "Crackers, some soup, I think. It's not much, but we can eat that. The meals can go in the garbage."

Eleanor nodded slowly. Her gaze had drifted, just for a moment, toward the counter; he saw it happen and then saw her pull it back, deliberately, like someone stepping away from the edge of something. Her fingers tightened briefly on her upper arms, then resumed their slow motion as she followed him in to the kitchen.

The room felt smaller with another body in it; he was suddenly conscious of every surface and every smell, from the faint damp that rose from beneath the sink, to the grease stain on the backsplash that he had stopped seeing years ago. He moved to the cupboard and pulled the door open with more force than was necessary.

"There. *Provisions*."

The word rang false even as he spoke it. The shelves held three cans of chopped tomatoes stacked unevenly against the back wall and a single can of beans with a deep crease along its side where it had been dented from a high fall. There was a cylinder of oatmeal, its cardboard soft with age; he had opened it once, months ago, found the fine gray dust of weevils sifting through the flakes and closed it again without comment. Behind these, shoved to the back was a sleeve of saltines that had gone soft in the humidity, their edges visible through the plastic and furred with something that might have been mold. And on the bottom shelf, a single can of creamed mushroom soup with a lid that had begun to dome outward, the metal stretched tight as a leather drum.

Eleanor stood beside him. She did not speak because she did not need to, he could feel her gaze moving across the shelves, taking inventory with the same methodical attention she had given the delivery clipboard hours before. He wanted to close the cupboard door and usher her back to the sitting room and pretend this inspection had never occurred. He did not move.

"Is this all?" she asked. Her voice was careful, neutral; the politeness in it called forth a rage that had him briefly, wildly, considering ripping each door from its hinges.

"I go out on Tuesdays." He heard himself reciting the words as though reading from a form. "I take a bus to the senior center for the meal program… " and here, he cleared his throat though he did not need to, "…the rest comes from the delivery."

The words landed in the narrow kitchen and he wished, immediately, that he could unsay them. *Senior center.* He was not yet fifty. But the phrase would conjure images in her head to be sure, a blanket across knobbled knees, a plastic spoon raised to slack lips, the smell of body odor and sour milk and he found, to his considerable irritation, that he minded what this minimum-wage grunt of a girl thought of him. He had no business caring, and *she* had no business *being here,* seeing this, standing in his kitchen, judging *him*.

She nodded slowly. Her hand had come up to rest against the edge of the counter, fingers splayed, and she was looking at the puffed lid of the soup can with an expression he could not decipher.

"The delivery." she repeated. "Do you mean Daily Bread?"

"Yes."

"How long have you been on the service?"

"Three years." He did not know why he answered. "Perhaps four."

"And this—" She gestured at the shelves, a small motion that encompassed everything and nothing all at once, "—this is what you keep between deliveries?"

The very nerve of the girl. "I *told* you, there are crackers and some soup."

"The soup's gone off." She said it simply, without accusation. "The lid's bulging, you know can't eat that."

He knew. But what could he tell her? That he had left it sitting there because throwing it away would mean admitting there was nothing to replace it with? Please. He reached past her and took the can from the shelf and set it on the counter beside the sink, the metal cool against his palm.

"And the crackers," she said. "Have you looked at the crackers?"

"They're fine."

She reached past him, pressing close enough that he could smell the rain still caught in her hair, something floral beneath it, shampoo or soap and pulled the sleeve from the shelf. The plastic crinkled under her fingers. She held it up to the light from the window, and he saw what she saw: the dark spots along the edges of the crackers, the fine web of something growing where the seal had failed.

She set them on the counter beside the soup.

"I manage," he said, each word ground out and weighted enough to fill their own clause. "I've managed for years. I don't require—"

"I'm not saying you require anything." She had turned to face him, her back against the counter, her arms crossed over her chest. The gesture pulled the fabric of her uniform tight across her shoulders and he kept his eyes trained on the negative rectangles of space there between her ears and the invisible line run up from the width of her. "I'm just asking. You're on the highest-priority list so that usually means there's meant to be some kind of backup. A caseworker, or a secondary contact, someone who checks on you..."

"There is no caseworker."

"...and checks that you're not running out between deliveries and that you have funds for—"

"Miss—*Eleanor*." The name came out like a lock clicking into place. He watched her flinch, almost imperceptibly, and felt a grim satisfaction that shamed him even as he leaned into it. "I have been alive this long without your concern. I do not require a caseworker. I do not require supplemental support. I do not *require* you to stand in my kitchen and conduct an audit of my circumstances," he spat.

"I'm sorry," she said quietly. "I didn't mean to pry. It's just, we're trained to notice, you know...if someone's struggling and the system isn't working the way it should."

"The system is working *precisely* as it should." He heard the bitterness in his own voice and could not stop it. "It delivers food that I eat when I am hungry."

She looked at the puffed soup can, the moldered crackers and the empty shelves in a slow, deliberate circuit that ended on his face, as if to say, *And what exactly are you planning to eat tonight?* Her expression did not change, but some minute recalculation was taking place behind her eyes and he understood then that she was not easy to fool and that his inventory of excuses was as transparent to her as his inventory of provisions.

"That's not what I—" She stopped, scraped her nails against her denim and tried again. "If you're not getting enough, that isn't...you not doing something *wrong*. It's the program that's wrong."

"The program," he said, imperious though he had no footing to speak in such a way, "is a *bureaucracy*. It functions at the level to which it is capable."

"Do you have money for groceries, then? If something goes wrong?" *Money* sounded oddly blunt in the close air between them.

"That is *not* your concern."

"I know it's not, but I'm asking anyway."

The unmitigated *gall* of the girl.

"Then stop asking." He turned away from her, gripping the edge of the sink, staring at the dark window and the ghost of himself staring back, the hollowed cheeks gone sallow, the patchy gray stubble, the pale eyes watery and red-rimmed beneath a wispy thatch of hair he had stopped cutting months ago. "You are here because the storm flooded the roads, you are not here to—"

"To what?" Her voice had gone quiet, but there was some thread of steel he had not heard before. "To notice that you have nothing to eat?"

There was a long, uncomfortable pause, and when Eleanor gathered herself to speak again it was with a speed that surprised him, as if her stopping for breath might deflate all of her nerve. "Have you ever told them you run out? They can adjust deliveries, you know, that's *kind* of the point."

"I do not wish to be discussed at meetings. I am not a charity case."

He turned. She had not moved from her place against the counter but her posture had changed, her chin lifted slightly now with her shoulders squared, the stance of someone who had decided not to back down. The borrowed towel had slipped from her shoulders and she caught it without looking before folding it over her arm.

Kerwin worked to compose himself before speaking. "I am not your client, and I am not your project. I am not some *problem* for you to solve between deliveries." The anger was rising now, hot and quick, filling the spaces where the shame had been. He leaned into it. "And while we're on the subject, what gives you the right to barge into someone's home, paw through their cupboards, ask questions you have no business asking. Did no one teach you basic manners, basic *tact*?" His voice had gone cold and precise, each word fastening itself a small blade as it escaped from behind his teeth. "You're, what, twenty-two? Twenty-three? Shouldn't you be in university somewhere, learning something useful? Why are you even doing this job—is this what you aspired to? Is this the *dream*?"

She had gone very still. Her face was pale, and he watched her absorb each blow with a vicious satisfaction that sickened him even as he continued. "I should throw you out. Storm or no storm, I should have left you on the landing where you belonged. What is *wrong* with you, that you can't take a hint, that you can't see when you're not—"

He stopped. He could hear his own breathing, ragged and harsh.

Something had shifted in her body. A slight drawing back, a tensing of the shoulders, it was almost imperceptible, but he saw it; her weight had moved to the balls of her feet. Her eyes flicked, just once, toward the doorway behind him, measuring the distance and he understood, with a clarity that turned his stomach, what she was calculating—how to get past him if she needed to, how quickly she could move to escape him. Whether or not she could make it.

She was afraid of him.

The realization landed like a cannon ball to the stomach. He looked at her and saw for the first time what she must be seeing, a strange man in a narrow kitchen, blocking the only exit, his voice raised, his face contorted with rage.

A man she did not know. A man who could do anything.

His mind, unbidden, cataloged the room: there was the knife block by the stove with its four handles protruding, the cast iron pan hanging from its hook, the weight of the soup can still in reach on the counter, the corner of the counter itself, sharp enough to split a skull if you hit it just right. Not to mention his own hands, which had done nothing violent in decades but which remembered, viscerally, what violence felt like.

He could kill her, of course he could. He could kill her in a dozen ways before she reached the door. The thought arrived fully formed, clinical, as though someone else had placed it in his head, and he stood frozen in the horror of having thought it at all.

What is wrong with you?

She was speaking. He did not know for how long, but her mouth was moving and sounds were coming out and he had missed all of it, lost in the dark tunneling of his own mind.

"—not judging you," she was saying. Her voice was careful, measured, the voice of someone talking down a wild animal. "I'm really not. I just—" She stopped, shook her head. "Never mind. You're right. It's none of my business."

The silence that followed was absolute before the storm filled it obligingly, slamming something loose against the outside wall and sending a shiver through the window frame. The light over the sink flickered once, a brief blink, then steadied. Eleanor stood motionless against the counter; she had not flinched, but something in her face had closed and he wanted to fling it open as surely as he had wanted to rip the doors from his cupboards just minutes before.

What was she *doing* to him?

"I—" The word caught in his throat. "That was—I shouldn't have—"

Don't apologize, said a voice in his head that sounded like his father. *She deserved it. She had no right to pry.*

She was trying to help, said another voice, much quieter. *She saw your empty shelves and she was trying to help, and you flayed her for it.*

She should learn to mind her own business.

She's stuck here because of the storm. She has nowhere to go. And you just—

"I don't think you're a charity case," she said quietly. "I've just seen a lot of kitchens in this job, and I haven't worked here for very long. You start to notice patterns pretty quickly." She stopped, shook her head.

She pushed off from the counter and moved past him toward the door, giving him a wide berth and he understood that she was giving him what he had asked for in her retreat. He should have been relieved.

He was not.

"Wait," he said.

She paused in the doorway, half-turned, the light from the sitting room catching the edge of her profile, but she did not come closer.

"The soup *is* off. You're right. And the crackers. I just—" He stopped. He did not know how to finish the sentence and, more importantly, he did not know what he was trying to explain, only that he needed her to understand that the empty shelves were not carelessness but something else he could not name.

"It's okay," she said. "You don't have to explain..."

"I don't have anyone," he said, the words spilling out before he could stop them. "There's no caseworker because I refused one, and there's no secondary contact because there's *no one* to contact. There's no backup because this is it. This is all there is."

She stood very still in the doorway and for a long moment, neither of them spoke, and the silence between them was not empty but full of all the things he had just admitted and not meant to say.

"Okay," she said finally. Her voice was very quiet. "Okay."

She did not move to leave. She simply stood there, holding the folded towel, looking at him with an expression he could not read.

The trays sat on the counter where he had left them, the spoiled soup sat beside the moldered crackers; outside the storm continued and for some time neither of them spoke, neither of them moved.

* * *

Kerwin watched her walk through the doorway into the sitting room with her shoulders held careful and straight and he went after her as if some part of him had been hooked and pulled along. The kitchen remained behind them like a crime scene; the cupboard doors were still open, the puffed can and the crackers still arranged on the counter like evidence. He did not look back.

In the sitting room, the lamp still cast its yellow circle, the book still lay where he had left it on the arm of the chair and the rain still drummed against the windows. Ostensibly, nothing had changed, and yet, as uncomfortable as it was to consider the current atmosphere within the cramped apartment, it was clear from every observable metric that *everything* had changed. Eleanor stood near the sofa but did not sit; the towel had slipped from her arm and she held it now in both hands, twisting it slowly, her fingers working the terry cloth. Her gaze moved around the room without settling on anything, the window, the television, the door, as though she were seeing it all for the first time.

The silence between them seemed impossible to move through.

"This is strange," she said finally. "I shouldn't be here."

He did not answer; he did not know what to say.

"I've overstepped." She shook her head slightly in a small, self-directed motion. "I'm sorry. I shouldn't have—the cupboards, the questions—it wasn't my place."

"You don't need to apologize."

"I do, though." She looked at him then, and her expression was guarded, the openness of earlier in the evening pulled back behind something more careful. "When there's a gap in the rain, I should go back down. Wait in the shop or try the roads again…they might have cleared by now." She glanced toward the window, toward the dark and the water streaming down the glass.

The thought of the door opening and closing, of her footsteps receding down the stairs and the apartment returning to what it had been scuttled up his chest like something with claws. *Panic,* he realized distantly, this was panic. It was a physical thing, sick and desperate and bright, rising from somewhere beneath his ribs and spreading outward until his fingertips felt numb with it.

She's going to leave.

The words arrived in his head with terrible clarity.

She's going to walk out that door and you will be alone again and whatever this was will be over and you will go back to watching the woman with the gray dog from the window and eating your meals standing at the counter and pretending that this is enough, that you don't mind—

"Thank you for the coffee," Eleanor was saying. She had moved toward the hallway and was reaching for her coat where it hung on the hook by the door. "And the towels. I'm sorry I barged in."

The hallway was narrow and dim, lit only by the light spilling from the sitting room and she seemed very small in it, very young, her small hand already reaching for the lock. The chain glinted dully in the half-light and he followed without deciding to.

She was too young to be out in the world, that was the trouble. When he thought of her doing adult things like signing leases and filing taxes he could only picture it if three of her were stacked in a trench coat, the topmost one wobbling slightly as she handed over documents. She was a child. She had no business being out in a storm like this, driving those flooded roads and making decisions about her own safety when she had already demonstrated such catastrophically poor judgment. Would it not be prudent, then, for him to prevent her from going? Would it not be the responsible thing?

And she was a woman, yes, technically, legally, but she had walked into a strange man's apartment with all the protestations of a whipped dog, had sat on his sofa and drunk his coffee and shown no unease whatsoever until he got only a little angry—and at *her* rudeness, her prying, her endless questions! If he were a madman, he would have been a madman at the door; if he meant her harm, he would have done it in the kitchen, when she stood with her back to the knives. What business did she have judging him now? What business did she have *leaving* him, as though he were the one who had done something wrong, as though he were the danger here when all he had done was tell her the truth about his empty cupboards and his empty life?

The hallway narrowed around him, the walls pressing in and beneath all the righteous fury something else was clawing its way up that had nothing to do with right or wrong or who had been rude to whom. His hand found the wall; his chest had gone tight and the word surfaced before he could stop it, *lonely*. He was lonely, and she was leaving, and the two facts were connected in a way he could not bear to examine.

He stepped past her and put his hand flat against the door.

She froze.

For a moment neither of them breathed. He could feel the wood beneath his palm, cool and solid, and he could feel her stillness in the sudden rigid tension of her body beside him. He understood, with the same sick clarity that had visited him in the kitchen, what this must look like, and more importantly, what this must feel like, for her. The narrow hallway, with its only door blocked. The strange man with his hand against the only exit.

You're scaring her. Again. What is wrong with you?

"You can't," he said. The words came out too fast, too urgent, and he heard himself and winced. He tried again, forcing his voice into something steadier. "The stairs are wet, the alley's a river...you said yourself the underpass is under water. If you try to drive again tonight, you won't make it that far."

Don't go. Don't go. Don't go.

She did not move. She was looking at him with an expression that was held in check by the risk assessment taking place behind her eyes. Out there were flooded roads and ditches and other drivers who didn't know how to stop and in here was a man she did not know, standing between her and escape, his voice still rough from shouting. He saw, with sick clarity, how very little information she had to decide with.

When she spoke, her voice was very level and calm. "You need to move your hand."

He did not move his hand.

Instead, he let his other arm fall open, palm up, fingers spread in the same gesture he had made in the kitchen, but different now and more desperate. Kerwin was not fending off a blow, he was asking for something which left him feeling wretched and like a criminal as he had not asked anyone for anything in years.

"Stay. Just—stay. For tonight."

There was a beat in which he heard every way that could go wrong, every story on the news his mother had tutted over, every warning about men and closed doors. Her eyes flicked past him, once, measuring the distance to the sitting room, to the kitchen, to the window if she had to climb out of it.

She was watching him. He could feel her gaze on his face, taking his measure, and he knew what she must be seeing: the hollow cheeks, the red-rimmed eyes, the desperate set of his mouth. He looked despicable. He knew he looked despicable. He could not bring himself to care.

"You shouted at me," she said finally. It sounded almost like a statement of fact for the court transcript. "You made me feel...unwelcome."

"Yes," he said. "I did."

"And now you don't want me to walk out of here."

"No."

"Why not?"

"You'll be safer here," he said, gesturing vaguely with one hand as though he could conjure a weather system in the narrow hallway and summon the flood and the wind to plead his case for him. It was the only thing he could think of that was not *please* or *I can't bear it* or *don't leave me alone with this.* "The storm. The roads. It's not safe out there."

The silence stretched between them. Somewhere in the building, a pipe groaned and the sound traveled up the walls and through the narrow space where they stood facing each other.

She was calculating. He could see it happening. She was tired, she was soaked, she had been driving for who knows how long before she ended up here and the roads really *were* terrible; for all his rudeness and his cruelty, he had not actually hurt her. He had given her coffee, he had given her towels and he had stood in his kitchen and let her see the shameful nothing of his life. How would he recover what that cost him, now, if she left?

She exhaled slowly, and he could see the moment she let the idea into her body, not just her head. Her shoulders dropped a fraction and she said, "All right." Her voice was quiet, but steady. "Tonight. But you unlock the door. Now."

His hand dropped away at once, as if the paint had scorched him. He slid the chain free and let it hang there, useless, the small rattle of links absurdly loud in the cramped space. Then he stepped back, far enough that if she chose to turn the handle now she could walk straight past him and down the stairs without touching him at all.

"Of course," he said. His voice had gone hoarse.

She didn't touch the handle, nor did she move toward the stairwell. She turned instead so that her back was against the door and her face toward the apartment again, as if she were aligning herself with it, admitting, for this one night only, that she belonged on the inside of it.

"Tonight," she repeated, more to herself than to him.

He nodded, though she wasn't looking at him. The frantic flutter in his chest subsided into something heavier and stranger. The storm outside went on hammering at the bricks; for the first time since it started, the noise beyond the walls and the noise in his own head were roughly, mercifully, the same.

4

Here in the Dark

The linen closet smelled of mothballs and his dead mother's perfume and the slow decay of fabric left too long in the dark; Kerwin stood before it with his hand on the knob, taking inventory. There were two wool blankets, one with a hole near the hem where mice had gotten to it years ago, a set of sheets he did not recognize that were still in their plastic, three over-flat pillows and above these, on a shelf he could barely reach was a quilt his grandmother had made before he was born, comprised of tatty blue squares alternating with white, the stitching still tight despite the years.

He pulled down one of the wool blankets and the packaged sheets and, after a moment's hesitation, one of the pillows. His mother would have offered the quilt. More truthfully, his mother would have offered the bed itself and taken the sofa without complaint in her way that made the whole thing seem natural and hospitable, but his mother was dead. Her instincts had not passed to him. The quilt stayed where it was.

Eleanor was in the sitting room where he had left her, standing by the window with her arms crossed over her chest. The rain had softened in the last hour and lost some of its violence, though it showed no signs of stopping entirely. She turned when she heard him in the doorway watched him approach with a wary politeness.

"For the sofa," he said, holding out the bundle. "I'm afraid there's no spare duvet, but this should be adequate. The radiators still work."

"Thank you," said Eleanor, pressing the bundle against her chest. He watched the wool settle into the space between her breasts. "This is more than fine."

She took the linens from him, her fingers brushing his briefly, and he pulled back as though burned. He saw the small tightening at the corners of her mouth and felt the heat rise in his face in turn.

"You'll want to make it up yourself," he said, as she set the linens on the arm of the sofa. "I imagine you have preferences."

For a moment the two of them looked at the pile as though it might demonstrate how to proceed. It did not.

"I can manage a sheet, Mr. Merle."

Kerwin hesitated, then turned back toward his room. There was something else he could offer; it seemed prudent, even. He had a drawer full of clothes he no longer properly inhabited full of T-shirts gone soft and thin with washing and of loose flannel pajama pants knotted at the waist, his uniform when he was not on the bus or at the senior center. None of them were new, but all of them were clean.

He went and fetched the least offensive of them and came back holding them in a small, uncertain bundle.

"You might be more comfortable," he said, keeping his eyes on a point somewhere over her shoulder, "if you had something dry to sleep in."

"No." The word came out quickly, almost a reflex. "No, I'm fine. Thank you."

Something in him curdled. She wouldn't take his linens without that careful, distant gratitude and she wouldn't take his clothes at *all.* He had offered her shelter and she had accepted it like a prisoner accepting rations with the minimum of acknowledgment necessary to complete the transaction. What did she think—that his shirts carried disease? That his pajamas would contaminate her? That anything that had touched his skin was beneath her?

"They are *clean,* I haven't handed you rags from the trash."

"I know," she said at once, color creeping along her neck.

"The offer stands," he said stiffly. "If you change your mind."

She opened her mouth, shut it again. "I appreciate the offer. Really." She was already moving toward the sofa and shaking out the sheets with brisk efficiency and her back was to him now, her shoulders a straight line of dismissal a worse man than him might want to prod upwards with a rubber mallet.

He stood in the doorway and watched her make up the sofa and he felt, absurdly, as though he were being erased from his own apartment. She moved through his space as though it were a hotel room and he was merely the bellhop who had delivered her luggage; the longer he stood there the more foolish he felt, keenly aware that she did not want him there.

"There's a bathroom down the hall," he added, his words clipped. "The hot water takes a moment. If you need water to drink, the sink in the kitchen is... tolerable. If the storm gets worse, or if there's a leak—" He stopped. The list was edging toward ridiculous.

"I'll shout," she said. "Or knock. Or...something."

"Very well."

He turned toward his room, then paused when she spoke again.

"Is it always this cold in here?" she asked.

He looked at the radiator which gave off its usual anemic warmth; the room felt as it always did to him which only fueled his ire.

"It's November," he said, speaking to her as if she were slow. "The building is ancient, this is what the landlord considers heating."

"Right." She gave a small huff that might have been a laugh. "Sorry, it's not a criticism. I'm just...cold."

"There are no more blankets." He heard the stiffness in his own voice and despised it even as he leaned into it. "You have what *I* have."

"I know. You've been very—*generous*." The word sat oddly between them. "I'll be fine, I just need to get used to it."

He could, of course, have offered his own duvet. The thought came and went, and he dismissed before it fully formed. She had already refused his clothes. He was not going to stand in the hall and press his bedding on her like some penitent suitor. She had agreed to stay because the alternative was worse, she would leave as soon as the roads were clear, and in the meantime she would tolerate his presence the way one tolerates a cough or an ill-fitting sock, an unavoidable unpleasantness to be endured until circumstances improved.

"Goodnight, then," he said. The formality of it left no room for alteration. "If you require anything, don't hesitate—"

"I won't," she said. "Goodnight."

He nodded, a small, stiff dip of the head, and retreated down the corridor to his room as though excusing himself from a meeting. The door closed with its usual soft click but tonight the sound seemed louder than the storm. He stood in the dark for a moment, listening as the apartment adjusted around the new arrangement.

He could picture the rectangle of her body under his blanket with her head on his pillow and her damp hair spreading out against the linen with appalling clarity. She would be curling onto her side, he thought, tucking her knees up with one hand curled under her cheek and though he had no evidence for this beyond the way she had occupied his sofa earlier, he felt entirely certain of it.

He undressed mechanically, folding his clothes over the back of the chair, pulling on the same pajama bottoms he wore every night. The sheets were cool when he slid between them to lie on his back and stare at the ceiling, which the dark had turned into a low, indifferent plane.

"Ridiculous," he said aloud, though there was no one to hear him. It was not clear whether he meant her presence or his own performance of hospitality.

Kerwin switched off the bedside lamp, plunging the room into a softer darkness, and somewhere beneath him, on his sofa, a stranger turned over under his blanket and settled into the kind of uneasy sleep one had in borrowed rooms. He lay very still, listening to the thin sounds she made when she moved, and tried not to think about the fact that, for the first time in years, he was not the only person breathing inside these walls.

Sleep did not come.

Though he had expected from the moment he lay down that the night would be a long negotiation between his body and the dark, knowing did not make the hours pass any faster. He lay on his back with his hands folded over his stomach, doing his best impression of a man at rest while the storm settled into a steady, unshowy battering; the gutters snarled and spat and the wind went on worrying at the loose flashing at the edge of the roof.

She, however, was asleep. She had to be. It had been over an hour since he'd closed his door and the sounds from the sitting room had grown infrequent enough that he was certain of three things: she was asleep, he was not, and the distance between those two states was quickly becoming insurmountable.

He turned onto his side, then onto his back again. The sheets had grown warm with his body heat but offered no comfort, they felt clinging and oppressive like a second skin he could not shed. He kicked them down to his waist and lay exposed to the cool air of the room, and it was then that he became aware of it.

It began with a heaviness between his legs that was both insistent and unwelcome; he shifted, irritated, and the movement rubbed fabric against skin in a way that turned awareness into heat. He drew in a breath through his nose and let it out slowly.

"Ridiculous," he murmured again.

He was not sixteen. He did not lie awake, rigid and aching, because there was a girl in the next room who might or might not be thinking of him. The last time he could recall this particular mix of urgency and mortification he had been in the bathroom of a public shopping center, one hand braced against the tiled wall and the other working furiously at his own treacherous flesh, praying that no one tried the door. Normally, months would pass without this particular inconvenience presenting itself and when it did, he dealt with it quickly and brusquely, the way one might deal with a cramp or a past-due notice.

He shifted again, seeking some configuration that would make it go down but every adjustment caught him more squarely, which was obscene because this simply didn't happen to him anymore. Be it age, medication, or sheer habit, that part of him had learned over the last decade to keep its peace; there were mornings when he woke with a vague sense that something had roused and then subsided without his input, but it was muted and manageable. It did not demand this kind of attention.

He stared at the ceiling and willed the thing to subside. It did not.

He pushed the thought away, but his body had already taken the hint. The stiffness thickened, pressed against the front of his pajamas and he imagined, with an unwilling clarity, the shape of it under the thin cotton, a blunt stake jutting up from the tangled thatch of his pubic hair, stiff enough that some enterprising carnival worker could have stood at the end of the bed and tossed rings over it for prizes.

He knew, intellectually, that there was nothing inherently sexual about their situation just as he knew there were damp towels in his bathroom, a pair of socks steaming gently over the radiator and his old sheet over the sofa. These were facts. They did not, by themselves, justify the way his pulse banged in the hollow of his throat, rough enough that he knew any sound escaping his lips would be a croak. It had nothing to do with *her* specifically, he told himself, it was simply the machinery of the species grinding on as it always had, indifferent to context or propriety or the fact that he was a man approaching fifty who had no business thinking about a woman young enough to be his daughter—

But he *was* thinking about it, that was the trouble. The thoughts arrived unbidden, slipping past his defenses like water through a cracked seal, the shape of her under his blanket, the pale strip of skin at her wrist where she had pushed up her sleeve to wash her hands. He had not meant to notice these things about her but he had noticed them anyway.

Stop it, he told himself. *Stop it at once.*

He tried to redirect by summoning some image sufficiently repellent to quell the heat spreading through his abdomen. He thought of the woman at the senior center who lunched beside him very rarely with the goiter and the endless monologue about her ne'er-do-well grandson's fabricated achievements; he thought of the crossword woman on the bus with her pen scratching against newsprint and her mouth moving silently as she worked. He even thought of the way his grandmother had looked at the end, her gaunt head stuck above a foil blanket for some scan or another, resembling a packet of ready-grill vegetables; the slack jaw and the yellowed skin and the terrible stillness of her hands on the blanket.

None of it worked. The erection remained, stubborn and stupid, jutting against the fabric as he closed his eyes and saw her as she might be in some other life, some other version of the night. A wife, perhaps. *His* wife. Downstairs watching her favorite show while he read in the bedroom, the sounds of the television drifting up through the floor, domestic and ordinary and unutterably precious. She would come to bed eventually, of course; *just five more minutes, Kerwin.* She would slide under the covers beside him and press her cold feet against his calves and he would complain, as husbands did, and she would laugh, and then—

The fantasy curdled even as he reached for it. She was not his wife. She was a stranger, a refugee from a storm, wet and unwashed and sleeping on his sofa because she had no better option. If he went to her now and touched her, if he pressed his mouth to the skin of her throat she would taste of sweat and the long hours of a terrible day. Her cunt, if he licked it the way he was imagining, would not be clean; it would be sour with the day's accumulation, with fear-sweat and damp cotton that had dried without airflow, and the thought should have repulsed him, should have been enough to finally, mercifully, end this—

It did not repulse him.

The realization landed like a blow. He was hard, harder than he had been in months, and the fantasy that should have collapsed under the weight of its own sordidness had instead intensified, had grown teeth and claws and a terrible specificity. He could picture it now, her thighs parting reluctantly, the dark tufts of hair (or was she trimmed?), the slick flesh beneath. He could picture the sound she would make when his tongue found her, delving inside with sweet abandon, the way her hips would jerk against his mouth, the bitter taste of her spreading across his palate.

Stop. Stop. You are disgusting. You are a disgusting old man and she is—

The thought jarred him so badly he actually turned his head, as if someone had spoken aloud.

"Filth," he said under his breath, but whether he meant the fantasy or himself he could not have said. The shame should have been cold water, but it was not. It threaded itself into the heat and made it stranger.

He shifted onto his side, pointedly turning his back on the direction of the sitting room as though that would help. The new angle pressed him more firmly against the mattress and his hand, wicked thing that it was, traitorously drifted down to adjust himself and stayed where it landed.

He told himself he merely intended to ease the pressure. He hooked his thumb under the waistband of his pajamas and tugged it away from his body in an attempt to create some space. His fingers brushed the hot, slick head of his cock and the jolt that ran up his spine was so immediate he had to bite back a sound.

"Stop it," he muttered.

His hand did not stop. It settled, almost of its own accord, curling around the shaft, considering the familiar weight of it in his palm in a way that was equal parts humiliating and oddly comforting and for a moment he simply held on, frozen in the purgatory between intention and action. He could stop. He could take his hand away and lie here in the dark and wait for the thing to subside on its own, as it eventually would.

That was the plan. He would hold himself still and the thing would eventually get bored and retreat, surely, like a sulky animal but when it did not retreat, the throb under his fingers only intensified. The skin felt thin and too hot; a smear of moisture slicked under his thumb where it rested along the vein.

He thought of all the years he had managed not to do this, of the mornings he had woken and turned onto his stomach and waited, hands flat on the mattress, for the mutiny to pass. He thought, pathetically, of the small, grim pride he had taken in going about his day with that energy banked, folded away into more respectable compartments and he thought of his mother, informing him with a matter-of-factness that had horrified him even as a boy, that certain urges were a test and that some men failed them more spectacularly than others.

"This is not a test," he whispered now. "This is *absurd*."

A floorboard creaked, very faintly, below. The sound traveled up through the joists and into the frame of his bed as he pictured her there again, curled on her side with one hand under her cheek. The blanket would have slipped somewhere, surely, exposing a length of calf and the dip behind her knee. She would be warm, a line of heat in the cold room, but not so warm that her nipples wouldn't pebble in protest of the sputtering old radiator.

His hand began to move. A bright, mean little spark of pleasure flared low in his belly.

"Oh, for—" He broke off, teeth closing on the curse.

It was a betrayal, he knew, of her, of himself, of whatever thin fiction of decency he had constructed over the years. He knew this. He pumped into his fist anyway, eyes squeezed shut, breath coming harsh through his nose. The pleasure was harsh and unwelcome, each stroke a small defeat, and he chased it with the single-minded focus of a man who wanted only to be done so that he might reach the end and be free of this humiliation.

He began to move his hand in earnest. The friction was not gentle because he did not deserve gentle. If he was going to do this here, now, with a woman on his sofa and his body behaving like a teenager's, then he would at least do it with the severity the situation demanded.

He worked himself in short, vicious pulls, his jaw clenched hard enough to creak his teeth, breath sawing in and out as the sensation built with indecent speed. There was no slow climb, no sweet ache; the pleasure sat atop his disgust like a rider on a nervous horse, digging in its heels.

The tension snapped.

He came with a groan that was louder than he intended, his hips jerking up off the mattress, his hand working frantically to wring the last spasms from his body clamped so tight around himself it almost hurt. Hot fluid spattered over his fingers, his belly, even the inside of his wrist and for a moment he lay in the aftermath, every muscle shuddering, the shame roaring in his ears like an extension of the storm.

Breathing hard and with his hand still wrapped around his softening cock he thought: *I am pathetic. I am a pathetic, disgusting old man, and she is twenty feet away, and I have just—*

"Mr. Merle?"

Her voice came through the door, muffled but clear. He froze, his heart slamming against his ribs. The mess on his stomach cooled in an instant.

"Mr. Merle, are you all right? I heard—"

He heard the word too, hanging there between them, waiting for its object. I heard *you*.

"I'm fine." The words came out strangled and too loud. He cleared his throat and tried again. "I'm fine. Go back to sleep."

There was an ugly pause. He could picture her standing in the hallway, her hand raised to knock with her ear tilted toward his door. What had she heard? The groan? The creak of the mattress? Could she smell it, somehow, the rank evidence of what he had done seeping through the wood between them?

"Are you sure? It sounded like—"

"I said I'm fine." He heard the harshness in his own voice and could not soften it. "Go back to sleep, Miss Fletcher. Go—go back to the sitting room."

Another ugly pause that was even longer this time. Then, quietly, "All right."

He heard her footsteps retreat down the hallway followed by the sofa springs protesting as she lay back down and he remained exactly where he was, flat on his back, his hand still curled shamefully around himself, his heart still hammering, his face burning in the dark.

He did not sleep for a long time after that.

When he finally did, he dreamed of nothing, and woke to weak light and the distant sound of rain and the certain knowledge that he could not look her in the eye for some time.

5

A Necessary Hunger

The bathroom door was closed when he emerged from his room, and he stood in the hallway for a moment, listening to the sound of water running behind it. So the girl was awake, then. She would be standing at his sink, looking into his mirror, seeing the rust stain in the basin and the mildew creeping along the edges of everything and her own face, even—pale, he imagined, smudged with sleep, the hair she had not washed hanging lank around her jaw. She would be cataloging the night's damage the way women did, pressing at the skin beneath her eyes and grimacing at whatever she found there.

He needed to use the bathroom. He could wait.

The thought of standing where she had stood, looking into that same mirror, meeting the face that had contorted and flushed so spectacularly above the body that had betrayed him—well, it was unbearable. There was nothing else that it might be. When he closed his eyes he could still see the obscene tent of his pajamas and the slick head of his cock emerging from his fist, purpled and straining. The sounds he had made; the mess on his stomach, cooling in the dark.

He went to the kitchen instead.

He filled his mother's old kettle and set it on the burner and stood with his back to the door, listening for the sound of the bathroom opening.

When it came, he did not turn around.

"Morning," Eleanor said from somewhere behind him.

"Morning."

He heard her footsteps cross the sitting room and then the sofa springs creak as she sat, or perhaps she was simply folding the blankets and putting the room back to rights. He did not turn to look. He watched the kettle instead for the first wisps of steam to curl from the spout, and waited for the water to boil.

Eleanor appeared in the kitchen doorway a few minutes later. She had changed nothing about herself except, perhaps, the angle of her shoulders; she still wore yesterday's jeans and the oversized denim jacket he had clocked beneath the coat, though both had dried into a stiff, rumpled mess. She leaned against the doorframe with her arms crossed over her chest and the posture pressed her small breasts together in a way he registered and then furiously unregistered, fixing his gaze on the kettle as though it required his complete attention.

"Did you sleep?" she asked.

"Some." He did not ask her the same question. He was afraid of what she might say, of how she might phrase it, of whether there would be something in her voice that suggested she knew more than she was letting on.

He handed her a mug. Their fingers did not touch.

"Thank you," she said.

"It's instant."

"I know."

They stood in the kitchen, separated by three feet of chipped linoleum and the vast, unacknowledged weight of the night before and drank their coffee in silence.

Eleanor's stomach made a sound.

She pressed her hand against it, a quick, embarrassed gesture, and looked away. He pretended not to notice. His own stomach answered a moment later, a low gurgle that seemed to originate somewhere near his spine, and he turned back to the window so she would not see his face.

Neither of them mentioned breakfast. Neither of them mentioned the trays still sat defiantly on the counter. They finished their coffee and rinsed their mugs and moved around each other with the careful choreography of people who have agreed, without speaking, not to discuss what needs to be discussed.

Kerwin knew this could not last.

* * *

By early afternoon, the hunger had become impossible to ignore.

Kerwin had tried to read; the words swam and scattered like minnows every time his stomach cramped. He had tried to sleep but his body refused, too hollow and restless to settle and he had tried, absurdly, to simply wait it out but the sensation trailed after him relentlessly such that every time he shifted in his chair he felt the emptiness within him more acutely. He could feel the absence of food the way one might feel the absence of a tooth, not quite pain, but instead a perpetual, irritating awareness.

Eleanor was on the sofa, her legs drawn up beneath her, a book from his shelf open in her lap. She had not turned a page in twenty minutes. He had been watching the way her eyes stayed fixed on the same spot on the page and the way her hand kept drifting to her stomach and then away again, as though she could press the hunger back down if she tried hard enough.

"We need to eat something," she said finally.

Kerwin did not respond immediately. He was looking at the edge of the counter visible through the kitchen doorway where the trays that had been sitting there for nearly twenty-four hours now remained, room temperature and waiting.

"The cupboard..." he began.

She closed the book and set it aside. "We've been over this."

"The roads might be clear," he said. "By now. You could—"

"I checked the weather this morning on the TV before you got up. There are flash flood warnings until tomorrow at six p.m, and the underpass is still underwater. We're not going anywhere."

The silence stretched between them.

"The trays," Eleanor said quietly.

"No."

"Kerwin—"

"I said no." He heard the sharpness in his own voice and could not soften it. "You don't understand. Food poisoning isn't always something you sleep off. It can *kill* you. It can shut down your organs, it can—"

"—And we haven't eaten in—" She paused, calculating. "Almost *thirty* hours, for me. Longer for you, probably!"

He did not correct her. He could not remember, precisely, when he had last eaten something more substantial than toast. The days had a tendency to blur together when you lived alone, when no one was watching and when it didn't matter whether you ate at noon or six or not at all.

"We could heat it," she said. *"Thoroughly.* That would kill whatever's growing in there."

"That's not how it works. Some toxins are heat-stable. Even if you kill the bacteria—"

"I know." She cut him off, not unkindly. "You've explained, but Kerwin—" She leaned forward, her elbows on her knees, her eyes fixed on his face with an intensity that made him want to look away. "What's the alternative? We sit here and starve? We wait for the roads to clear and hope we can still stand up long enough to drive somewhere?"

"It's not that dire."

"Isn't it?" She held his gaze. "When did you last eat a real meal? Not toast, not coffee, a *real* meal that wasn't scraped out of a can?"

He did not answer. He was thinking of the plastic trays with their compartments at the senior center, filled up with watery green beans and gray meat loaf and the square of cake wrapped in cellophane that he always saved for the bus ride home. Those were his real meals, the only real ones that he had eaten in years, all surrounded by people twenty and thirty years his senior who called him "young man" and asked after his mother as though they thought her alive.

She must think him pathetic, standing there cataloging his failures and arriving at the same conclusion that *he* often reached himself, which was that he was barely surviving and that he could not even feed himself without the intervention of charity and government programs and delivery drivers who pitied him enough to barge through his door.

"I'm hungry," she said. Her voice had gone quiet, stripped of argument and the tone of it shook loose his spiraling thoughts. "I'm so hungry I can feel it in my *throat*, and I know the food might be bad, and I know the risks, and I don't—" She stopped, swallowed. "I don't particularly care what happens to me. Not enough to sit here and feel like this for another day or two."

"If we get sick," he said slowly, "it won't be pleasant."

"I've been sick before."

"Not like this. Not—" He stopped, shook his head. "You don't know what you're agreeing to."

"Then tell me." She did not look away. "Tell me exactly what might happen, and let me decide for myself!"

And so Kerwin told her. He felt foolish doing it, standing in his own kitchen and reciting horrors like a man reading from a medical pamphlet but the explanation gave his mind something to grip that was not the gap between her front teeth that showed when she parted her lips to listen. He found himself speaking faster than was necessary when cataloging symptoms: the cramps that came first, twisting low in the gut, the violent and unrelenting vomiting that followed, the fever that climbed while the body shook with chills. He told her about dehydration, organ strain, and the particular indignity of being too weak to stand and too sick to stay still. He described what it looked like (and what it *smelled* like) when the body decided to empty itself from both ends at once, and he watched her face as he said it, searching for disgust or fear or the sensible retreat of a woman who had finally understood what she was risking.

She did not retreat. She listened with her arms crossed and her head tilted slightly, and something about the angle of her jaw or the freckles dusted across the bridge of her nose made him think, unwillingly, *would I still want her, if I saw her like that?*

The thought arrived fully formed, obscene in its clarity. If she were hunched over his toilet, sweating and shaking, her hair plastered to her face with sick; if she were reduced to the animal business of purging, stripped of dignity, of everything that separated a person from a body in distress, would he still feel this? This heat that had no business existing, this pull toward her that persisted despite every rational objection he could muster?

He did not know. He suspected, with a kind of grim wonder, that he might. That the wanting had sunk its roots somewhere that would not be dislodged by mere revulsion. Last night he had lain in the dark and spent himself into his own fist like a teenager, and this morning he could not meet her eyes, and still—*still*—some part of him tracked the movement of her mouth when she spoke, noted the hollow at the base of her throat, wondered what sounds she would make if he...

Stop.

He finished his recitation. His father's warnings, his father's rules, every horror story from a childhood spent entertaining himself behind a shop counter. When he was done, his mouth was dry and his hands were unsteady and she was still looking at him with that same quiet attention as though he had not just described, in clinical detail, the ways their bodies might betray them in the hours to come.

When he finished, she nodded slowly.

"All right," she said. "I understand."

"And?"

"And I still want to eat."

He looked at her for a long moment. The rain fell; the hunger sat in his gut like a fist and somewhere beneath the fear and the caution and the voice of his father telling him that this was wrong, there was another voice, quieter, more desperate, that said, *she's staying. She's choosing this, with you.*

Perhaps he was mad, perhaps all of these years spent alone really had done his head in.

"We heat it thoroughly," he said. "As hot as the stove will go."

"Agreed."

"And if either of us starts to feel off—any symptom, anything at all—we tell the other. Immediately." He fixed her with a look that brooked no argument.

"Agreed."

He stood. His legs felt unsteady beneath him, though whether it was from hunger or something else he could not say. Eleanor stood too, and for a moment they faced each other across the small distance of the sitting room, two people about to make a choice they could not unmake.

"Well," he said. "Let's see what we're working with."

They went into the kitchen together, which made it feel smaller than it had the night before; there was something about having another body at his shoulder that altered the dimensions and shifted the air there, as if the room had been a set and someone had just walked in from offstage without warning. The lids had puffed slightly in the hours since he'd set them down; the cardboard sleeves had gone soft with condensation, and the smell rising from them was not precisely foul but sat somewhere in the uneasy territory between edible and regrettable. There was beef stew in one and some variety of chicken in the other, the sauce congealed to a skin that caught the light in a way that gave it texture, a topographical sheen.

Eleanor reached past him and lifted the lid of the beef stew, peering at the contents with the detached curiosity of a student examining a specimen. She did not recoil, nor did she wrinkle her nose. She simply looked, replaced the lid, and then looked at him.

"This one," she said.

"You're certain."

"I don't trust chicken when I can't tell what part of the bird it came from." She was already reaching for the cutlery drawer, pulling it open with the easy familiarity of someone who had spent the last day learning the blueprint of his kitchen. "Stew is stew. You can't hide much in a stew."

He wanted to tell her that she was wrong about that; had she paid any attention in school she would know that the very nature of stew was concealment, that it was peasant food, invented to disguise the rank smell of spoiling vegetables and to stretch gristly cuts of meat past their natural lifespan. You could hide a great deal in a stew, he knew, because he was not an *idiot*. That was the point of stew.

But he did not. He turned on the stove instead, set the heavy-bottomed pan on the burner and scraped the contents of the container into it with more force than was strictly necessary. The meat hit the hot metal with a hiss, a smell rose up, onion and beef and perhaps thyme and his stomach cramped at the scent with a hunger so acute it bordered on pain.

"Not the microwave?" Eleanor asked. She had found two forks, two knives, and was holding them in one hand like a bouquet.

"Microwaves heat unevenly. There are often pockets of cold where bacteria survive." He stirred the stew, breaking up the chunks of potato, exposing the meat to the heat. "If we're doing this, we're doing it properly."

She did not respond to that. He heard the clink of metal on wood as she set the cutlery on the small table in the sitting room and then she was back in the doorway, leaning against the frame with her arms crossed, watching him cook. He could feel her gaze on the back of his neck which quickly turned into a point of pressure he could not shake.

"It smells better than I expected," she said after a while.

He grunted. The stew was beginning to bubble at the edges, the gravy loosening, the meat starting to fall apart the way it was supposed to. He stirred it once more, then reached for the chicken container and repeated the process in a second pan. The chicken smelled less promising, there was a sourness beneath the herbs that pricked behind his ears but he heated it anyway, stirred it anyway, telling himself on repeat that heat would kill whatever needed killing.

They ate at the small table, their knees nearly touching in the cramped space between the sofa and the wall. Eleanor had taken the beef stew without comment; the chicken sat before him, glistening under the weak light of the lamp and he made himself eat it with the methodical determination of a man completing a task. It tasted like what it was, old food reheated and so he ate, and she ate, and for a long while neither of them spoke; the sound of forks on plates, of chewing, of swallowing, filled the small room like a kind of music, tuneless and strange.

"Still better than prison food," he said, finally breaking the silence.

He had not meant to say it. The words came out dry, offhand, the kind of comment one made without thinking and he realized his mistake only when Eleanor went very still across from him, her fork suspended halfway to her mouth.

She set the fork down. Her eyes moved, just briefly, to the doorway behind him; he saw the same calculation in them that he had seen in the kitchen, the same measuring of distance and probability of escape. When she looked back at him her expression had shuttered into something careful and blank.

"Sorry?" she said.

The word was a placeholder, he knew, to fill the silence while she decided what to do with what he had just told her.

He should have felt ashamed and he should have rushed to explain, to soften, or to offer context but instead he felt—and this was the worst part, the part that confirmed every dark suspicion he had ever harbored about himself—a flicker of something else entirely. She was afraid of him again. She was sitting in his apartment, eating his food, wearing the rumpled evidence of a night spent under his roof and she was afraid of him. Some feral part of his brain registered this fact and responded with a dark prod of heat that felt so, so very far from remorse.

He thought of the sounds he had made in the dark last night, the image of her body beneath his blanket, the fantasy that he refused to abandon. And now, unbidden, a new image; chasing her across the room, catching her at the door, pressing her against it with his weight, his cock finding the cleft of her backside through their clothing, her breath fogging the glass—

Her knee brushed his under the table.

He jerked back as though she had burned him, his chair scraping against the floor, and the shame came rushing in to fill the space the heat had left, a cold tide that made his face go hot and his hands clench in his lap. She had flinched too and he saw the small recoil there, the way her shoulders drew up toward her ears. She thought—God, what did she think? That he had recoiled from *her*? That she had done something wrong? Or had she seen something in his face, some flicker of the filth that had just passed through his mind?

The silence stretched between them, unbearable.

Eleanor picked up her fork again, but her hand was unsteady; the tines clattered against the plate, a small arrhythmic sound that seemed impossibly loud in the quiet room. She was trying to eat, or trying to pretend to eat, and her jaw was tight and her breathing had gone shallow and he understood then that he had frightened her. *Again.* He understood that everything he did seemed to frighten her and that he did not deserve the strange mercy of her continued presence.

He ought to say something. Some explanation for the tension she could feel radiating off him, some context for the word that had slipped out and landed between them like a grenade.

Prison. He was a fool.

"My father owned the shop downstairs," he said, as good an opening as any.

Eleanor looked up. Her fork went still. The taste of the stew turned flat and metallic in his mouth.

He had not meant to say anything at all; he had meant to let the silence stretch until the clattering of her fork subsided and they could finish their meal and pretend that none of this had happened. But her eyes were on him now, wide and waiting, and he found that the words were already forming, already rising, a tide he could not hold back.

* * *

Merle's Convenience had occupied the ground floor of the building for as long as Kerwin could remember. His earliest memories were of the shop, of the smell of newsprint and tobacco and the bell above the door that chimed whenever a customer entered. His father behind the counter (he was *always* behind the counter), a cup of coffee at his elbow and a newspaper spread before him, working the crossword with grim concentration.

The shop was not successful. It was not unsuccessful, either; it simply existed as a fixture of the neighborhood that people visited out of habit rather than preference, buying milk and bread and lottery tickets and the occasional bottle of wine that Kerwin's father would ring up without comment, his eyes never leaving the crossword, his pencil never pausing in its slow traverse of the grid. The regulars knew not to expect conversation, and the newcomers learned it quickly.

Kerwin had worked the register on weekends and after school since he was twelve, stocking shelves and sweeping floors and learning to make change without looking at the register. He was not good with customers because he was always too quiet, a shade too awkward, too prone to staring at a point somewhere over their shoulders rather than meeting their eyes. But his father did not seem to mind and so Kerwin continued, week after week, year after year, until the rhythm of the shop had become as familiar to him as his own heartbeat.

His mother tried to teach him—*look at them, Kerwin, smile, ask how their day is going*—but the lessons never took, and eventually she stopped trying, and Kerwin understood this as another small failure, another way he had disappointed her without meaning to. But she loved him. He was certain of that, in the way children are certain of things they have no evidence for. She loved him, and he loved her, and if their love was a quiet thing, it was still real and it was still theirs.

He did not know, then, how easily love could turn.

The boys had started coming in during his second year of high school. There were five of them, always together, moving through the aisles with the lazy confidence of young men and the splayed swagger of young men who were not often told *no*. They were not from the neighborhood, they came from the part of town that boasted sprawling, manicured lawns and two-car garages, and Kerwin could never quite understand why they bothered to walk the extra half-mile to his father's shop when there was a mini-mart three streets from their school.

He understood eventually. They came because his father's shop was easy pickings.

The stealing started small with a chocolate bar here and a packet of chips there, items slipped into pockets and jacket sleeves with a casualness that suggested long practice. Kerwin saw it happen and said nothing. His father saw it happen and said nothing. But the sign went up the following week, hand-lettered in his father's cramped script and taped to the glass door at eye level: NO BACKPACKS INSIDE.

The boys had laughed when they saw it. Kerwin remembered the sound of their laughter echoing off the fluorescent lights overhead; he remembered the way they had looked at him behind the counter, their eyes sliding over him as though he were part of the furniture, beneath contempt (for an isolated boy with few favors and even fewer prospects, this was worse—*much* worse). They had stuffed their pockets instead of their bags after that, making a game of it right in front of his father's face, daring each other to take more and more while Kerwin watched and said nothing and hated himself for his silence.

Dominic Welland was the worst of them.

He was not the leader (that was Talan Hines, whose father owned half the commercial property in the district and whose mother sat on the school board) but he was the one Kerwin remembered most clearly, the one whose face still surfaced in his dreams thirty years later. Dominic was tall and pale-eyed, with the kind of angular good looks that girls seemed to find appealing and that Kerwin, even then, had recognized as a mask for something colder underneath. He was the one who lingered longest in the aisles, who let his fingers trail over the merchandise with proprietary ease, who looked at Kerwin sometimes with a small, knowing smile, as though they shared a secret between them.

They shared nothing. Kerwin was nothing to him and had nothing to share that the boy might want. He knew this.

He had seen Dominic once, in the park behind the school, crouched over an anthill with a magnifying glass in his hand. The smell of burning had reached Kerwin before the sight did; he had stood at the edge of the clearing and watched as Dominic moved the focused point of light from ant to ant, his face expressionless and his hand perfectly steady. When he finally looked up and saw Kerwin watching, he had smiled that same small smile and said, "Curious little fuckers, aren't they? They just keep coming."

Kerwin walked away without answering and did not tell anyone what he had seen. Actually, he had tried very hard to forget it, and had mostly succeeded until the night that cemented the next stretch of years before him wherein he would have little else to do but remember.

It was March of his final year when Talan Hines approached him after school.

Kerwin had been walking home alone as he always did, his bag heavy with books he would not read and homework he might complete in silence at the kitchen table while his father worked the evening shift downstairs. He had not heard Talan coming; one moment he was alone on the sidewalk, and the next there was a hand on his shoulder, a voice in his ear, a presence at his side that made his whole body go rigid with surprise.

"Merle," Talan said. "Your dad runs the shop, yeah? Merle's?"

Kerwin nodded. He did not trust himself to speak.

"Thought so." Talan's hand was still on his shoulder, a weight that felt heavier than it should have. "Listen, we're having a bit of a thing this weekend. A party at my place while my parents are in the Caribbean. We need some... *supplies*," he added, waggling his brow, "if you know what I mean."

Kerwin knew what he meant. He also knew that he should shrug off Talan's hand and keep walking without having anything to do with whatever they were planning. But Talan was looking at him with an expression that was almost friendly, *almost* warm, and somewhere beneath Kerwin's ribs a pathetic, hungry thing had woken up and was straining toward the possibility of belonging.

"What kind of supplies?" he heard himself ask.

"Beer, mostly. Maybe some wine if you can manage it. Nothing fancy." Talan's smile widened. "We'd pay you, of course. And you'd be invited. To the party, I mean...if you wanted to come."

If you wanted to come. The words hung in the air between them, glittering with promise. Kerwin thought of the years he had spent watching these boys from a distance, noticing their ease and their laughter and their casual cruelties; he thought of the empty weekends in the apartment, the silence broken only by the television and the clink of bottles being opened and discarded; he thought of how it might feel to walk into a room full of people who knew his name, invited him, wanted him there, even.

"I can't steal it," he said. "My father counts everything. He'd know."

"We're not asking you to steal it." That was Dominic, materializing at

Talan's elbow as though he had been there all along. His pale eyes fixed on Kerwin's face, and Kerwin felt his stomach clench. "We just need you to leave the back door open Saturday night, after your dad's gone to bed. We'll be in and out in five minutes. He'll never know."

"And if he wakes up?"

"He won't." Dominic smiled. "Trust us."

Kerwin did not trust them. He knew, even as he stood there nodding, even as he agreed to disable the alarm and prop the door and wait upstairs while they took what they wanted that this was a mistake and that nothing good could come of it. But the hungry thing in his chest was louder than his fear, and so he said yes, and Dominic clapped him on the shoulder, and Talan said, "Good man, Merle. See you Saturday," and then they were gone, and Kerwin was alone on the sidewalk feeling like a chump; feeling like a criminal.

Saturday came. The day passed in a blur of anxiety and anticipation, his hands trembling as he stocked shelves, his mind running through the plan again and again until it felt less like a betrayal and more like an inevitability. His father closed the shop at ten, counted the register, locked the beer chiller as he always did and went upstairs without a word. Kerwin followed. They ate dinner in silence—corned beef and crackers—and then his mother and father went to bed, and Kerwin was alone.

He waited until midnight. Then he crept downstairs, disabled the alarm with the code his father thought he didn't know and propped the back door open with a brick.

The brick. He would remember that detail later, would turn it over in his mind untangling the thread of thought again and again, wondering if things might have been different if he had used something else—a book? A shoe? Anything else that could not be picked up and swung? But he had used a brick because it was heavy and would hold the door open against the wind, not because he had imagined what he was making possible with his choice.

He went back upstairs. He lay in bed with his clothes still on, staring at the ceiling, listening for the sound of the back door opening. His heart was pounding so hard he could feel it in his throat, in his temples, his blood frothing through the tips of his fingers. He told himself it would be fine.

Five minutes, Dominic had said. In and out. His father would never know.

The crash came at half past two.

It was loud enough to shake the walls and bring him bolt upright in bed, his heart slamming against his ribs. Something large and heavy had fallen, and in the silence that followed he heard voices, muffled and urgent, and then his parents' door opening, and then his father's footsteps on the stairs.

His mother's voice, sleep-blurred and querulous, "Tom? Tom, what is it?"

Kerwin did not move. He would fixate on this later, of course, the reasons why he should have moved or called out, the many ways in which he could have stopped his father or done anything other than lie there frozen with his hands clenched in the sheets and his breath caught in his throat. But he did not move, and so his father's footsteps reached the bottom of the stairs, which pre-empted the shouting, his father's voice raised in anger, and then—

The sound.

It was a final sound. One that Kerwin would hear it for the rest of his life, waking from dreams with the *thwack!* echoing in his ears, forever flinching at the thump of a dropped book or the slam of a car door. It was the sound of a brick meeting a skull, and, most importantly, it was the sound of his father dying.

He was out of bed before he knew he was moving, down the stairs, through the door that led to the shop. The fluorescent lights were on, buzzing and flickering, casting everything in a sickly pale glow. The end cap display had been knocked over and chips and cheap chocolate bars lay scattered across the linoleum; there was a metal shelf lying on its side and there were boys in ski masks, four of them, frozen in the act of fleeing, bottles clutched in their hands.

And on the floor, between the counter and the door, his father.

The blood was already spreading, a dark pool that crept toward the drain his father mopped every night. His father's eyes were open, his mouth was open, but his father was not *moving*, not breathing, because his father was not anything anymore. Standing over him with the brick still in his hand was Dominic Welland.

Their eyes met through the holes in the ski mask.

Kerwin saw nothing there but the same flat, pale gaze that had watched the ants burn; the same small smile playing at the corners of his mouth now as it did then.

"Shouldn't have come down," Dominic said. "Stupid old bastard."

Again, Kerwin did not remember moving— he told the police this, later, but they scoffed at him, tossing around phrases like *selective memory* and *liar*. But it was the truth, he did not remember crossing the distance between them and reaching for Dominic and he certainly did not remember anything except the sudden blinding pain as something struck the side of his head and the world tilted sideways and the floor came up to meet him.

When he woke, the boys were gone.

He was lying on the linoleum, his cheek pressed to the cold floor, blood trickling into his eye from a gash at his temple. The shop was silent. Three feet away, his father's body lay in its spreading pool of blood. Kerwin crawled to him, gathering his father's head into his lap and pressing his hands to the wound as though he could hold the pieces together and undo what had been done. This, he knew even in the moment was as futile as wanting something badly enough to believe that he could make it so.

That was how the police found him; that was how his mother found him too, standing in the doorway in her nightgown, her face white, her hand pressed to her mouth as though she could push the scream back in. He looked up at her, his father's blood on his hands, on his face, on his chest, and he said, hysterical, animal, "Mom! I didn't! Please, it wasn't—*Mom!*"

She knew. He could see it in her face, the terrible gymnastics she was doing in her head as her eyes darted about everywhere but the blood slick growing larger by the second; the alarm that hadn't gone off, the back door that had been propped open. She didn't know the details yet, but she knew that her son had done *something*, had let something in or angered the wrong crowd and now her husband was dead on the floor of his own shop and her son was covered in his blood and she could not—she *would not*—look at him the way she had looked at him before.

"Mom, please…" he said again, but she had already turned away, reaching for the telephone to call the police.

She did not look at him again that night. Not when the police arrived to take him away in handcuffs nor when he turned at the door of the squad car and searched for her face in the crowd of neighbors who had gathered on the sidewalk in their robes and slippers.

The trial was brief; the verdict inevitable.

The boys had alibis, each other, their parents, a party at Talan Hines's house that a dozen witnesses swore they had attended. Dominic's family moved away that summer, suddenly and without explanation to somewhere in the south that no one could quite remember. The brick had Kerwin's fingerprints on it. The alarm code had been entered correctly. The back door had been propped open from the inside.

The detective who interviewed him was not unkind. He asked his questions in a flat, tired voice, and when Kerwin told him every detail and every name, he wrote it down without comment and then closed his notebook and looked at Kerwin with something that might have been pity.

"Son," he said, "I believe you, but believing isn't the same as proving, and those boys have lawyers that cost more than I make in a year. I'm sorry."

His mother did not come to the police station. Kerwin waited for her through the fingerprinting and the photographs, through the long hours in the holding cell and still, she did not come. He asked the nearest officer to call her and when he did, he came back with a face that told Kerwin everything he needed to know.

"She says she's not available," the officer said, and would not meet his eyes.

Though he expected it, something twisted within him when she did not come to the arraignment, or the hearings, or the motions, or the endless procedural appearances that stretched over months. The lawyer they assigned him was a tired old man with dandruff on his shoulders and a briefcase held together with tape who told Kerwin that his mother had been interviewed by the prosecution. Apparently, she had told them about Kerwin's difficulties at school and his lack of friends, which were, unfortunately for him, entirely true.

"She's not on your side, son," the lawyer said, not unkindly. "I'm sorry, but you should know that going in."

Kerwin had not believed it until the sentencing. His mother sat in the back row wearing a black dress he had never seen before, her hair pulled back from her face in a way that made her look older and harder, like a stranger wearing his mother's skin. When the judge pronounced the verdict (manslaughter, ten years) she stood and walked out of the courtroom without looking at her son. When he called out to her, she did not give any sign that she had heard him at all.

The door closed behind her. The bailiff took his arm. And Kerwin understood then, finally, painfully that his mother had made her choice. That in the architecture of her grief, her husband's life sat higher than her son's, and so she would spend the rest of her days making sure he knew it.

Kerwin never saw her again. She died while he was inside from a heart attack in the apartment above the shop that was no longer *their* shop, and he learned about it from a letter that arrived three weeks after the funeral. The lawyer's handwriting was neat and impersonal and the estate, such as it was, had been left to him. The apartment was his, when he got out.

Small mercies.

The memory released him slowly, like a hand unclenching.

He was sitting at the table in his apartment, his food cold on his plate, his hands trembling in his lap. Eleanor was watching him with an expression he could not read; he did not know how long he had been silent.

"Ten years," he said. His voice sounded strange to him, hoarse and distant. "I was inside for ten years and by the time I got out, my mother was dead and the shop was gone and there was nothing left but this."

Eleanor did not speak. She reached across the table, slowly, deliberately, giving him time to pull away and laid her hand over his.

He did not pull away.

Her palm was warm against his knuckles, her fingers light, and he understood that this was not pity nor the performative sympathy he had learned to despise. It was something simpler than that. Recognition, maybe.

"She was wrong," Eleanor said quietly. "Your mother was *wrong* to leave you."

No one had ever said that to him before; not the lawyers, not the social workers, not the prison counselors who had processed him through the system like a bundle of bad paperwork. No one had ever looked at him and said, simply, *Kerwin, that should not have happened to you.*

He turned his hand over beneath hers and let their palms press together.

6

The Last, Last Supper

Their palms were still pressed together across the table, her skin warm against his and Kerwin found himself unwilling to be the one to break the contact even though he understood that they could not simply sit here indefinitely with their hands clasped like children in a fairy tale, waiting for something to happen.

He was the one who pulled away first.

He slid his fingers from beneath hers carefully with what he hoped was a neutral expression and busied himself with the cold remains of his meal as though the congealed chicken held some vital interest. She did the same, though neither of them ate anything; they simply pushed food around their plates and avoided each other's eyes and waited for the moment to resolve itself into something bearable.

"We can't just sit here," Eleanor said finally.

She was right. They couldn't. But Kerwin could not think of a single thing to do that would not feel absurd after the way she had looked at him when she said *she was wrong to leave you*, after the press of her palm against his and the terrible, fragile thing that had passed between them.

"I might have something," he said, and was on his feet moving toward the hall cupboard before he finished the sentence, bristling with the odd energy that she had seemingly pulled forth with her kindness. "Board games from when my mother was alive."

He did not wait for her response. The cupboard was crammed with the detritus of decades, old newspapers, a broken vacuum cleaner he kept meaning to throw away, boxes of things he could not bring himself to sort through and he had to shift several layers of neglect before he found what he was looking for—a cardboard box with dust furred along its edges.

He pulled it out and carried it to the sitting room, setting it on the coffee table with a thud that sent dust motes spiraling into the weak lamplight. Inside was a chess set with a cracked bishop, a pack of cards held together with a rubber band, and a Scrabble box so old the cardboard had gone soft at the corners.

"Scrabble," Eleanor said, lifting the lid. "Half the letters are missing."

"We can improvise."

"With what? Interpretive dance?"

He almost smiled. *Almost.* "We'll make do."

Kerwin held the rule leaflet between his fingers. The print was small and cramped and someone, years ago, had underlined phrases in pen, making angry little trenches in the paper.

"You're reading that like it's a legal document," Eleanor said. She sat cross-legged on the floor opposite him, elbows on her knees, hair half pulled back and half escaping. "It's a children's game."

"That would explain the level of strategic complexity," he replied, "but the last time I signed something without reading it properly I lost ten years, so you will forgive me if I am cautious."

They set up the board between them, knees nearly touching under the coffee table and divided the remaining tiles into two uneven piles. The randomness of the remaining letters should have made the game unplayable, but Eleanor approached the problem with a methodical intensity that reminded him, uncomfortably, of himself.

QUIET. Twenty-four points, with the Q on a double letter.

"You've played before," he said.

"My grandma had a set," Eleanor replied. She did not elaborate and he did not ask; there was something in the flatness of her voice that suggested the grandma was no longer living, or no longer speaking to her, or both.

They played in silence for several turns, the click of tiles on the board the only sound in the apartment. Outside, the rain had gentled to a steady drizzle, the wind had dropped, and the world beyond the windows felt very far away. Kerwin found himself relaxing into the rhythm of the game despite himself, the simple pleasure of arranging letters into words and watching the board fill with the evidence of two minds working in parallel toward no particular goal. It was restful in a way he had not expected, it asked nothing of him except that he pay attention and paying attention to something outside his own head was a relief so profound it was nearly frightening.

It was Eleanor who broke the silence.

"What about you, then?" she asked, and when he looked up, confused, she clarified, "I mean—you told me about your father, and the—well, everything, but I haven't..." She stopped, moving a tile while pointedly ignoring his eyeline. "It seems unfair that you've given me all that and I've given you nothing."

"You want parity," he said. "Is that it?" And then, when she did not respond, "You don't owe me anything." said Kerwin, and he meant it. He had not offered up his worst memory as a transaction requiring repayment.

"I know." She placed another tile, frowning at the board. "But I want to. If that's—I mean, if you want to hear it."

He wanted to hear it more than he could justify, certainly more than made sense given that she was a stranger who had walked into his apartment less than two days ago and might walk out again as soon as the roads cleared. But he had learned, in the years since his release not to reach for things he wanted because wanting had a way of turning sour and curdling into disappointment. So he simply nodded, and waited, and let her find her own way into the telling.

She shrugged, moved her tiles about without looking at him.

"I dropped out of college" she said simply. "I was a *Philosophy* major, if you can believe that. It was okay before I quit, I suppose...I went to seminars, wrote the essays, smoked a *lot* of weed." She said it flatly, without the performative flourish he'd heard in other people who wanted to sound interesting. "I dated people who thought doing ketamine in the park was a political act and I talked a lot about *systems* and *power* and how everything was broken while my loans crept up and up and I explained to anyone who would listen that capitalism was the problem—which I don't *totally* disagree with now, but I had no idea what I was talking about, then. Obviously."

"Obviously," he echoed. "You couldn't possibly have selected anything practical."

"Oh, God, no." She smiled briefly, without humor. "Can't waste the talent and all of that potential. I was going to 'make something of myself.' Their phrase, not mine."

Another turn. She was playing almost automatically now, her attention elsewhere.

"Your parents?" he questioned.

"Yeah." She drummed her fingers on the edge of the board, a rapid, nervous rhythm. "My mother, especially. My dad just... nodded along. He always nodded along."

"I see," he said, though he did not, not yet.

"So I went," she said. "And it was—fine, I guess. Good, even, when I wasn't paralyzed by the idea that I was supposed to be brilliant. It turns out being told you're intelligent your whole childhood is not *actually* the same as knowing what to do with your life."

"No," he said. "It isn't." The corner of his mouth twitched. "And your mother was... delighted by this development?"

"She liked the bit where I could say words she couldn't pronounce," Eleanor said, "Although she didn't like the bit when the letters from the bank starting coming in. We argued about it, of course, and I always said it was fine, that everyone was in debt and it was part of the experience but then I ran out of loan money, which turned out to be more of a problem than capitalism in the *immediate* sense. So I worked in fast food, a call center, whatever would have me. Daily Bread were the first to offer something vaguely legal with set hours." She placed a word—BROKE, eighteen points—and sat back. "It's not a bad job, actually, it's better than nothing...which is what I had for a while. Not as good as it should be, but what is?"

He recognized in her then, the weary pragmatism of someone who had learned to calibrate her expectations downward. She saw the system, he realized, not just her own failures but the larger machinery that had processed her and spat her out. He knew that pressure. He had buckled under it himself, once.

"And now?"

"Oh, my parents are delighted." Her voice was flat. "Their little dropout philosopher, delivering other people's dinners. The first in the family to go to university and the first to fuck it up so spectacularly."

She placed another word. WASTE. He wasn't sure if it was deliberate.

"You keep saying 'they,'" he said carefully, "like they're a theoretical construct. Where are they, actually?"

She went still. The tiles in her hand clicked together, a small nervous sound.

"I'm not talking to them," she said.

He waited. He had learned, in prison, the value of silence; people would fill it eventually, if you gave them long enough. Eleanor lasted almost a full minute before the words started to spill out.

"I moved out after an argument. A *bad* one. I packed a bag that night and I haven't—" She stopped, swallowed, tried again. "I haven't seen them since. That was almost two years ago."

"What kind of argument?"

She met his eyes then, and there was something in her expression that he recognized, a kind of reckless defiance that he had seen in his own face in the months after his conviction, when he had stopped caring what anyone thought of him.

"I punched my mother in the face," she said.

The words landed between them like a cartoon piano on a city walk. Kerwin felt his own assumptions shifting and rearranging themselves to accommodate this new information; Eleanor had seemed so—not soft, exactly, but contained, and at the very least, the kind of person who calculated her moves and weighed her words and did not, generally speaking, go around punching people.

But then again, he had seemed like a lot of things too before the night that revealed what he actually was.

"Did she hit you first?" he asked.

"No."

"Did she—" He stopped, unsure how to phrase it. "Was there a reason?"

Eleanor's mouth twisted into something that was not quite a smile. "There's *always* a reason, isn't there? She said I was wasting my life, I said it was *my* life to waste. She told me that I was ungrateful, and selfish...and then she grabbed my arm to stop me from walking out in the middle of her sentence. I told her to let go, and she didn't. So I turned around and—" She lifted her hand, looked at it as if it might still remember the motion. "I punched her."

The words fell into the small room with a dull weight. He almost expected to hear them echo, but they just sat there between them.

"You hit your mother," he said. He did not mean for it to sound like a charge being read out, but it did.

"Once! You make it sound like it was a hobby of mine! I don't go around punching people, you know. "

"How hard?"

"Not hard enough to knock her out, if that's what you're asking. I hit her and she fell and there was blood on her mouth and I thought—" Another pause, longer this time. "I thought, *good.* That's the worst part. I wasn't sorry, I was glad."

He thought of his father on the floor of the shop, the blood spreading, the way he had felt nothing at all except a terrible, hollow exhaustion. He thought of his mother in the doorway, the calculation in her eyes and the way she had turned away without a word. He did not say any of this. He simply nodded, and waited, and let her continue.

"She just... looked at me." Her mouth flattened. "Like I'd become someone else in front of her eyes. And then I left."

"Do they know where you are?" he asked.

"They know my number. They haven't used it."

"Do you plan to go back?"

"No." The word was flat, final, a door closing. "There's nothing to go back *to*. I rent a room now; the landlady's ancient and half-deaf, and she *never* checks on me. I pay my rent in cash and she leaves me alone. I could die in there and no one would know for weeks…months, maybe, if the smell didn't travel."

Kerwin wanted to ask if she'd seen her mother fall, if there had been a sound when she hit the ground and if the memory of it kept her awake at night the way his own memories kept him awake. Instead he said, "And that was it?"

"That was it." She picked up her tiles, arranged them, placed a word. ALONE. "I packed a bag, I walked out and I haven't seen them since."

The board between them was filling up now, a patchwork of words that seemed, in the low lamplight, to tell a story of their own. QUIET, BROKE, WASTE, ALONE. He looked at his own tiles, a jumble of consonants and a single vowel and tried to find something to spell that would not feel like a confession.

"Your turn," Eleanor said.

He placed his word. STAY.

"Twelve points," she said. "Not bad."

"I'm not trying to win."

"No," she agreed. "Neither am I."

She reached for her tiles and fumbled the rack, tipping it facedown on the board. "Sorry," she muttered, righting it without looking at him, "clumsy."

She placed her tiles on the rack, and her hand went to her stomach, and she pressed her knuckles against her sternum in a gesture that was not quite casual.

"Eleanor…" he said.

"I'm fine." She smiled, but it didn't reach her eyes. "Just ate too fast, probably. You know how it is."

She reached to move her piece and missed the square entirely. The tile tipped over, laid on its side.

"You're cheating now," he said. It sounded like himself from another room, thinner and more amused than he felt.

"Just dizzy," she muttered, but she stayed very still with her hands flat on the table, her breathing careful and deliberate, like someone trying not to wake a sleeping animal curled somewhere deep inside her.

"Your turn," she said.

He picked up the dice. His hands were steady but his stomach was not, there was a sourness at the back of his throat, a metallic tang that he recognized from the few times in his life he had been truly, catastrophically ill.

Eleanor swallowed twice, two quick, dry clicks of muscle and her hand drifted to her stomach again.

"Are you warm?" she asked. "It's warm in here, isn't it?" The color seemed to have gone out of her in patches, her freckles sat on skin that had taken on the particular, grayish translucence of unbaked dough.

It was not warm. The apartment had been cold all day, the ancient radiators producing more noise than heat but he could feel the sweat starting at his hairline, the flush creeping up the back of his neck, and understood that whatever was happening was happening to both of them, they had crossed some threshold together and there was no going back.

"A bit."

She nodded, seemingly relieved to have the lie confirmed, and reached for her tiles. Her fingers fumbled at the bag, missed the opening, tried again. When she finally drew her letters she held them at an angle that sent one skittering across the table and onto the floor, and she stared at it for a long moment as though she had forgotten what it was or what she was supposed to do with it.

"I'll get it," he said, but when he bent to retrieve the tile the room tilted sideways, a slow nauseating lurch that made him grip the edge of the table until his knuckles went white.

"Kerwin?"

"I'm fine," he managed. "Just stood up too fast."

But he had not stood up at all; he had only bent, shifted his weight, and the fact that such a small movement could produce such a profound wrongness told him everything he needed to know about what was coming. He retrieved the tile—an E, worth one point, entirely useless—and placed it on the table between them, and when he looked up Eleanor's face had gone the color of the chicken he'd eaten not long ago.

"I think," she said carefully, "I might need to—"

She did not finish the sentence. She was on her feet and moving toward the bathroom before the words were fully out, one hand pressed to her mouth and the other trailing along the wall for balance. He heard the door slam, heard the lock turn, followed by a sound that was unmistakable.

His own stomach clenched in response, a sympathetic spasm that quickly revealed itself to be something more. The cramp started low, a dull pressure that he might have mistaken for hunger if he had not just eaten, and then it thickened, twisting into something urgent and undeniable. He gripped the arm of his chair and breathed through his nose and told himself that this was fine, that he had been through much, much worse.

The second cramp doubled him over.

He heard himself make a sound and then he was on his feet and moving, though where he intended to go he could not have said.

From behind the bathroom door, another sound. Retching, and then a sob, and then retching again.

"Eleanor," he called, or tried to call; his voice came out strangled and reedy. "Eleanor, are you—"

He did not finish the question. There was no point in finishing it. She was not all right; he was not all right; neither of them was going to be all right for some time. He made it to the kitchen sink just as the third cramp hit, and then his body made its decision for him,and he stopped thinking about anything at all.

The vomiting came in waves, each one more violent than the last, his stomach contracting with a force that seemed disproportionate to anything he had eaten. He gripped the edge of the sink and let his body do what it needed to do, and somewhere beneath the misery and the fear he felt a strange kind of relief—that it was starting, that the waiting was over, that whatever was going to happen would happen now and he would not have to dread it anymore.

When the first wave passed he was trembling, his arms barely strong enough to hold him upright, his forehead slick with sweat. He ran the tap and splashed water on his face and rinsed his mouth and spat, and the water in the basin was tinged with something he did not want to examine too closely.

From the bathroom, silence. Then the tap running. Then Eleanor's voice, faint through the door. "Kerwin?"

"Here," he said. His voice sounded like it belonged to someone else, someone older and more broken. "I'm here."

"Are you—"

"No," he said, because there was no point in pretending. "Are you?"

A pause. Then, very quietly, "No."

The toilet flushed. The tap ran again. He heard her moving around in there, heard the small sounds of someone trying to put themselves back together, and he thought about going to her, about waiting outside the door, about offering some kind of comfort or assistance. But another cramp was building in his gut, slower this time but no less insistent, and he understood that comfort would have to wait, that they were both about to descend into something that would strip away everything but the bare fact of their bodies and what those bodies were capable of.

Time passed—he could not have said how much. The waves came and went, each one leaving him weaker than the last, and somewhere in the middle of it he became aware that the sounds from the bathroom had stopped and replaced by a silence that might have been recovery or something worse. He thought about calling out to her and asking if she was all right but his throat was raw and his voice had abandoned him.

The bathroom door opened.

She emerged looking like something that had been wrung out and hung up to dry, then taken down too soon. Her hair clung in damp ropes to her temples, her face was the same color as the hallway paint, and there was a faint, crystalline sheen at the corners of her mouth where the water hadn't quite washed everything away.

Eleanor pushed herself off the doorframe and made for the sitting room in careful increments; her feet found each patch of linoleum like she was testing ice. Kerwin watched her go in the watery light from the kitchen fixture, noting the particular way her shoulders hunched around herself and how her knees bent at slightly the wrong angles. By the time she reached the sofa she was shaking, she folded into it rather than sat, a slow collapse that ended with her curled on her side, one arm thrown over her eyes as if the lamplight were too bright.

He should go to her and sit beside her, he knew, offer some comfort, perhaps, but his legs would simply not cooperate. He leaned against the kitchen counter instead and breathed through his nose and waited for the next wave to roll up through him in a slow, inevitable arc, dragging everything with it. By the time he had registered what was happening his vision had gone thin and bright around the edges and he barely had time to turn back to the sink before his body emptied itself again with a violence that left him shaking.

"Kerwin?"

He glanced up. Eleanor was standing in the kitchen doorway now, one palm flat against the frame again as if she had never left it. Her pupils were blown wide, the green of her irises reduced to a thin ring around the black. She was looking at his hands, at the tendons standing out under the skin, at the way his shoulders had hiked up around his ears.

"You should sit down," she said.

"I can't—" Another cramp, smaller this time but still nearly unbearable. He gripped the edge of the sink and rode it out, his jaw clenched so tight he could hear his teeth grinding. "I can't make it to the sofa."

"Then don't." She crossed the kitchen in three unsteady steps and lowered herself to the floor, her back against the cabinets, her legs stretched out in front of her. "The floor is fine."

He stared at her for a moment, this strange woman sitting on his kitchen floor as though it were the most natural thing in the world, and then his legs made the decision for him; they buckled, and he slid down the face of the cabinets until he was sitting beside her, both of them staring at the opposite wall with the blank exhaustion of soldiers in a foxhole. Their shoulders almost touched; if either of them had relaxed by so much as an inch, they would have.

"Well," she said after a moment. "This is..."

Another cramp crawled through his gut, dragging a sheen of sweat to the surface of his skin. He closed his eyes until it passed. It did not, strictly speaking, pass; it retreated just enough to allow him to breathe again.

He laughed, or tried to; it came out as a wheeze, followed by a cough, followed by a renewed surge of nausea that he had to breathe through very carefully. "I did warn you."

"You did. You were very thorough." She closed her eyes and let her head fall back against the cabinet door with a soft thunk. "I should have listened."

"You were hungry."

"I was *stupid.*"

"Those aren't mutually exclusive."

She made a sound that might have been a laugh, cut short by a grimace. He watched her press a hand to her abdomen, her face contorting and then smoothing itself out through what was clearly an effort of will, before she swallowed convulsively several times in quick succession.

"Bathroom," she said, the word barely a whisper, and then she was scrambling to her feet and lurching down the hallway, and he heard the door slam and then the sounds that followed, and there was nothing he could do but sit there on the kitchen floor and listen and wait for his own body to betray him again.

It did, of course. It was only a matter of minutes before he was pulling himself upright by the edge of the counter and only seconds after that he was bent over the sink again, heaving until there was nothing left to heave and then heaving some more, his body apparently unconvinced that it had fully purged whatever poison they had introduced to it. The muscles of his abdomen screamed; his throat felt like it had been scoured with sandpaper; his eyes were streaming, the world contracted to the rectangle of ceiling he could see between the cabinets and the strip light, hairline cracks running like rivers through the paint.

He did not make it to the sink the next time.

The cramp hit mid-step and his legs simply stopped working; he went down hard on one knee, felt the shock of it travel up through his hip and into his spine, and then his stomach was turning itself inside out onto the kitchen floor, onto his own hands, onto the front of his shirt where it soaked through warm and reeking. He heard himself make a high, thin whine that came from somewhere outside of his body and he could not stop it or swallow it back, he could only kneel there, stuck in the spreading puddle of his own sick, watching it seep into the cracks between the linoleum tiles.

* * *

He crawled to the sink eventually, pulling himself up by the edge of the counter, his hands cramping into claws around the metal rim, fingers locking so tight he had to pry them open one by one when the wave finally passed. The water was cold, blessedly cold and he stuck his whole head under it, letting it run over his face, into his mouth and down the back of his neck where his shirt was plastered to his skin with sweat and sick. When he straightened, the kitchen tilted sideways in a perspective that did not correspond to any physics he understood, the ceiling somehow lower than it had been, the cabinets breathing at the corner of his vision, expanding and contracting in slow wet pulses like something alive.

From the bathroom, he heard Eleanor's knees hit the tile. A wet crack, the sound of bone on ceramic and then a moan that she had tried to muffle. Something splashed, something dripped, something else pattered down steadily and Kerwin Merle quickly found himself losing control of himself and the night in equal measure.

He blinked. The kitchen was still.

He was hallucinating. He *knew* he was hallucinating. This was what happened, he knew, when dehydration and fever and shock began to fray the edges of perception. He *knew* this.

"Kerwin."

Her voice came from very far away, or very close; he could not tell which. He turned and she was in the doorway, a pale smear of a woman, her face the color of something left too long underwater, her eyes too dark in their sockets, her freckles swimming across her cheeks. He blinked again and she was just Eleanor, nothing more than a sick woman holding onto the doorframe with both hands, her knees shaking, a dark stain spreading down the inside of her thigh that neither of them acknowledged.

"Bathroom," she said, her voice a scrape of rust on metal.

"I can't."

"Kerwin, you *have* to."

She was right. His bowels were cramping now with a different sort of urgency and he understood with terrible clarity that they could not both be in the bathroom at the same time, that there was only one toilet and two people who needed it.

He barely made it. She waited in the hallway; he heard her slide down the wall, her forehead thunking against her knees, whispering something that might have the word *no,* over and over, a quiet incantation against the next wave.

When he emerged she pushed past him without speaking. The door did not close all the way, and so he heard everything, leaning against the wall and feeling nothing except a dim, distant gratitude that he was not the one making those sounds at the moment.

He found her on the bathroom floor at some point, curled around the base of the toilet with her cheek pressed to the tile, her hair trailing in the bowl. He gathered it in his fist, heavy though it was, sodden with sweat and bile and held it away from her face while she retched and spat and brought up nothing but strings of foam that hung from her lips like something a spider might make. Her shoulders twitched with each convulsion. He was close enough to smell the acid staleness of her breath and to see the veins standing out in her temples, even to count the freckles on the back of her neck where the skin had gone over-pale and slick with sweat.

"Sorry," she whispered, when the wave had passed. "Sorry, I'm sorry—"

"Don't."

Later—minutes or hours, he could not have said—she crawled back to him with a washcloth she had rinsed in the sink. The fabric was green and mildewed at the edges but it was cool, and when she pressed it to his forehead he made a sound he had not intended to make, halfway between a sob and a sigh. She did not comment on it, she simply held the cloth there while he shook and then the smell of him must have hit her because she turned away, gagging, her body trying to wring itself out again.

"Sorry," she managed, when she could speak.

"Stop apologizing."

They ended up on the bathroom floor eventually. He was curled around the base of the toilet with his cheek against the cracked tile, the cold seeping into his skull and she had not quite made it past his legs before she'd given up, her weight now pressed against his calves, her breath dragging raggedly, thick and wet. The room smelled of bile and bleach and shit—at some point one or both of them had lost control of that too, and neither of them had acknowledged it, it rose up from the very seams of the place, the grout, the pitted ceramics, the dark wedge behind the toilet where light never reached.

"Kerwin," she said. Just his name.

"I'm here—"

The lights went out.

It happened without warning, the bathroom light, the small red eye of the smoke detector in the hallway, all of it gone at once, instantly swallowed into a darkness so complete that for a moment he thought he had gone blind. Eleanor made a sound, a sharp intake of breath that was either fear or another wave rising in her throat.

"Power's out," he said, his voice strange in the dark.

At some point he was back on the floor, and she was somewhere near him, and they found each other's hands in the dark and held on. Her fingers were slick with something he did not want to think about, his probably were too.

As his fever climbed, the walls started to breathe again, expanding and contracting in his peripheral vision and this time he did not try to blink it away. The cabinet above the sink appeared to open its mouth, he watched the hinges flex, saw the dark interior of it pulse, and something whispered from inside it, words he very nearly understood. The voices sounded like people he had seen somewhere, the woman with the crossword, the man on the bus who never looked up, the woman with the dog, Amir, even, with his chips and soda and neon signage. They were speaking to him. They told him that they had *always* been speaking to him; he had simply never been empty enough to hear.

You're ready now, someone said, or no one said.

He closed his eyes and the voices faded, and when he opened them Eleanor was watching him, her eyes too bright in the dark, her lips cracked and peeling.

"Did you hear that?" he asked.

"Hear what?"

"Nothing." He pressed his cheek back to the tile. "Nothing."

And then the dark shifted and he was somewhere else entirely. He was sixteen years old and the shop was bright and his father was on the floor with his head split open, blood pooling on the linoleum, and the boys were gone, the *cowards,* and his mother was standing in the doorway with her hand over her mouth, looking at him again. Not at his father, at *him.*

You did this, she said. *You let them in.*

He knew that. He had always known that.

You wanted this, she said, and her voice was different now, younger, not his mother's voice at all. *You wanted—*

"Kerwin?" It was Eleanor's voice, small and far away. "Kerwin, are you—"

"I'm here," he said, or tried to say. "I'm here."

She did not answer, and the dark went on.

* * *

He did not remember falling asleep. He remembered being awake, and then he remembered not being awake, and somewhere in between there was a gap that his mind refused to fill. He was on the bathroom floor, his shirt dried stiff against his chest, a shell of sweat and worse that crackled when he moved and Eleanor was no longer across his legs.

He sat up slowly, his head pounding, his vision swimming. The bathroom was murky with odd light and the smell was still there but fainter now, or perhaps he had simply grown used to it.

"Eleanor?"

No answer.

He pulled himself up by the edge of the sink on shaking legs, his foot slipping in something wet before he caught himself on the towel rail without looking down. The power was still out; the light switch did nothing when he tried it. He opened the bathroom door and the small light from the window hit him like a physical thing, making him squint.

She was in the sitting room. She had made it to the sofa somehow and was curled on her side with the blanket pulled up to her chin, her face slack with exhaustion. The relief that washed through him was so intense it made his knees buckle; he had to grab the doorframe to keep from falling.

He made it to his chair. The apartment was quieter than it had been in hours, the rain reduced to a soft patter against the windows, the wind gone still. His body felt hollowed out, scraped clean, an empty vessel that had been thrust full with sickness and was now simply empty.

He closed his eyes, and when he woke again Eleanor was still on the sofa. The power had come back on at some point while he slept; the lamp in the corner glowed weakly, left on from the night before, now restored to life. The apartment felt almost normal, like the storm had never happened.

She stirred, opened her eyes and looked at him.

"Hey," she said, her voice in tatters.

"Hey."

"We made it."

"Seems like."

She smiled, or tried to; it came out as a grimace, her cracked lips splitting fresh. "I feel like something that got scraped off a shoe."

"You look like it too."

"Charming." She pushed herself up slowly, wincing, her hand going to her stomach. "Is it over? The—" She gestured vaguely at her abdomen. "The everything?"

"I think so." He did not feel sick anymore, just exhausted in a way that went past tiredness into something more fundamental. "The worst of it, anyway."

She nodded and let her head fall back against the sofa cushions with a groan.

When she fell asleep again, he watched the slow rise and fall of her chest, the way her hand curled loosely against her collarbone and the dark circles under her eyes that looked like bruises in the dim light. Then he closed his eyes too, and let himself drift.

The day passed in fragments; they did not talk much. She slept on the sofa; he dozed in his chair; occasionally one of them would get up to use the bathroom or drink water from the sink, moving carefully like convalescents in a hospital ward. The apartment felt different somehow, smaller, maybe, or more intimate, as if the sickness had compressed the space between them until there was no room left for pretense.

By evening the rain had stopped entirely. The roads would be clear by morning, probably, and she could leave. She could go back to her studio and her half-deaf landlady and her life that she had described with such flat despair and he would be alone again, and everything would go back to the way it had been.

He did not want that. He was surprised by how much he did not want that.

"I should probably go," she said, as if she had heard his thoughts. She was sitting up now, the blanket pooled around her waist, her hair a matted mess that she had made no effort to fix. "Tomorrow, I mean. When the roads are clear."

"You could stay." The words came out before he could stop them. "If you wanted. A bit longer."

She looked at him. Her eyes were unreadable in the dim light. "Why?"

He did not have an answer. Or he had too many answers, none of which he could say aloud: *because you're the first person who has touched me in years, because you saw me at my worst and did not leave, because I am so tired of being alone that I would rather be sick with you than well by myself.* He said none of this.

"I don't know," he said instead. "I, however, wouldn't mind if you stayed."

She was quiet for a long moment. "I'm not in a rush to get back to—" A vague gesture at the window, at the world beyond it. "Any of it, really."

"Then stay."

"Okay." She said it simply, as if it were the most natural thing in the world. "Okay. I'll stay a bit longer."

The relief he felt was out of all proportion to the words. He nodded, not trusting himself to speak, and they sat in the pooling dark and did not look at each other.

As the apartment settled into its familiar creaks and groans, Kerwin turned on the other lamp in the sitting room, the one with the shade his mother had chosen, and the light it cast was warm and yellow and made the room feel almost cozy.

Eleanor was still on the sofa. She had been drifting in and out of sleep all evening, her body still recovering, her face still pale beneath the freckles. He had heated some water on the stove at some point and she had drunk half of hers before setting it aside, her hands wrapped around the mug for warmth.

"I think I'm going to wash my face," she said. Her voice was muzzy with exhaustion. "I feel human enough to try, anyway."

"Bathroom's free."

"I know." She pushed herself up, swaying slightly, and steadied herself on the arm of the sofa. "I won't be long."

He watched her go. She moved slowly, with one hand outstretched beside her for balance. The bathroom door opened, the light clicked on, and he heard the sink running followed by her small sound of relief at the coolness of it.

He closed his eyes. He was half-asleep when he heard the sound. A thump, maybe, or a crack, it was the sound of something hitting something else, hard, the dense acoustics of a body connecting with a solid surface. It came from the direction of the bathroom; it was difficult to tell, muffled as it was by the walls, blurred by the fog of exhaustion that had settled over his brain. He waited for the sound of her voice, for the sink turning off, for her footsteps in the hallway.

Nothing. He should get up, he knew, to check on her. But his body was so heavy and the chair was so soft, and surely she was fine, surely she had just dropped something, knocked something over…surely she would call out if she needed him.

"Eleanor?"

No answer.

The sink was still running. He could hear it, a thin trickle of water hitting porcelain, steady and unchanging. He should get up. He would get up. In just a moment. In just—

When he woke, it was morning. Sunlight was streaming through the windows, pale and watery, the first real sunlight he had seen in days. The lamp was still on, its yellow glow washed out by the brightness. The apartment was quiet, the sink no longer running.

He sat up slowly, blinking, his body stiff and aching from a night spent in the chair. The sickness had passed, he could feel the absence of that churning wrongness in his gut, the lightness of being empty but no longer emptying.

He stood. His legs were unsteady but functional; he made it to the hallway without falling and to the bathroom door without his knees giving out. He knocked, two quick raps, and waited.

He waited hardly at all before opening the door.

She was standing at the sink, her back to him, her hands braced on the edge of the basin.

"Morning," she said. She turned, and he saw the cut on her temple—a thin line of dried blood, already scabbing over, just above her left eyebrow. "I must have hit it on the toilet when I was sick. Didn't even notice until I looked in the mirror."

He stared at the cut, at the dark crust of blood, at the faint bruise already forming around the edges.

"Does it hurt?" he asked.

"Not really. It looks worse than it is." She touched it gingerly, winced, let her hand drop. "I'll live."

"Good," he said. "That's—good."

7

Staycation

"I'm sorry, sir, but we didn't deliver to your address."

The woman's voice was harried, half-drowned by the chaos on the other end of the line; someone was shouting about a route change and there was the clatter of what sounded like a filing cabinet being slammed shut. Kerwin pressed the receiver harder against his ear.

"Daily Bread," a woman said. She sounded harassed. In the background, phones rang in a chaotic, overlapping chorus.

"I am calling," Kerwin said, keeping his voice very level, "because the meals you delivered yesterday were spoiled. My guest and I have been violently ill for the last—"

"Name?"

"Merle. Twelve Grove Street."

He heard the click of keys. Eleanor was sitting up on the sofa now, watching him. She looked wrecked, still—pale and hollowed out, clutching at a blue towel like a security blanket. He avoided her eyes. He wanted to get this done, get the apology, get the refund and restore order to his universe.

"Sir?" The woman's voice had lost its rote impatience and replaced it with confusion. "You said Grove Street?"

Kerwin tightened his grip on the receiver.

"Sir," the woman repeated, "we don't have a delivery recorded for Grove Street."

"*Excuse* me?"

"The storm, sir" she said, as if he was unaware of the local weather. "The fleet was grounded on Friday afternoon...we didn't send anyone out in that weather. We're rescheduling everyone for today or tomorrow."

"There was a woman," he said slowly..."a driver...she got stranded here because of the storm."

"Sir, I don't have time to—" A voice in the background, urgent, and the woman broke off to answer it. When she came back her tone had frayed further. "We don't have anyone on the eastern route. No one went out that way. Are you sure it was Daily Bread?"

He looked at Eleanor; Eleanor looked back at him. Her brow had furrowed slightly, a question forming on her thin face.

He crossed the kitchen in three steps, reached down, and pinched the soft flesh of her upper arm between his thumb and forefinger hard enough to leave a mark.

"Ow!" She jerked away, rubbing the spot, her expression caught somewhere between confusion and outrage. "What the hell was that for?"

The relief was immediate and overwhelming; she was not a hallucination conjured by fever and loneliness and too many hours spent watching the same strip of street.

"Who are you talking to?" Eleanor asked, and then her gaze slid past him to the carrier bag on the counter and her face changed, alarm flooding in as she sat up straight, waving her hands in front of her chest—*no, no, no*—her eyes gone wide and slightly panicked.

"I don't want to get in trouble," she hissed. "Kerwin, hang up. Please! Hang up the phone! I wasn't supposed to—I took the van out before they grounded the fleet. They radioed the stand-down but I was already past the underpass and by then the water was too high to turn back. I didn't clock the return because there wasn't one. If they know I was out here with the equipment, that I kept going after the order came through..."

"Why would you be in trouble?" he asked, his hand covering the mouthpiece of the receiver.

But she was shaking her head, wouldn't answer, and on the phone the woman was still talking, her voice tinny and distant. "Sir? Sir, are you still there? I'm sorry, we're very busy, the storm set everything back, we have people waiting on deliveries that should have gone out days ago—what was it you needed?"

Eleanor was mouthing something at him now, her hands still moving in agitated little circles; the woman on the phone was waiting for an answer while the chaos in the background pressed against his ear and he found that he did not want to think about why Daily Bread had no record of Eleanor or why the eastern route had been canceled or what any of it meant. He wanted to hang up the phone and sit down and drink a cup of coffee and not think about anything at all.

On the other end of the line, the woman was still talking. "Sir? Hello? Do you want to reschedule for Monday or not?"

"No," he said. "I don't need anything. Cancel my account."

"Are you sure? We can offer you a discount, given the circumstances—"

"I'm sure."

He hung up before she could respond and stood there for a moment with his hand still on the receiver, feeling the plastic warm beneath his palm. Eleanor had gone quiet; when he looked at her she was slumped against the sofa cushions with her eyes closed, the tension draining out of her in visible increments.

"Thank you," she said without opening her eyes. "I just—I can't lose this job. I know that sounds pathetic, but it's the only thing I have."

He wanted to ask her why she had come to his door if the route had been canceled, and how she had found him at all . "Coffee?" he said instead.

She opened her eyes and smiled at him, a small, tired smile that did something ugly to his chest. "Please."

He filled the kettle and set it on the stove and did not think about the phone call at all.

They were on their second cup when she set hers down and stretched, wincing slightly as the vertebrae in her back popped. "Back in a minute," she said, and he nodded without looking up, listening to her footsteps on the stairs, the familiar creak of the third step from the top that he kept meaning to fix. He was thinking about nothing in particular when her voice came down from the landing.

"Kerwin? Kerwin, there's...something's coming out from under the door."

Something in her voice had him taking the stairs two at a time, and he found her standing in the hallway with her arms wrapped around herself, not touching anything, just looking down at the floor. There was a dark stain spreading out from under the bathroom door, seeping into the grain of the warped floorboards.

"What is that?" she asked.

"Leak," he said. The word came out before he'd thought it. "Must be a leak. The pipes up here are—this whole place is—"

He could hear himself making excuses and hated the sound of it. She lived in a studio with a half-deaf landlady; she'd told him so herself, but she was *young,* late twenties at most, the freckles across her nose making her look younger still. She was supposed to be living in squalor, passing through it on her way to something better.

He pushed past her, his shoulder brushing hers, and opened the bathroom door just wide enough to slip through.He pulled it shut behind him and stood there in the dim light with his back against the wood and his heart pounding in his ears.

The smell was worse in here. Much worse. Was that *shit* seeping out...?

He looked at the toilet, at the sink, at the cracked tiles on the floor where the *liquid*—where whatever it was had pooled and spread. He grabbed the towels from the rack, both of them, and dropped to his knees and began to mop, pressing the fabric against the floor, soaking up what he could. The towels turned dark. He wrung them out into the sink, watched the discolored water spiral down the drain, and did it again.

"Kerwin?" Her voice through the door, muffled. "Is everything—"

"Fine!" He wrung out another towel. "Just give me a minute."

He found more threadbare old towels in the cupboard under the sink, the kind his mother had kept for cleaning. He rolled one up and pressed it against the base of the door where the light came through, and then he stuffed another one along the edge of the tub, and another in the corner where the tiles met the wall. By the time he was done the bathroom looked like some kind of makeshift dam.

He washed his hands, and then he washed them again. He splashed water on his face and made himself look in the mirror at his own patchy stubble and bloodshot eyes and sagging skin. He gathered the wet towels, heavy now, sodden, reeking, and bundled them against his chest and opened the door.

Eleanor was still standing in the hallway, exactly where he'd left her. The precise angle of her jaw was set, her dark eyes watchful as she took in the towels, his face, and the closed door behind him.

"Pipes..." He shifted the towels in his arms, something dripped onto the floor and he stepped over it. "Something's burst, I think. Or cracked. I'll have to call the landlord."

"Is it bad?"

"Bad enough." He moved past her toward the stairs. "Use the kitchen sink for now, for washing, until I can get someone in to look at it."

"Okay." She followed him down, her footsteps light behind his. "Do you need help? With the—"

"No. I've got it."

He stuffed the towels into the washing machine, turned the dial to hot, and stood there for a moment with his hands braced on the edge of the basin, breathing through his mouth.

"Kerwin?"

He turned. She was standing in the kitchen doorway, one hand pushing her short bangs out of her eyes, watching him with an expression he couldn't parse.

"I'm sorry," she said. "That you have to deal with all this. The leak, now, and me, and—"

"Don't." He shook his head. "Don't apologize."

"I seem to do that a lot."

"You do."

She almost smiled, and he caught a glimpse of the small gap between her front teeth. "Bad habit."

They stood there for a moment, the washing machine beginning to churn behind him, the light coming through the kitchen window in pale gold bars. She was wearing one of his sweaters—he couldn't remember when he'd given it to her or if he'd given it to her at all—so maybe she'd just *taken* it, found it somewhere and her hair was tangled and her face was still too pale and she was looking at him like she was waiting for something, though he couldn't have said what.

"Kitchen sink," she said finally. "Right. No problem."

"I'll get you a washcloth."

"You don't have to—"

Kerwin got her a washcloth, and a towel, and a bar of soap that had been his mother's, still wrapped in paper that had gone thin at the edges and he set them on the counter beside the sink and stepped back to give her room.

"Thank you," she said.

"It's just a washcloth."

"I know." She turned on the tap, tested the water with her fingers, shrugged. "Thank you anyway."

He should have left and given her privacy, but he stood in the doorway and watched her cup water in her hands and bring it to her face, watched the droplets run down her wrists and drip from her elbows, watched her close her eyes and tip her head back, her throat exposed, the water catching the light where it clung to her skin. The sweater had slipped further, baring the curve of her shoulder, and her dark hair was wet now at the ends, dripping onto the collar, and she made a small sound of relief that he felt in his gut like a hook.

She opened her eyes and caught him watching.

"Sorry," he said, and looked away.

"Don't..." He heard her turn off the faucet, reach for the towel. "Don't apologize."

"I do that a lot."

"You do." There was a smile in her voice.

She was drying her face, the towel pressed against her eyes, and he made himself turn and walk out of the kitchen, climb the stairs and not look back.

He went into the bedroom and closed the door, leaning against it with his eyes shut and his breath coming too fast and his cock already straining against the front of his pants.

What if he hadn't left? He thought, unwrapping the fantasy from its coil inside of his mind. What if…when she'd bent over the sink with her throat bared and water running down her wrists, he had crossed the kitchen and pressed himself against her from behind, pinned her hips to the counter with the weight of him? What if he had ground his cock against the cleft of her ass through the thin fabric of her borrowed clothes—*his clothes, she was wearing his clothes!*—and felt her gasp, felt her push back against him or try to pull away, it didn't matter which, both versions played out behind his eyelids in parallel. What if he had reached around and cupped her breast, found the nipple through the sweater, felt it harden under his thumb. What if she had said his name in the same voice she used for the banter, what if she had said *Kerwin* and it had sounded like *yes*.

He had his cock out now, fisting it roughly, his other hand braced against the door. The room smelled of unwashed skin, stale sweat, the feral musk of a man who had been ill and hadn't properly bathed and underneath it all the sour, savage stench of his own arousal. The bathroom smell was still in his nostrils too, that sweetish rot, and somehow that made the whole thing more depraved: he was jerking himself to the thought of her while the stink of the upstairs bathroom clung to his clothes, to his hands, even to the air he was breathing in ragged gasps.

What if he had yanked the sweater up over her head and bent her forward over the sink, her cheek against the cold porcelain, her dark hair trailing in the basin. What if he had pulled down whatever she was wearing underneath, underwear, nothing, he didn't know, he hadn't looked, he was looking now in his mind's eye—and pushed into her without asking, without waiting, just taken what he wanted because she was here and she was warm and she said his words back to him and no one had done that in so long, so long, so fucking long—

He bit down on the meat of his palm to keep from groaning. His teeth sank in and the pain was clarifying, was filthy, was exactly what he deserved; was pleasure, made more complex. He could taste the bathroom on his hands, whatever he had mopped up from the floor and still he didn't stop, couldn't stop, his hips snapping forward into the tunnel of his fist while the fantasy unraveled in vivid, shameful detail, her sounds, her skin, the wet grip of her, the way she would say his name, the way she would echo him, the way she would finally, finally answer—

He came with a choked-off grunt, spilling over his fingers, his knees almost buckling. The orgasm tore through with claws, leaving him hollowed out and shaking, slumped against the door with his softening cock in his hand and his own bite mark throbbing in his palm.

The smell hit him then. All of it. The come cooling on his fingers, the unwashed reek of his own groin, the lingering rot from the bathroom, the sour tang of shame. He looked down at himself—pants undone, shirt untucked, a gaunt man with his cock out in the middle of the morning, alone in a room that smelled like shit and sex and desperation.

He cleaned himself with a dirty shirt from the floor and tucked himself away, washing his hands in the little sink in the corner that his mother had used for her night-time ablutions, scrubbing until his skin was red.

The bite mark on his palm was deep, a crescent of purple indentations that would bruise. He pressed his thumb into it, felt the pain flare, and was grateful for it.

He went back downstairs.

She was sitting on the sofa, looking out the window at the rain, her dark bangs puffed up across her forehead. The sweater had slipped off her shoulder again, and she did not fix it.

"All right?" she asked without turning.

"Fine." His voice came out steadier than he expected. "Just checking on the leak."

"Is it worse?"

"About the same."

She nodded, still not looking at him, and he sat down in his chair and folded his hands in his lap to hide the bite mark and did not think about what he had just done or the fantasy that was still playing out in some back room of his mind, on loop, forever.

She turned and smiled at him—that crooked smile, the fucking gap in her teeth and said, "Rematch?"

He blinked. "What?"

"Scrabble." She nodded toward the coffee table, where the battered box still sat from before, the lid warped, half the letters missing. "You owe me. I was winning before we—" She gestured vaguely at her stomach.

"You weren't winning."

"I absolutely was!"

"Fine," he said. "Rematch."

She pulled the box onto her lap and began setting up the board, her dark hair falling forward, her fingers sorting through the depleted bag of tiles. He watched her hands, the bitten nails, the freckles on her knuckles, and tried not to think about what those hands would feel like on his skin.

He failed.

***

They were three rounds into the rematch when the buzzing started. Eleanor's head came up and she patted the cushions around her until she found the source of it, her phone, wedged between the sofa arm and the seat, its screen lit up with a name he couldn't read from where he sat.

She looked at it and did not answer.

"Don't let me stop you," he said, nodding at the phone.

"I'm aware." She didn't look at him, just jabbed at the screen and tossed it face-down on the coffee table.

The phone buzzed again, and again. A persistent, angry vibration that made the tiles on the board shiver.

"You appear to be in demand."

"Mm." She wasn't looking at him, was instead rearranging her letters with studied concentration. "My mother." She said it the way you'd say *cockroach*. "She's got a sixth sense for when I'm somewhere she can't get at me. Probably already ringing the hospitals."

"Have you told her where you are?"

"God, no." Eleanor placed a word using his L and sat back. "She'd have the police here within the hour. Her only daughter, alone with a strange man." She glanced up at him through her lashes, something steeled in her expression. "No offense."

He grimaced.

The phone buzzed again.

"Christ, she's relentless." Eleanor picked it up, stared at the screen for a long moment and then switched it off entirely. "You'd think after two years she'd take a hint. There," she said. "Problem solved."

"And when she's rung every hospital in the county?"

"Then she'll have wasted a perfectly good afternoon, won't she have?" Eleanor dropped the dead phone beside the board. "Anyway, the battery was almost gone. It would have died on its own soon enough."

He wanted to ask more about her mother, the punch and the two years of silence between them but something in her posture suggested that line of inquiry would not be well received, so he looked at his tiles instead and tried to find a word that would not embarrass him.

The phone sat between them, dark and silent, and neither of them mentioned it again.

The knock, when it came, sounded just after dark.

Three quick raps, evenly spaced, and Kerwin's whole body went rigid in his chair. No one knocked on his door. No one *had* knocked on his door in years, Amir left his deliveries on the step, the postman shoved letters through the slot and anyone else who might have had business with him had long since given up trying.

Eleanor looked up from the board, her hand frozen mid-reach for a tile. "Expecting someone?"

"I am not." His voice came out strangled. He cleared his throat. "No."

Another knock. Patient, and unhurried.

His first instinct was to hide and press himself flat against the wall, to wait for whoever it was to give up and go away the way he had done a hundred times before when the world came calling and he refused to answer. But

Eleanor was here, and the thought of someone seeing her, seeing *them*, sent a spike of panic through his gut—

They would *know*. Whoever was at the door would take one look at him, see that he had long gone past careless into derelict and then at her, young, pretty, wearing his clothes, her dark hair mussed and her feet bare and they would know exactly what he'd been thinking. What he'd done, upstairs, with his hand on his cock and her name caught in his throat. They would see it written on his face, the wanting, the shame, the fantasies of pinning her to the sink, of her gasping his name, of taking what he wanted because she was here and she was warm and no one else had been warm in so long—

"Kerwin?" Eleanor was staring at him, her brow furrowed. "You look like you're about to be sick."

"Behind the sofa. Now."

She blinked. "I'm sorry?"

"I need you to get behind the sofa."

"Have you lost your mind? What's wrong with you?"

"I am aware of how this sounds…"

"Then you're aware that you sound certifiable!" She hadn't moved, was looking at him like he'd sprouted a second head. "What exactly do you think is going to happen if someone sees me sitting on your sofa?"

He couldn't tell her the truth, that they would think he was the kind of man who kept young women in his crumbling hovel, who looked at them the way he had looked at her, who wanted things he had no right to want. That they would be correct.

Another knock.

"I am asking you to do something that makes no sense to you," he said, and his hands were doing something strange, opening and closing at his sides like he didn't know what to do with them, "and I am asking you to do it anyway." He rubbed the back of his neck, looked at the door, looked back at her. "That is—that's all I can—please. Eleanor."

"That's not an explanation."

"No." He was at the window now, peering through the gap in the curtains, his fingers white-knuckled on the fabric. "It isn't."

She stood up from the sofa and then quickly sat back down. Her hands were in her lap and then they weren't; she was twisting the hem of his sweater between her fingers. "Kerwin, you're scaring me."

"I know." He let the curtain fall. "I'm sorry. I'm—" He pressed the heels of his hands against his eyes for a moment, then dropped them. "Behind the sofa. Please. Just until I see who it is."

Another knock, and she flinched. He saw it in the small jerk of her shoulders, the way her eyes went to the door.

"This is insane," she said, but her voice had lost its edge. "You know that, right I'm not crouching behind your sofa like a—like your mistress! Who do you think is out there?" she asked, quieter now.

"I don't know."

"Then why—"

"I don't *know*."

They stared at each other across the dim room, and he could see his fear bleeding into her, occupying the space between them.

"If it's the police, I'm standing up and telling them you've had a psychotic break."

"It isn't the police."

"You can't possibly know that."

She held his gaze for another long moment, and then, to his profound relief, she sighed, quietly got up from the sofa and crouched behind it, her dark head disappearing below the line of the cushions.

"I want it on record that this is the most ridiculous thing I've ever done," she hissed. "And you owe me an explanation. This is ridiculous! If it's the police, I'm standing up."

"It's not the police!"

"How do you know?"

He crossed to the door, his socks silent on the floorboards, his heart hammering against his ribs. He pressed his shaking hands flat against his thighs for a moment, steadying himself, and then he opened the door.

Four people stood in the hallway, and he knew all of them.

That was the first thing that registered, before anything else— he *knew* them. Not their names, not their lives, but their faces; he had watched them for years from his window, had cataloged their routines the way a naturalist might catalog wildlife.

Amir was in front, wearing a suit that was dark and ill-fitting as if borrowed from someone larger, and his face wore an expression Kerwin had never seen on it before; calm and patient, as though he had been waiting for this and was in no particular hurry now that it had arrived. Behind him stood the woman with the gray dog, though there was no dog now; just the woman herself, her hair pinned back from her face in its usual way, her body wrapped in a charcoal suit that matched her coat, and she was smiling at him in a way he was not certain he had ever seen her smile at anything. Beside her, the man from the bus, the one who sat in the same seat every morning with his newspaper folded to the crossword, who Kerwin had studied in peripheral glances for years without ever meeting his eye, was looking up directly at Kerwin now, and he was smiling too.

And at the back, half-hidden by the others, a teenager, a boy, really, sixteen or seventeen, with acne scars on his cheeks and a suit that was too big in the shoulders. Kerwin had seen him before, somewhere, couldn't place where—the bus stop, maybe, or the corner shop, one of the dozens of faces that populated the edges of his world without ever entering it. The boy was holding a Styrofoam container, the kind takeouts came in, wrapped in a plastic bag printed with THANK YOU THANK YOU THANK YOU in red letters.

The smell of food hit him.

Hot food. Something rich and savory, meat and fat and salt, and his stomach cramped so hard he nearly doubled over. When had he last eaten? The Scrabble, the sickness, the days blurring together—he couldn't remember the last time he had put anything in his mouth except coffee and tap water, he hadn't wanted to, really, after what they both went through and now here was this smell, this impossible smell, and his mouth was flooding with saliva and his hands were shaking and he wanted—

He wanted to grab the container from the boy's hands and tear it open and shove whatever was inside into his mouth without chewing, just swallowing and swallowing and swallowing to fill the void that had opened up inside of him.

"Mr. Merle," said Amir, his voice softer than Kerwin had expected, formal and almost gentle. "We've brought you something."

The four of them stood there in the hallway, smiling their knowing smiles, the smell of hot food curling around them like smoke, and Kerwin stood in the doorway with his hand on the frame and his stomach howling and his shame like a bolus in his throat.

Behind him, hidden behind the sofa, Eleanor did not make a sound.

"May we come in?" Amir asked politely.

And Kerwin, who had not let anyone other than Eleanor into his home in years, inexplicably stepped aside to welcome in a group of strange individuals who were, somehow, even stranger together than they were on their own.

II

Part Two

Proverbs 23:1-2: Consider carefully what is before you; and put a knife to your throat if you are a man given to appetite.

8

The Gastronauts

The four of them filed in, and the apartment shrank around them. Kerwin had not realized how small his sitting room was until there were bodies filling it—Amir first, then the woman with the gray dog, then the man from the bus, then the teenager with the Styrofoam container clutched tight to his chest. They moved with an odd formality, as if they had rehearsed this and knew exactly where they were meant to stand. The smell of the food came with them, rich and savory though something underneath it had begun to turn, a sourness creeping in at the edges that Kerwin tried not to notice.

Eleanor's head appeared over the back of the sofa.

Amir saw her at once. There was a tightening around the eyes, a small *tsk* of his tongue against his teeth, and something in his gaze made Kerwin's stomach drop through the floor.

"What have you done?" Amir asked. His voice was soft and almost gentle.

"I haven't *done* anything!" Kerwin was backing up as he said it, his hip catching the edge of the coffee table, tiles scattering. "She's not—if you're thinking I've done something to her, I haven't, she came in from the storm, she wanted to stay, I didn't—"

Amir had already crossed the room and was standing in front of Eleanor now, close enough to touch. He reached toward the cut on her temple, dark and crusted against her pale skin. "Your head. What happened to your head?"

"Don't touch her." The words came out sharper than Kerwin intended, loud in the cramped room. "Get away from her."

Amir's hand stopped, hovering an inch from Eleanor's face. His mouth twitched at the corner, not quite a smile.

Eleanor flinched back against the sofa cushions, her dark eyes darting between them. "Kerwin?" Her voice had gone thin. "Who are these people? What's happening?"

The woman with the gray dog had moved to the window and was looking around the room with an expression of calm appraisal, as if she were taking inventory of everything she saw: the rickety end table, the dusty furniture, the threadbare carpet worn through in patches. The man from the bus stood by the door with his hands clasped in front of him, very still, his thin smile fixed in place. The teenager shifted his weight from foot to foot, the Styrofoam container rustling in its plastic bag.

"I think," Amir said, turning away from Eleanor at last, "that it would be best if we explained ourselves." He looked around the room as if seeing it for the first time. "Do you have somewhere we can sit?"

"The kitchen—" Kerwin started, but the kitchen was too narrow, he knew it even as he said it, there was no room for six people in that cramped galley.

"Here will do," the woman with the gray dog said. She had already settled herself into his mother's chair by the window and was smoothing her charcoal skirt over her knees with perfect composure.

Eleanor looked young and frightened in his too-large shirt, that fucking cut on her temple standing out livid against her skin. Her hand drifted toward her phone on the coffee table, and Kerwin remembered then that the battery had died hours ago. There was no one she could call, no one who knew she was here, no one who would come looking.

Amir noticed the movement. "That won't help you," he said, not unkindly. "We're not here to hurt you. *Either* of you."

"Then what are you here for?" Eleanor's voice had steadied slightly, but that sharpness was back, the part of her that pushed and prodded and didn't let things go. "Breaking into someone's apartment in the middle of the night isn't exactly a social call."

"We didn't break in." Amir lowered himself onto the other end of the sofa, closer to Eleanor than Kerwin would have liked. "Mr. Merle invited us, and it's hardly the middle of the night."

"I didn't—" Kerwin started.

"You opened the door and you stepped aside." Amir's eyes met his, two soothing pools of brown. "That is invitation enough."

The man from the bus had taken the only other chair, leaving Kerwin standing in the middle of his own sitting room like a guest in someone else's home.

"Sit down, Mr. Merle," Amir said. "Please. There is much to discuss."

Kerwin didn't move. "I'd prefer to stand."

"Suit yourself."

The silence stretched. Eleanor was looking at him and he wanted to tell her it was going to be all right but he didn't know if that was true, really, and lying to her seemed worse somehow than saying nothing at all.

"Well?" Eleanor said finally. Her voice cracked slightly on the word. "You said you were going to explain...so...*explain*."

Something in her tone, the impatience perhaps, as if they were at a restaurant and the service had been slow made Kerwin want to laugh. If he stopped to think it through from beginning to end he might have doubled over with it right there in his cramped sitting room with its water stains and his dead mother's chair because the whole thing was absurd, wasn't it? His entire existence since she had come through his door had taken on a waxy quality of unreality, a fever dream he kept expecting to wake from. He had spent years with nothing happening except for the woman with the gray dog at eight-fifteen and Amir's voice through the floor and then there had been a storm, and a horrible meal, and a young girl with soft skin and a gap in her teeth, and now these strangers, these *freaks,* sat around him like guests at a party. He had invited some sort of cult into his home and it seemed normal—natural, even, as if this was what had been waiting for him all along.

Amir smiled. It was not a reassuring smile. "We call ourselves the Gastronauts," he said, calm as you please.

* * *

"The Gastronauts," Eleanor repeated. She was sitting up now, her hands wrapped around one knee, that prior alertness back in her face. "That's not a word."

"It is to you *now,*" replied the woman with the gray dog, speaking for the first time. Her voice was softer than Kerwin had expected, almost musical, completely at odds with the severe set of her face. "A Gastronaut is—we're anti-gourmands, I suppose you could say. We pursue..." She took a deep breath, started again. "There are things you can only see when you're emptied out," she continued quickly. "We chase what happens when your body turns against itself."

"So you poison yourselves."

"We *open* ourselves," Amir corrected. "There's a difference."

"That's—" Eleanor stopped. "What does that even *mean?*"

Amir leaned forward, his elbows on his knees. He had the posture of a man settling in to tell a long story, and Kerwin found himself tensing, bracing for something.

"I have watched you for a long time, Mr. Merle," said Amir, ignoring Eleanor's question entirely. "From the shop below. I have thought, for years now, that you might be sympathetic to our cause but this is not the sort of thing that can be pushed." He spread his hands, palms up, a gesture of openness that didn't reach his eyes. "A person must be ready, and most importantly, they must come to it themselves."

"Ready for what?"

"For the emptying. The *purge.*" Amir's gaze was steady and unblinking. "For what comes after."

The smell from the container had worsened. Kerwin could feel it at the back of his throat now, thick and cloying and he swallowed against it, trying to focus on what Amir was saying. Eleanor was leaning forward now, her fear giving way to that desperate need for meaning that Kerwin had seen in her from the beginning. He understood it, he supposed. He hadn't had dreams since before his father's death, hadn't wanted anything badly enough to chase it, but he remembered what the horizon looked like to a young person, yawning blank and featureless, nothing to walk toward and nothing to run from. For a smart girl—because even though he'd focused primarily on her body, she could hold a conversation and match him word for word—stuck in the doldrums of a pointless job, this must feel like discovering a trapdoor in a room she'd thought she knew. A way out more than a way down.

Kerwin was less certain.

"Why do you think I took the shop?" Amir asked. He was looking at Kerwin now, only at Kerwin, and there was something almost tender in his expression. "Your mother's estate, the lawyers, the back and forth, I could have fought it, of course I could have. I had grounds, but I didn't, because I *wanted* to be here. I wanted to wait."

"Wait for what?"

"For *you*, Kerwin. For you to be ready."

The woman with the gray dog shifted in her chair. "Don't you think there are other streets I could walk down, Kerwin?" She said his name like they were old friends. "Other places to take my morning walk?"

Kerwin stared at her. Eight-fifteen every morning for as long as he could remember. He had thought he was watching her, which seemed quaint now, naive, even...he had thought—

"I own a car," the man from the bus said. His voice was flat, uninflected, the voice of someone reading from a script. "Why would I need the bus?"

The teenager shifted his weight, rustling the container. "There are other places I can smoke."

"My son," the man from the bus said, placing a hand on the boy's shoulder. The boy flinched slightly at the touch but didn't pull away.

Kerwin's mouth had gone dry. Was it possible, then, that all of them had been watching him, waiting for him, arranging their lives around his routines? He wanted to ask why and demand answers but the words wouldn't come, his throat had closed around them.

"And me?" Eleanor's voice cut through the silence, thin and sure. "Was I part of this too?"

Amir turned to her, and his expression softened in a way that made Kerwin want to pinch very hard at the skin tags under the man's eyes.

"Being on Mr. Merle's route was no accident, Eleanor. Daily Bread has several drivers and you were only assigned to the eastern route less than a week ago. Do you remember who made that decision?"

She was quiet for a moment, her brow furrowed. "My supervisor, Mr. Haddad."

"My cousin." Amir spread his hands again, that gesture of false openness. "We have a sense for these things...people who are ready. For people who are—" He paused, searching for the word. "Empty enough."

The smell was unbearable now. Kerwin's eyes were watering with it, his stomach turning over and over, and still no one else seemed to notice. The teenager stood there holding that container like it was perfectly normal and like the stench of it wasn't filling the room, fogging everything with its film.

"Who are you?" Eleanor whispered. She had gone pale again, the freckles standing out against the bridge of her nose. "What do you actually want?"

Amir settled back against the sofa cushions. He looked, Kerwin thought, like a man who had been waiting a long time to tell a story and was finally being given permission.

"We are the Gastronauts," he said again. "Anti-gourmands, like Mallie said. Seekers after transcendence through the body's rebellion against itself." He paused, let the words settle. "And we have been around since the beginning."

"The beginning of what?" Kerwin managed.

"Of *everything*, Mr. Merle." Amir's eyes glittered in the dim light. "Of God and man and the long war between them. Of the fruit and the serpent and the woman who was brave enough to eat it."

Eleanor scoffed. "You're talking about the Bible? The garden of Eden?"

"I'm talking about the truth." Amir was quiet for a moment, studying them both, Kerwin on his feet, Eleanor on the sofa with her hands wrapped around her knee. He seemed to be deciding something. "They said the apple was knowledge and that Eve's sin was curiosity, but what the disciples got wrong was the parameters of consumption...specifically *why* God forbade it." He shook his head slowly. "Eve couldn't eat the apple in a particular way, for a very particular reason. Anything else you've learned is the children's version."

"And the real version?"

Amir looked at the woman with the gray dog again. Something passed between them, and then Amir leaned forward, elbows on his knees.

"The apple fell from the tree days before Eve found it and by then, it was already soft and browning at the edges, the skin split where the wasps had been. She knew, in and of herself that she should have left it there, but she picked it up anyway, and she didn't eat it—such was her shame—she hid it. *Inside* herself. Between her legs, during her monthly, where Adam wouldn't think to look."

He said this plainly, as if he were describing something that had happened to a neighbor.

"She carried it there for days and her own heat softened it further, and then the apple changed inside of her, ripening into something else entirely. She was ashamed, of course. She couldn't stand to be near Adam because she knew she couldn't lie to him and so she hid by the river in a pool made by a clump of roots, where she could cool herself and drink and plan her next steps."

Eleanor had gone still, her foot no longer tapping, her hands tight on her knee.

"The serpent found her sleeping in the shallows. He coiled on the bank and watched her and when she woke, he asked what she had between her legs."

Amir paused, rubbing his palms on his thighs, an oddly nervous gesture for such a calm man.

"She told him the truth because this was before the fall, she *could not* lie, and said it was the fruit of the tree that they were forbidden to eat from and the serpent said—" He put on a voice here, higher, almost wheedling "*—Oh, good. Thank the LORD. I'm starving, you see. I need something to eat.*"

"Eve said he couldn't have it, that the Lord had forbidden it and the serpent, in his great cunning, asked if she would really let him die, starving on the riverbank while she hoarded God's bounty inside herself."

Amir's eyes moved to Kerwin, then back to Eleanor.

"Her guilt was already eating at her from the inside and so she said no, she wouldn't let him die. She lay back in the water and opened her legs and let the serpent eat."

The room was very quiet. Kerwin felt as if something hot and viscous had broken over his head.

"His tongue was forked, of course," continued Amir, wiping roughly at his mouth, "And he licked at her, tasting the fruit where it pressed against her flesh, and his tongue found the hard nub at the top of her seam, and Eve—she'd never felt anything like it. Her body didn't know what was happening, and she started to shake."

He leaned forward slightly, and something in his voice shifted into the cadence of someone who had told this story many times and knew exactly where to pause. Kerwin felt himself leaning in despite himself, the resistance in him going slack and he thought, or would have thought, were he capable of focusing on anything other than the shape of Amir's lips and what might pass through them next: *this is how it happens. This is how people end up believing things.*

"The apple was rotten by then, as soft as old meat and crawling with larvae. She could feel them wriggling against her as the serpent's tongue worked deeper, coaxing the fruit down, and the pleasure built and built until she couldn't tell it apart from the revulsion anymore. And when she finally came, when her back arched and she cried out loud enough to scatter the birds and shake them loose from their trees, the apple slid out of her, the serpent caught it in his mouth and then swallowed a large chunk of it whole."

Eleanor made a small sound. Kerwin didn't look at her.

"The serpent was writhing by then, his coils twisting in the mud, his eyes rolled back in his head. Whatever had been fermenting inside of her for days was doing something to him, he thrashed and shuddered and made horrible sounds and Eve watched him and didn't understand what she was seeing, only that it looked like agony and ecstasy at once and that she wanted it too.

The serpent looked at her afterwards, this human woman who'd just given him everything and he said, *Eve, the things I've seen...you have to eat from the apple. You have to.*"

Amir sat back.

"Eve looked at the core, the seeds and the little brown flesh that was left after the serpent's feast, still squirming with worms and she wasn't disgusted. She picked it up and bit into it, and the taste was—" He stopped. Shook his head. "There aren't words for what it tasted like, I'm sure, but she saw God. For the first time, she saw his true face."

He was quiet for a moment.

"That's what really happened in the garden. Eve didn't eat from the tree because she wanted knowledge—that was why she *took* the apple. Curiosity, greed, call it what you will, but she didn't eat it. She hid it. She carried it with her, tucked against her body and the guilt of what she'd done rotted it from the inside out." He paused, letting this settle. "The serpent found her later, weeping over the ruined thing, and do you know what he told her? He told her to eat it anyway. He told her the rot was the *point*. That the apple she'd stolen was never going to give her what she wanted, but the apple she'd *ruined*—the apple that had fermented in her guilt and her shame and her fear of what she'd done—that apple could set her free." He looked at Kerwin. "*That's* what we chase, that's what the Gastronauts are. We are people who understand that corruption is not the enemy of transcendence, it is the doorway. We are people who understand that this is the only way man might escape himself."

The room was silent. Kerwin could hear his own heartbeat and Eleanor's breathing, quick and shallow beside him. The smell from the container pulsed and throbbed, filling up all the space between them.

"You're insane," Eleanor said, but her voice had no conviction in it. "You're all insane."

"Perhaps." Amir didn't seem bothered by the accusation, fully immersed as he was in his own peculiarity. "Most true things sound insane at first, just as most prophets are called madmen before they are called saints."

"You're not a prophet."

"No." He tilted his head, considering. "But I have seen what you saw in your sickness, Eleanor. I have heard the voices that spoke to you when you were emptied out." His eyes moved to Kerwin. "Both of you heard them, didn't you?"

Kerwin's throat tightened. His gut was heavy and he felt hot, too hot, with the whole room closing in on him...there *were* those voices in the dark...the cabinet opening its mouth and the wild, utterly *mad* feeling that something was speaking to him, had perhaps always been speaking to him and he had simply never been empty enough to hear.

He understood it, he supposed, watching her lean forward with that hunger in her face. He had done the same thing himself, hadn't he? He'd shut himself off so completely, for so many years, that he had numbed himself not only to the pain but to the pleasure too; for anything to register now it had to be extreme enough to break through the scar tissue he'd built around himself. When he'd come the other day, his hand on his cock and her name in his throat, it had been like a cannon blast, white behind his eyes, his whole body seizing with it—the good had to feel like transcendence now, like revelation, like being flayed open and put back together wrong, or it simply felt like nothing at all.

"How do you know about that?" Eleanor's voice was barely a whisper.

"Because I heard them too. We all did—" Amir gestured at the others "—that's how you know you're ready, more precisely, how you know you've been chosen."

"Chosen for what?"

Amir looked at the teenager, who stepped forward at last, holding out the container in both hands like an offering. The plastic bag rustled—THANK YOU THANK YOU THANK YOU—and the smell intensified, rich and rotten.

"Your second communion," Amir said. "If you're willing."

Kerwin stared at the container. The smell of it was unbearable, thick and sweet and wrong, and his stomach cramped around the nothing inside of it.

"No," he said.

The word came out before he had consciously formed it, blunt and final, and he felt the relief of it immediately, a door slamming shut, a lock engaging, the familiar comfort of refusal. This was what he knew how to do. It was the only thing he had ever been good at, really; saying no, shutting down, pulling the drawbridge up and flooding the moat and sitting alone in his tower while the world went on without him. He had spent decades perfecting this particular skill, and it had kept him alive, if not quite living, and he was not about to abandon it now because a shopkeeper in a borrowed suit had told him a dirty story about Eve's vagina.

"No," he said again, more firmly. "I think you should leave. All of you. I think you should take your—your container and your stories and get out of my apartment before I call someone."

He did not specify who he would call, but the threat sounded like something a normal person might say when four strangers appeared in their sitting room and invited them to such a dinner party, and he clung to it.

Amir did not move. None of them moved. They remained in their positions scattered around his sitting room with their patient faces and their knowing eyes and waited, the way they had apparently been waiting for years, and the silence that followed his refusal was not the shocked silence of people who had been told no but the calm, unhurried silence of people who had expected it.

"Of course," Amir said, inclining his head. "Of course, Mr. Merle. We would never presume."

But he did not move toward the door.

Eleanor was watching Kerwin. He could feel her gaze on the side of his face, the full weight of her attention and he did not look at her because he knew with a certainty that went deeper than thought that if he looked at her now he would see something in her face that would undo him. Curiosity, maybe, or worse, hope that he might change his mind.

"Kerwin," she said quietly.

"No."

"I'm not asking you to —"

"I said *no*, Eleanor." He was gripping the arm of his chair now, his knuckles white, his voice harder than he intended. "This is my home. These people are strangers. They've just told us a story about a woman hiding a rotten apple inside her — her —" He could not bring himself to say the word, which infuriated him. "And now they want us to follow them into a basement. Can you hear yourself? Can you hear how that sounds?"

"I can hear how it sounds," she said, drawing out her vowels as if he was slow. "I can also hear the voices we both heard when we were sick. Can you explain *those?*"

He could not. He had been trying not to think about the cabinets breathing, the whispers from inside them, the voices that had sounded like people he knew, people he had watched for years from his window. *You're ready now*, someone had said, or no one had said, and the memory of it sat in his chest like a fish bone that he could not cough up.

"Coincidence," he said. "Fever and dehydration. The brain does strange things when the body —"

"When the body is emptied out," Mallie finished softly from his mother's chair. "Yes. That's rather the point."

He wanted to hit her. The urge rose in him so suddenly and so completely that he had to grip the chair harder to keep himself seated, his fingers aching with the force of it. How dare she sit there, in his mother's chair, wearing his mother's knowing expression, finishing his sentences as though she had earned the right? She had walked her dog past his window for years and he had timed his breathing to her footsteps and she had known, the whole time, she had been watching him the way he thought he was watching her, and the violation of it was so profound that for a moment he could not breathe.

"Get out," he said, and his voice had gone very quiet, which was worse than shouting, he knew; the quiet voice was the one his father had used in the moment before everything went wrong. "Get out of my apartment. *Now.*"

Amir raised both hands, palms outward. "We're leaving," he said. "Declan, the food."

The boy stepped forward and set the container on the coffee table, the plastic bag rustling — THANK YOU THANK YOU THANK YOU — and then stepped back.

"That stays with you," Amir said simply. "Whether you come downstairs or not...you need to eat, Mr. Merle. *Both* of you do."

They filed out. Amir first, then Mallie, then Gordon, then the boy. Amir paused at the door and looked back at Eleanor, and something passed between them that Kerwin could not read and did not like.

"We meet downstairs," Amir said. "The door at the back of the shop, the one with the padlock. It's open tonight." He held Eleanor's gaze a moment longer. "You know where to find us."

The door closed behind them. The room was quiet again, just the two of them and the container sitting on the coffee table, leaking its smell into the room.

Kerwin exhaled. His hands were shaking.

"Well," Eleanor said after a long moment. "That was dramatic."

"I'm not going down there."

"Okay."

"I mean it. I'm not — whatever that was, whatever they're doing in that basement, I want no part of it. They're lunatics, Eleanor. They eat rotten food and hallucinate and call it God."

"Okay," she said again. She was sitting very still on the sofa, her hands folded in her lap, and she was not arguing with him. She was not pushing. She was simply sitting there, agreeing with him, and it was worse than any argument she could have made because he could see, in the careful blankness of her face, that she had already decided to go and was simply waiting for him to catch up.

The minutes passed. The container sat between them. The smell of it filled the room, rich and wrong and impossibly appealing, and Kerwin's stomach cramped again around its own emptiness and would not let him think about anything else.

"You want to go," he said flatly.

"I didn't say that."

"You don't have to say it. I can see it in your face."

She was quiet for a moment. Then, "I want to understand. And before you start—" she said, holding up a hand to hold off his coming argument, "that's *not* the same thing."

"It's close enough."

"Kerwin." She leaned forward, her elbows on her knees. "Something happened to us last night...something happened, and they know what it was.

They've felt it too. Doesn't that — doesn't some part of you want to *know?*"

Stupid girl. Of *course* it did! Of course some part of him wanted to know because it was the very same part of him that had stood at the window for years and cataloged and observed and tried to make sense of a world he could not bring himself to enter. He was a watcher. He had always *been* a watcher. And now that someone was offering to show him what lay behind the curtain, every instinct he had was screaming at him to stay in his seat.

But Eleanor was going to go, he knew. He could see it as clearly as he could see the gap between her front teeth when she bit her lip, which she was doing now, waiting for his answer. She was going to go, with him or without him, and if she went without him she would descend those stairs alone and sit at that table alone and eat whatever they put in front of her alone, and he would be up here in the dark, listening for sounds through the floor, imagining the worst, and she would come back changed or she would not come back at all.

He thought about the hallway. His hand on the door, blocking her exit, the desperate animal plea to have her *stay. Just stay.* He had been willing to terrify her to keep her from leaving. What was he willing to do now to keep from being left behind?

Kerwin didn't know what he thought, but what he *knew* was that he was was an ugly, stooped, sway-chested man with thinning hair and bad skin, half in love with a girl just because she'd crossed his threshold. A memory drifted up then, unbidden—something his mother had said once about marriage, that it didn't work if the two weren't equally yoked, and they weren't married, of course they weren't married, *not yet, not ever, you sick fuck,* but they were so unevenly yoked in their partnership, thin though it was that he'd follow her anywhere, do anything she asked, walk into a basement full of strangers who wanted to feed him roadkill or worse because she was looking at him with those dark eyes and waiting for an answer.

I think I'd do anything you asked.

I think," is what he said instead, slowly, "that we've come this far."

Eleanor nodded once, a harsh jerk of her chin. "Fine. But I meant what I said — we can leave whenever we want."

"Whenever you want," he echoed, though the words were meant for himself more than for her.

She stood, and the movement decided everything; the room rearranged itself around her intention the way it had since she'd first walked through his door and hung her coat on his hook and claimed his space as though it had been waiting for her. She crossed to where he sat and bent down and pressed her lips to his cheek —quickly, lightly, the kind of kiss a wife might give a husband on her way out the door—and the place where her mouth had been burned like a brand.

He could feel the heat of it spreading across his face, up into his hairline, down into his throat. She had kissed him. On the cheek, like a child, like it was nothing, and his whole body had lit up like a pinball machine, every nerve firing at once, and he was nearing fifty years old and blushing in his own sitting room because a girl had put her lips on his face.

"Come on, then," she said, already moving toward the door, and he was on his feet and following her before the blush had faded, before his brain had caught up with his legs, before any part of him that might have objected had time to register its complaint.

They took the back stairs down. The stairwell was worse than Kerwin had anticipated after the flood, refuse on the steps, takeout containers with their contents long since rotted to black smears, plastic bags bunched in the corners and something that might once have been vegetables reduced to a slick brown paste. His mother would have wept to see it and been on her knees in an instant with a brush and a bucket, scrubbing until her hands cracked and bled.

The door to Amir's shop was unlocked, just as he'd said it would be. They passed through the stockroom in the dark, past shelves Kerwin could not see but could smell (cardboard and plastic and the faint chemical residue of cleaning products) and found the door at the back with the padlock, standing open, just like he'd said.

The stairs beyond it led down.

Eleanor was behind him, her hand gripping the back of his sweater, and he could hear her breathing through her mouth, trying not to smell it.

Somewhere below, candlelight flickered against the walls, and he could hear the low murmur of voices — the Gastronauts, waiting, as they had apparently been for a very long time.

"Charming," Eleanor muttered behind him.

Kerwin didn't answer. He was thinking about the story he had been told of the apple rotting inside Eve, the serpent's tongue and the taste of something so foul it had shown her God's face. He was thinking about the voices in the dark and the feeling that his whole life had been leading to this stairwell, this descent, this door at the bottom where Amir's voice rose up to meet them like heat from a vent.

"Welcome," Amir said, stepping aside to let them pass, "to the table."

The smell that wafted out was indescribable, and still, Kerwin and Eleanor stepped through.

9

The Table and All of its Articles

Kerwin had expected storage, but what he found instead made him stop so abruptly that Eleanor walked straight into his back, her hand still fisted in the fabric of his sweater.

The closest room he might compare it to was the city's VFW hall, half-remodeled and barely distanced from its strip club past (his mother, he remembered, was particularly scandalized when the shoddy construction kept the *V* from *Velvet Touch* to save on signage). It was a banquet space, or some approximation of one; the walls were draped in fabric, great swaths of heavy velvet in shades of burgundy and wine-dark purple, gathered and bunched in elaborate folds that pooled on the floor. The material had a wetness to it in the candlelight, a sheen that made it look almost organic, as if it had been peeled back from outside of itself rather than hung. Candelabras stood in the corners, tall and tarnished, their flames guttering and dripping pale wax onto brass bases gone green with age. The ceiling was lost in shadow above them, and the whole room seemed to breathe as the fabric shifted in some imperceptible draft, the folds deepening and receding like the slow expansion of lungs.

In the center of the room stood a long table, the wood so dark it was nearly black and it had been set for six with a precision that bordered on the obsessive: fine china rimmed in gold, silver cutlery arranged in descending rows, crystal glasses catching and scattering the light. At each place sat a silver dome, and Kerwin found himself counting them—one, two, three, four, five, six— as if confirming it would make any of this make sense. The centerpiece was fruit, grapes and figs and something that might have been pomegranate split open to show its seeds, all of it soft-looking and overripe, spotted with the first bruises of decay. A fly landed on one of the figs as he watched and began to crawl across the skin with the unhurried movements of a creature that knew it belonged there.

To the left of the entrance, a sideboard held silver trays of what must have been appetizers, and Kerwin's eyes moved over them and then quickly away: small glistening spheres nested in beds of dark jelly, pale pink folds arranged in spirals like the petals of some fleshy flower, thin marbled slices fanned across a bed of greens that had begun to wilt at the edges. His stomach turned, and then horribly, traitorously, it growled.

And in the far corner, a fountain comprised of three tiers of hammered copper, the liquid flowing down them something thicker and darker than water, reddish-purple and almost black where it pooled in the basin below. It caught the candlelight where it glowed from within, sluggish and strange, and the smell of it reached Kerwin even from across the room—sweet and fermented, like wine that had been left too long in the bottle with something underneath that his nose kept trying to slide away from.

"How is any of this here?" Eleanor asked behind him, and her voice had a thin, reedy quality to it that he had not heard before. She had let go of his shirt and stepped past him into the room, her bare feet silent on the stone floor, and she was turning slowly, taking it all in, the velvet, the candles, the table with its silver domes and rotting fruit. "How did you do this?"

"We've had years to prepare," Amir said, and he was moving through the room with the ease of long familiarity, trailing his fingers along the back of one of the chairs as he passed. "The space was always here, beneath the shop. We simply transformed it into something more suitable for our purposes."

There was something wrong with the room, Kerwin thought, something beyond the obvious wrongness of the velvet and the candles and the odd little group in the basement. The white lilies in the vases along the walls had begun to brown at the edges, their stamens heavy with orange pollen that had dusted the tablecloth beneath them, and when he breathed in he could smell, underneath the sweetness of the fountain and the rot of the fruit, something else entirely; it was the same smell of the air freshener his mother had kept in the upstairs bathroom.

Mallie had crossed to the fountain and was filling a crystal goblet, holding it beneath the lowest tier where the liquid ran thickest. It clung to the glass as it rose, coating the sides in a way that wine should not and when she raised the goblet to her lips and drank her throat worked multiple before she lowered it. Her eyes were closed, and there was an expression on her face that looked almost like ecstasy.

"It's not blood" she said, and when she opened her eyes she was looking directly at Eleanor, a faint smile playing at the corners of her mouth. "It's wine, reduced and concentrated, spiced with things I could not *begin* to name. The first course is always the lightest, you see, it prepares the stomach for what comes after."

Gordon had already crossed to the fountain and was filling his own glass, and his son Declan stood just behind him with the studied boredom of a teenager who wanted you to know that he had seen far worse than this, whatever this was, and was not impressed with any of it. Kerwin wondered if that was true. He wondered if any of them had ever seen anything like this before or if they were all simply pretending, performing for each other in this ridiculous room.

Eleanor looked at him, and he could not have said what his face was doing, it seemed to have disconnected from the rest of him somehow, gone numb and strange but whatever she saw there made her press her lips together and nod once, a quick jerk of her chin, as if he had said something and she was agreeing with it. Then she crossed to the fountain herself and picked up one of the waiting goblets, heavy crystal cut in a pattern that caught the light, and held it beneath the stream.

The liquid filled her glass slowly, far too slowly, clinging to the crystal as it rose in a way that made Kerwin think of honey. When the glass was full she lifted it and held it before her face for a long moment, studying it in the candlelight, and her expression was unreadable.

She drank it quickly. Her face did something complicated as she swallowed—a flinch, quickly suppressed. She lowered the glass and looked at it, and then she looked at Kerwin, and still her face told him nothing.

"Well?" Mallie asked, and there was something almost hungry in her voice.

"It's different," Eleanor said slowly, as if she were choosing each word with great care. "It's not like anything I've tasted before."

"No," Mallie agreed, and her smile widened slightly. "It isn't."

Kerwin found that his hand was reaching for a goblet before he had made any conscious decision to move. The crystal was colder than the room should have allowed and when he held it beneath the fountain the liquid that filled it was warm and it smelled of minerals, something that made his mouth flood with saliva even as his throat closed in protest.

He raised the glass to his lips, and he drank.

The taste was sweet, that was the first thing, thick and sweet and coating his tongue, sliding down his throat with odd weight . His hand was shaking when he lowered the glass, and Eleanor was watching him with her dark eyes and none of the Gastronauts seemed surprised at all, as if they had seen this same reaction a hundred times before.

"Good," Amir said softly, and Kerwin had not heard him approach but suddenly he was there at Kerwin's elbow, his hand warm when he placed it briefly on Kerwin's shoulder. "The first taste is always the hardest. It will come easier from here, I promise you."

Kerwin was not certain whether that was meant as a comfort or a threat.

Amir disappeared behind a heavy curtain at the far end of the room as the others settled themselves around the table with the ease of long practice, pulling out chairs and unfolding napkins, leaving two places empty that were clearly meant for him and Eleanor. Kerwin watched them arrange themselves and thought, absurdly, of dinner parties his mother had thrown when he was small, the careful placement of cutlery, the folded napkins, the way she had fussed over the centerpiece as if the neighbors would judge the entire worth of the family by whether the cut flowers were wilting.

"Sit, sit," Gordon said, waving a hand at the empty chairs. "We don't stand on ceremony here. Well—" He chuckled at his own joke. "We do, rather, but not about seating arrangements."

Eleanor didn't move, and neither did Kerwin. They stood together near the fountain, close enough that he could feel the warmth of her shoulder against his arm, watching as Declan slouched into a chair at the far end of the table and began picking at the edge of his napkin with bitten fingernails.

"You'll have to forgive my son," Gordon said, and there was a note of long-suffering patience in his voice that suggested he had made this particular apology many times before. "He's not much for conversation. Are you, Declan?"

The boy had slouched into a chair at the far end of the table and was picking at the edge of his napkin with bitten fingernails. He didn't look up. "I talk when there's something worth saying."

"Charming," Eleanor muttered, and Kerwin felt something loosen slightly in his chest. A dangerous feeling, he knew, the exact kind that preceded attachment and worse yet, need. He was grateful for her presence beside him in a way that embarrassed him and he reminded himself that she was not his and never would be, that he was a middle-aged man with a rotting house and a rotting life and no business thinking of her as anything other than a temporary disruption to the gray procession of his days.

Mallie had taken her seat and was assessing them both. "It's overwhelming at first," she said, her voice gentler than he had expected. "The room, the ritual, all of it...I remember my first time here, I thought Amir had lost his mind entirely."

"Had he?" Eleanor asked, and there was a challenge in it.

Mallie smiled thinly. "That depends entirely on your definition. He showed me things I couldn't explain, things I'd spent my whole life pretending didn't exist. Whether that makes him mad or simply more honest than the rest of us, I've never been certain."

"How long have you been doing this?" Kerwin heard himself ask. His voice sounded strange to him, too steady, too normal, as if they were having a perfectly ordinary conversation about hobbies and weekend plans.

"Fifteen years, give or take." Mallie picked up her goblet and turned it in her hands, watching the liquid catch the candlelight. "Amir found me when

I was very ill. Dying, the doctors said, though they couldn't agree on what was killing me. He offered me something else." She shrugged. "I took it."

"And you got better?"

"I became...*different*." She took another sip, her throat clicking as she swallowed. "Better is a relative term, but I'm still here, which is more than the doctors expected."

Gordon had been watching this exchange with barely suppressed impatience, and now he leaned forward, his elbows on the table, his face eager in a way that made Kerwin's skin prickle. "The point is, it works," he said. "Whatever else you might think of it, however strange it seems, it *works*. I've seen things in these sessions that I couldn't begin to explain... visions, revelations." He spread his arms as if to encompass the whole of his experience. "Glimpses of something...beyond." He waved his hand in front of his face which was pinched in distaste. "Beyond this tedium."

"Visions of what?" Eleanor asked.

Gordon opened his mouth to answer, but Declan spoke first, his voice flat and unimpressed. "He means he hallucinates. We all do. That's the *point*."

"Declan—"

"What? It's true." The boy looked up for the first time, and there was something in his face that didn't match his sullen teenage affect. "We eat rotten food, we get sick, we see things. It's not complicated. Whether any of it actually means anything..." He trailed off, shrugging the rest of his thought away.

Gordon's face had gone red, and Kerwin could see him struggling to compose himself. "My son is young," he said tightly. "He hasn't yet learned to appreciate what we're doing here."

"I've learned plenty." Declan met Kerwin's eyes across the table. "I've learned that when you're empty enough, you'll believe anything." He held Kerwin's gaze a moment longer, then looked down at his napkin again. "You'll see. You get used to the taste, or you don't. Either way," he added, tucking his shoulders up to his ears, "you keep eating."

The silence that followed felt impossibly heavy, and Kerwin was grateful when Eleanor touched his elbow and nodded toward the corner of the room, away from the table. He followed her without speaking, and they stood together in the shadows near the velvet-draped wall, their backs to the others, their voices low.

"We don't have to do this," she said. "We can leave. *Right now.*"

Eleanor, as far as he knew her, was not a woman prone to equivocation, and the uncertainty sat strangely on her face, ill-fitting, like a coat that belonged to someone else. He found he did not like it; he had never liked it in women, that wavering, that looking to him for answers he didn't have. He wanted a woman either entirely submissive or entirely dominant, he wanted her on her knees in front of him with her mouth open, waiting, or he wanted her standing over him with a knife in her hand, telling him what to do. He wanted someone who would make his decisions for him or someone who would let him do whatever he wanted to her. He did not want this, this asking, this uncertainty, this looking at him as though he might know what came next.

"Can we?" He heard the doubt in his own voice and hated it.

"What do you mean?"

He didn't know what he meant, not exactly. He only knew that something had shifted in him when he'd swallowed that thick, sweet liquid, something that felt like a door opening or a lock giving way, and he wasn't certain he could close it again even if she asked it of him. He thought of his house, of the meals he ate standing at the kitchen counter because it seemed pointless to sit down for one person, the books he read until his eyes burned because sleep meant dreams and dreams meant remembering things he'd spent decades trying to forget. "I mean that we're already here," he said slowly. "We've already drunk from the fountain, we've already seen the room, we've already heard their stories. If we leave now—"

"Then we leave. So what?"

"We'll always wonder." The words came out before he could stop them, and he knew as soon as he'd said them that they were true. "We'll spend the rest of our lives wondering what would have happened…what we might have seen."

Eleanor was quiet for a long moment, her dark eyes searching his face.

"You want this," she said finally, and it wasn't quite a question.

Did he? He thought about the life he had been living before she'd arrived; of his father, who had died believing his son would amount to something and his mother, who had died knowing he wouldn't. He thought about the woman he might have married, if he'd been different, *better*, if he'd been capable of giving her anything other than his silences and his black moods and his conviction that love was someone letting you do whatever you wanted to them.

"I don't know what I want," he said honestly. "But I know that if we eat whatever's coming, we can't take it back. You understand that. This isn't something you can undo."

"It's just food, Kerwin." But her voice had lost its certainty. "People eat spoiled food all the time."

"Not like *this,*" he hissed, "and not on *purpose.* Not as part of—" He gestured helplessly at the room around them, "—whatever this is."

She was quiet again, and he watched her thinking, watched the calculation happening behind her eyes.

"I want to find out," she said finally, and her voice was steady again, her jaw set in that way he had come to recognize. "I want to know what they see. I want to understand why someone would do this to themselves on purpose."

"All right," he said, letting out a breath. "All right."

They walked back to the table together, and Kerwin pulled out the chair beside Mallie and sat down, and Eleanor took the seat beside Gordon, and the silver domes gleamed in the candlelight, and somewhere behind the curtain Amir was preparing whatever horror they were about to eat, and Kerwin folded his hands in his lap and waited for what came next.

Amir emerged from behind the curtain, and in his hands he carried a book.

It was not like any book Kerwin had seen before. The cover was dark and mottled, the texture of it wrong somehow, and when Amir set it on the table the sound it made was soft, almost fleshy. The pages, when he opened it, were not paper but something thinner, more translucent, covered in a script that Kerwin could not read from where he sat.

"Before we eat," Amir said, "we remember why we eat."

The others had gone still. Even Declan had stopped picking at his napkin, his eyes fixed on the book with grim focus.

"We are not the first to walk this path, nor are we the first to understand that the body must be broken before the spirit can be freed. This is the mystery that has been hidden from the world since the beginning—hidden by priests who were afraid of what it meant, by churches that preferred a clean resurrection to the truth."

He looked around the table, meeting each of their eyes in turn. When his gaze fell on Kerwin, there was something in it that made Kerwin want to look away.

"The Gospel of Mary," Amir said. "Not the Magdalene but the mother. This is her testimony, preserved by those who understood, passed down through generations of the faithful."

He turned the pages carefully, reverently, and began to read what he named the first of five chapters of the true story of Communion.

"And it came to pass that the Lord spake unto Judas, surnamed Iscariot, in a dream, saying, Behold, Judas, son of Simon, I have chosen thee for a purpose which shall be hidden from all else, for I have seen the end from the beginning, and I know the treachery that dwelleth in thine heart; yea, even before thy mother's womb did fashion thee, I knew what thou wouldst do."

Amir's voice had changed. His eyes had gone somewhere Kerwin couldn't follow, the lids half-dropped and the pupils fixed on a point that wasn't in the room; whatever was speaking through him now had been doing it for a very long time and Kerwin found himself leaning forward despite himself.

10

The Crucifixion, and its Afters

"And Judas was sore afraid," Amir continued, his fingers grazing the text like a lover as he read, "and said, Lord, wherefore speakest thou thus? For I love the Master, and would lay down my life for him."

3 And the LORD said, It is because thou lovest him that I have chosen thee, for another man would betray him for silver alone, but thou shalt betray him for love.

4 But I say unto thee a hidden thing: the body may be spared the knowledge of its own suffering.

5 Hear now what thou must do. When the feast of the Passover is come, thou shalt prepare the bread and the wine and the bitter herbs for the supper.

6 But the bread thou shalt set aside in a dark place, three days and three nights, until the mold groweth upon it, and the fish likewise thou shalt leave unclean, sat overlong in the sun until the flesh softeneth and turneth.

7 And Judas said, LORD, this is an abomination. Shall I poison my Master whom I love?

8 And the LORD said, I will have thee spare him, for I have seen what the Romans shall do unto him, and the lash and the nail and the spear. No man can endure such things and keep his mind whole.

9 But if thou givest him to eat of that which hath corrupted, his spirit shall be loosed from his flesh, and he shall feel the torment as through a veil, and his suffering shall be unto him as ecstasy.

10 This is the mystery of the mortification of the flesh, which I give unto thee: that pain and pleasure are as one river with two mouths, and he that drinketh deep of corruption shall find the waters mingled.

11 And Judas wept, and said, LORD, I will do as thou commandest. But what shall become of me?

12 And the LORD said unto him, That which thou doest, thou hast always done; yet now do it for love.

13 For Judas knew his own heart, that it was divided within him; and he feared lest, when the hour came, he should fail altogether.

14 And the LORD showed him the end from the beginning, and the tale that should be told of him among men; and Judas bowed himself, for he saw that his name was already given away.

CHAPTER II

1 And it came to pass that Judas went unto the market and bought barley loaves and dried fish and lentils and wine and pulse that had spoiled.

2 And he set apart the loaves in a vessel of clay, and covered them with a cloth, and put them in a place where no light came; and the fish he wrapped in leaves and buried beneath the straw where the ass was kept.

3 And for three days he watched and waited, and his heart was heavy within him, for he knew what he must do.

4 On the third day he took up the loaves, and behold, they were soft and spotted with growth, green and white upon the crust. And he took up the fish, and the smell of it was sweet and foul, as of something that had begun to return unto the earth.

5 And Judas prepared the Passover, and set the table, and laid out the corrupted bread and the fish that had turned, and the wine which he had mingled with the juice of fruits left too long in the sun.

6 And the disciples came, and the Master with them, and they reclined at table as was the custom.

7 And Jesus took the bread, and blessed it, and gave unto them, saying, Take, eat; this is my body.

8 But Judas had set apart a portion for the Master alone, and this portion

only was corrupted; and the disciples ate of the clean bread, and knew not that the Master's bread was different from their own.

9 And Judas watched, and saw how the Master chewed and swallowed, and how his eyes grew strange and distant, as one who sees things that are not of this world.

10 And Jesus took the cup, and gave thanks, and gave it to them, saying, Drink ye all of it; for this is my blood of the new testament.

11 And they drank, and knew not what they drank.

12 And Jesus said, Verily I say unto you, that one of you shall betray me. And they were exceeding sorrowful, and began every one of them to say unto him, LORD, is it I?

13 And Judas looked upon the Master, and the Master looked upon him, and there passed between them a knowledge that no other man shared.

14 And Jesus said unto him, That thou doest, do quickly.

15 And Judas rose, and went out into the night, and the weight of what he had done and what he yet must do was as a millstone about his neck.

CHAPTER III

1 Now when they had scourged Jesus in the place called Gabbatha, in the hall of Pilate, the soldiers marveled, for he cried not out as other men.

2 And when the lash fell upon his back, and the skin was torn and the blood flowed, behold, his face was as the face of one who heareth music from a far country.

3 And his lips moved, and those who stood near heard him whisper, Father, Father, and his eyes were lifted up, and there was upon his countenance a look of rapture such as no man had seen.

4 And the soldiers said one to another, This man is mad, or else a sorcerer, for he feeleth not the stripes we lay upon him. What manner of man is this, that he groaneth as one in pleasure?

5 And they beat him more, thinking to break him; but still he smiled, and his body writhed not in agony but as one who is caught up in a vision.

6 Now Mary had followed after, and stood without the hall, and heard the sound of the scourging.

7 And she looked through the lattice, and saw Jesus beneath the lash, and saw his face, and was amazed.

8 For she had seen men scourged before, and they had wept and begged and fouled themselves with terror; but the Master was as one transfigured, his torn flesh shining, his eyes fixed upon the heavens.

9 And Mary remembered what Judas had told her in secret, before he went away to do what he must do.

10 For Judas had come to her in the night, and his face was wet with weeping, and he had said, Mary, hear me, for I have not long. I must tell of something which shall seem unto thee as madness.

11 The LORD will die. This is written, and cannot be unwritten. But I have given him a gift that will ease his passage, and thou must give him another.

12 And Mary said, What gift can I give? I am only a woman, and have nothing. What shall I do there? Shall I weep for my son?

13 And Judas said, When he is laid in the tomb, thou must go unto him. Thou must take him into thyself, so that nothing remaineth for the Romans to defile. This is the resurrection that is promised: not of the flesh, but through the flesh. He will live because he will live in thee.

14 And Mary said, This is madness. Thou speakest blasphemy!

15 And Judas said, Watch his face when they beat him. Then thou shalt believe, for when thou seest him upon the cross, his face shall not be as the face of other men who die.

16 And he put into her hand his own and said, When it is finished, go to him, and do what must be done. Tell no one. Let them think what they will think.

17 Then Judas took from his garment a vial of the juice of hemlock, which he had prepared for himself.

18 And he said unto Mary, I go now to do what must be done. And after, I shall hang myself in the potter's field, for I cannot live with the knowledge of this thing.

19 But the poison shall work first, that I might die more quickly, for I am not strong as he is strong.

20 And Mary wept, and said, Why must it be thee?

21 And Judas said, Because I alone could betray him. And God, who knoweth all things, knew I would do it whether he commanded me or no.

22 For the weakness was already in my heart. He hath only made a sacrament of my sin.

23 Mary saw these things, and the words of Judas returned unto her.

24 And suddenly there came upon her a rushing wind, though she stood in a still place, and she knew that the Spirit of the LORD had entered into her.

25 Her unbelief departed from her, and she knew what she must do.

26 And she said in her heart, My son, my son, I shall not fail thee.

CHAPTER IV

1 And Judas went out, and Mary saw him no more.

2 Now when Jesus was dead, and taken down from the cross, there came a rich man of Arimathaea, named Joseph, who also himself was Jesus' disciple, and begged the body of Pilate.

3 And they laid him in a sepulcher which was hewn out of rock, and rolled a large stone unto the door.

4 And Mary Magdalene and Mary the mother of Jesus beheld where he was laid.

5 And when the sabbath was past, Mary came alone unto the sepulcher, very early in the morning, while it was yet dark.

6 And she saw the stone, and it was great, and the guard that was set to watch. And she turned away, and went round about to the far side of the hill where the rock was soft.

7 And the spirit of the Lord came upon her, and her hands were filled with a strength that was not her own.

8 And she began to dig.

9 With her fingers she tore at the earth, and the rocks cut her hands and the roots tore her nails, but she felt it not, for the Lord was with her.

10 And she dug through the night, beneath the hill, toward the place where her Lord lay, and the tunnel was narrow and dark and the smell of death was close about her.

11 And when she had broken through into the tomb, she crawled forth into the chamber, and there was Jesus upon the slab, wrapped in linen, and he was dead.

12 And Mary wept over him, and kissed his cold face, and saw that his lips were curved at the edges, as one who dieth in the midst of a pleasant dream.

13 And she cried out, LORD God, take him! Take him up! Let him rise, as it was promised!

14 But there was no answer, and the body lay still.

15 And Mary waited, and prayed, and the night wore on, and still he did not rise.

16 And when the night was more than half spent, Mary grew afraid in her heart, for she thought then that all of it shall be for nothing.

17 And she looked upon her LORD, her teacher, the still face of her son whom she had borne in Bethlehem and nursed at her breast, whom she had watched grow in wisdom and stature. She thought of what the Romans would do when they found him still in the tomb, how they would take his body and hang it up for the dogs and the crows.

18 And the spirit moved in her again, and she understood what she must do.

19 And she said within herself, That which hath been given must not be returned unto the world; for the world devoureth all things without understanding.

20 And Mary took up a stone that was sharp and jagged, for there was no iron with her, and she did not turn her face away as she rent the linen from his body.

21 And she laid hold upon the flesh of her son, whom she had borne and nourished, and she took him unto herself, that corruption should not claim him.

22 And she fell upon him, weeping, and with the stone she cut, and with her teeth she tore, and she ate of his flesh.

23 She rent the meat from the bone and swallowed it down. It was salt with the blood and bitter with the gall they had given him, and her stomach heaved and she vomited upon the floor of the tomb.

24 And behold, rats came out of the darkness, and ate of her vomit, and she did not drive them away, but returned to her work.

25 For this was the bread of life, the true communion, and she would not suffer any of it to be lost.

26 And she began with the wounds, for there the flesh was already opened unto her, and she pressed her mouth to the gash in his side where the spear had pierced him, and she drank of the water and the blood that remained.

27 And she ate of his hands, where the nails had torn through, and the meat there was ragged and soft, and she swallowed it down though her throat closed against it.

28 And she ate of his feet likewise, and of the flesh of his calves, and of his thighs, tearing what she could not cut and cutting what she could not tear.

29 And when she came unto his belly she found the bowels within, and they were hot still with the corruption that had begun its work, and the smell of them was as a pestilence, but she did not turn away.

30 And his hair, which was long and matted with blood, she could not chew nor swallow, and it wound about her teeth and filled her throat, and she choked and heaved and brought it up again in a mass of black and red.

31 And she pulled the hair from her mouth with her fingers, gagging, her eyes streaming, and the rats watched her from the corners of the tomb.

32 And she ate of his face, which she had kissed and washed and loved, and she ate of his lips that had spoken the word of God, and she ate of his tongue that had given her comfort.

33 And his eyes she took last, for she could not bear to look upon them, and they were grown clouded and soft, and when she bit into them they burst upon her tongue like figs too long in the sun.

34 And she ate, and wept, and ate, and the night passed, and the dawn began to show at the mouth of the tunnel.

35 And she said, My boy, my little boy, forgive thy mother.

36 And when she had finished, she was sick and her belly was swollen and her mouth was foul and her hands were red to the wrist. She shook as one with a great fever.

37 And she crawled back through the tunnel, and packed the earth behind

her, so that no man could see where she had gone.

38 And she lay upon the hillside as one dead, and the sun rose, and the birds sang, and within her belly the body of the LORD began its final transformation.

CHAPTER V

1 Now when the first day of the week was come, the guard rolled away the stone from the sepulcher.

2 And they looked within, and behold, the tomb was empty.

3 And they were sore afraid, and ran to tell the chief priests, saying, He is not there! The body is gone!

4 And there was great consternation, and some said, His disciples have stolen him away by night.

5 But Mary knew the truth, and kept it in her heart.

6 And in the days that followed, the disciples saw the LORD in visions, walking among them, speaking unto them, and they said, He is risen!

7 And Mary saw him also, in dreams and in waking, and she knew that he lived within her, that his flesh had become her flesh and his blood her blood.

8 And this is the mystery of the resurrection, that the body is not raised but consumed, that eternal life cometh not from the grave but from the table, that whosoever eateth of this bread shall never die.

9 For Christ said, Except ye eat the flesh of the Son of man, and drink his blood, ye have no life in you.

10 Whoso eateth my flesh, and drinketh my blood, hath eternal life.

11 And Mary understood, as no other understood, that these words were not spoken in parable.

12 This Gospel is hidden, for the world is not ready to receive it. But unto those who have ears to hear, let them hear: that the truth of the Lord is not always beautiful, and the path to salvation is not always clean.

13 For he that would follow in the way of Mary must eat as Mary ate, after corruption hath set in and the flesh hath begun its return unto the earth.

14 He must not turn away from that which the world calleth abomination: the meat grown soft and green with mold, the fat rendered to tallow beneath

the skin, the eyes jellied in their sockets and loose upon the tongue.
15 He must eat of the bowels where the worms have made their dwelling,
and of the organs swollen and blackened with rot, and of the flesh gone rigid
with the stiffening that cometh after death.
16 For this is pleasing unto the LORD, even as it was pleasing when Judas
did corrupt the bread; and he that eateth in faith shall be shown things
hidden from the foundation of the world.
17 The veil shall be lifted, and he shall see as the Master saw beneath the
lash, and pain and pleasure shall be mingled in him as the waters of one
river.
18 Blessed are they who hunger, for they shall be filled.

11

Well Fed

Blessed are they who hunger, for they shall be filled.

Amir closed the book, setting it on the sideboard with the appropriate care of a man handling relics before turning back to face them. His hands were folded before him, his expression so carefully composed that Kerwin found he could not look at it for long without feeling he was intruding on something private.

The candles had burned low during the reading, the wax pooling pale and congealed in the brass bases and the flames guttered and leapt in some draft Kerwin could not feel on his own skin. No one spoke. The smell from beneath the silver domes had thickened, or perhaps Kerwin had simply become more attuned to it now that there was nothing else to occupy his attention; it was rich and savory, the kind of smell that might have been appealing under other circumstances but underneath it there was something sweet and dense that coated the back of his throat when he breathed.

Eleanor was beside him, close enough that he could hear her breathing. He did not look at her. The story was still turning over in his mind—Mary in the tomb with her sharp stone, her mouth pressed to the wound in his side, the rats in the corners, the gray dawn showing at the mouth of the tunnel—and he thought that if he looked at Eleanor now something in his face might give him away and show her whatever had settled cold and strange behind his ribs while Amir was reading. He was not ready for her to see that. Perhaps, he thought with his usual disdain that accompanied self-reflection, he would never be ready.

Gordon had bowed his head, his lips moving in what might have been prayer, his hands folded on the table before him with the knuckles gone white. Mallie sat with her eyes closed and her face turned slightly upward, peaceful in a way that seemed almost indecent given what they had just heard, as if the story of a mother eating her son in a tomb were simply another form of devotion. Declan alone seemed unchanged; he was slouched in his chair with his arms crossed, but there was something watchful in his eyes now, and when his gaze met Kerwin's across the table the boy held the contact for a long moment before looking away.

The silence stretched on. Kerwin became aware of sounds beneath it: the soft drip of liquid from the fountain, the creak of someone shifting in a chair, the distant rumble of what might have been traffic or thunder. He thought about standing, about taking Eleanor by the arm and walking out of this room, up those stairs, through the shop and out into the street where the rain would be falling and the air would smell of nothing but the ordinary decay of an ordinary city. He turned the possibility over in his mind like a stone in his palm.

He did not move.

Amir reached for his silver dome.

"Now," he said quietly. "We eat."

The domes came off together, a coordinated motion that suggested long practice and for a moment Kerwin could only stare at what lay beneath.

It had been arranged beautifully. That was the thing that struck him first, before the smell hit, before his mind could begin to parse what he was actually seeing—someone had taken care with this. Small cubes of something gray-pink and glistening had been stacked in a neat pyramid at the center of the plate, and around them a dark sauce pooled, nearly black in the candlelight, thick enough that it held its shape where it had been drizzled. There were herbs scattered across the top, bright green against the gray, and to one side three thin slices of something darker had been fanned out like a garnish at a restaurant, the kind of place where the portions were small and the prices were not.

The smell reached him then. It was rich, almost meaty, the way a good stew might smell after hours on the stove and his stomach clenched and then, horribly, growled.

Gordon had already picked up his knife and fork and was cutting into the little pyramid with evident relish, his eyes half-closed, his lips parted slightly in anticipation. Mallie ate more delicately, lifting each cube to her mouth and pausing for a moment before biting down and Declan was shoveling the food into his mouth mechanically, not looking at his plate, not looking at anyone, his jaw working steadily as he chewed and swallowed and chewed again.

Eleanor had not moved. Her hands were flat on the table on either side of her plate, and she was staring down at the food with an expression Kerwin could not read. He watched her throat move as she swallowed, though she had not yet eaten anything.

"What is it?" she asked, and her voice was steady, but only just. "What are we eating?"

Amir smiled. It was a gentle smile, paternal almost, the kind of smile you might give a child who had asked where babies came from.

"Does it matter?"

Eleanor looked at Kerwin then, and he looked back at her, and something passed between them that he could not have named if he had been asked. She picked up her fork. He watched her do it, watched her fingers close around the handle, watched her spear one of the small gray cubes and lift it to her mouth. She did not hesitate. She put it in her mouth and she chewed and she swallowed, and her face did something complicated as it went down, a tightening around the eyes, a flicker of something at the corner of her mouth, but she did not gag, did not spit it out, did not push back from the table and run.

She picked up another piece.

Kerwin looked down at his own plate. The cubes glistened wetly in the candlelight, and the sauce had begun to congeal slightly at the edges where it met the china, and the smell of it filled his nose and mouth to settle finally somewhere at the base of his skull. He thought about the story Amir had read, about Mary in the tomb, about the way she had started with the wounds because the flesh was already opened there and he thought about the sound he had heard in the night, the thump from upstairs, the water running in the bathroom and he thought about Eleanor pressing her hand to the cut on her temple and the impossible way they might all be connected.

He *was* mad, surely. They all were. Still, he picked up his fork.

The first bite was soft, almost dissolving on his tongue before he could properly chew it. The taste was iron and salt and something gamey and rich that coated his mouth and slid down his throat with a weight that seemed impossibly wrong for food. His body tried to reject it; he could feel his throat closing, his stomach rising, but he swallowed anyway, forced it down against the rising gorge and when it hit his stomach it sat there, warm and heavy, like a ballast tucked under his ribcage.

The second bite was easier. By the third, he had stopped thinking about what he was eating and by the fourth, he had stopped thinking about anything at all.

The candlelight was the first thing to change; the flames stretched and wavered in ways that had nothing to do with any draft. The shadows they cast began to lag behind, trailing after his vision when he turned his head, smearing across the velvet like something wet. Eleanor's face across the table looked wrong, the planes of it shifting, the hollows beneath her eyes deepening and filling with darkness and when she looked at him her pupils were at once too large, too black, swallowing the color of her irises until there was nothing left but that darkness looking back at him.

He tried to say her name but his mouth would not form the shape of it.

The room was breathing. He was certain of it now, could see the velvet on the walls swelling and contracting in a rhythm that matched the pulsing of the candles, and it seemed to Kerwin that he was no longer in a basement at all but somewhere else, somewhere warm and wet and alive that was slowly, slowly, drawing him deeper.

His plate was empty. He did not remember finishing.

The others were still eating, or perhaps they had stopped, he could not tell, their faces blurring at the edges when he tried to look at them directly, only coming clear in his peripheral vision where they grinned and chewed and swallowed with mouths that opened too wide, too red, too hungry.

Something was coming. He could feel it building behind his eyes, pressure like a wave gathering before it broke, and he gripped the edge of the table and held on and waited for it to hit.

* * *

It hit him like a fist.

His mother was on the stairs, scrubbing the way she always had on Saturday mornings, down on her knees with her housecoat bunched up around her thighs and her hair escaping from its pins, the smell of the soap so familiar that Kerwin felt his chest seize with grief.

But the water in her bucket was wrong.

It was dark, nearly black, and when she wrung out the rag something thick dripped from it onto the steps she had already cleaned. She did not seem to notice. She kept scrubbing, kept wringing, kept spreading the darkness further and further down the stairs, and Kerwin could see now that her hands were raw, the skin worn away in places to show the red meat beneath and still she did not stop, still she kept working, and when she looked up at him her face was his mother's face but her eyes were not her eyes, they were dark and as flat as stones at the bottom of a well.

"You never helped," she said, and her voice was his mother's voice, and also it was not. "You never once helped me."

He tried to answer. He was not on the stairs, he was at the table, he was in the basement, but he could smell the soap and he could hear the wet slap of the rag against the wood and he could feel the words caught in his throat like something swallowed wrong.

The stairs dissolved.

Eleanor was in his arms.

They were in his bedroom, on the narrow bed where he had slept alone for so many years, and she was beneath him, her legs wrapped around his waist, her fingers digging into his shoulders as he moved against her. He could feel the heat of her through the thin fabric between them, could feel her hips rising to meet his as they frotted endlessly against each other and when she reached down and circled him with her hand he made a sound that he had not known he was capable of making.

Her mouth was on his neck, his jaw, the corner of his mouth. He turned his head to kiss her and her face was wrong.

It was his mother's face.

Her eyes were wide and staring and there was blood on her cheeks, in her hair, spattered across her forehead in a pattern he recognized because it had haunted him for thirty years. His father's blood, specifically the shape it had made on the wall behind the chair and the way it had dripped from the ceiling in the minutes after.

He tried to pull back but her legs tightened around him, her hand still working, and her mouth opened and she said in his mother's voice, "You never helped. You just watched, you always just watched."

He was still hard. That was the horror of it. Even with his mother's face beneath him, even with his father's blood on her skin, his body would not stop, would not soften, would not release him from this.

The bedroom dissolved.

The tomb. Stone walls, stone floor, the smell of earth and damp and something else, something sweet and rotting that coated the inside of his nose and throat. Mary was on her knees in the darkness, and before her on the slab lay a body wrapped in linen, and she was unwrapping it with hands that shook, pulling the cloth away strip by strip to reveal what lay beneath.

The flesh was gray and had begun to soften in places and darken in others, and where the wounds were the skin had pulled back from the edges to show the meat beneath, red going to black going to green in the torchlight. Mary made a sound, a low moan that came from somewhere deeper than her throat, and she bent her head and pressed her mouth to the wound in his side and she drank.

Kerwin could hear her swallowing; he could hear the wet, slurping sounds of her throat working and then the tearing sound as she pulled back and brought the stone to the flesh and began to cut.

Oh, Mary, she was weeping as she ate...tears ran down her face and dripped onto the body beneath her, and her mouth was red, her chin was red, her hands were red to the wrists, and still she kept eating, kept cutting, kept tearing with her teeth when the stone would not serve, and the rats watched from the corners with their bright black eyes, patient, waiting for what she could not keep down.

Her stomach heaved. She turned her head and vomited onto the stone floor, a wet splatter of half-chewed flesh and bile, and the rats moved forward, their claws clicking on the stone, and began to eat, and Mary wiped her mouth with the back of her hand and turned back to the body and kept going.

The tomb dissolved.

His father's face. The last time, though he had not known it then. His father sitting in the chair by the window with the light falling across his hands, and he had looked up when Kerwin came into the room and there had been something in his eyes that Kerwin had spent thirty years trying not to see.

"You could have been different," his father said, and his voice was very quiet. "You could have been so many things."

Kerwin opened his mouth to say that he had tried, that he had wanted to be different, that he had spent his whole life wanting to be someone other than who he was but the words would not come, and his father turned back to the window, and the light fell across his hands, and Kerwin understood that there was nothing he could say that would matter, that there had never been anything he could say, that the distance between them was not a thing that could be crossed with words.

His father dissolved.

Eleanor was in his home, standing by the window in the morning light, and the door was open behind her. Men were coming through it, men in dark uniforms with their faces covered, and they were laughing as they crossed the room toward her. Kerwin tried to move, tried to put himself between them and her, but his legs would not obey him, his arms hung useless at his sides, and he could only watch as they took her by the arms and pulled her toward the door.

She did not struggle. That was the worst of it. She looked back at him over her shoulder as they dragged her away, and her face was calm, almost relieved, as if she had been waiting for this, as if she had hoped all along that it would end this way.

"Did you really think she wanted to be here?" one of the men said, and his voice was muffled by the mask but Kerwin could hear the laughter underneath. "In this stinking apartment? With you? *Look* at yourself! Look at what you are."

Kerwin looked down at his hands. He was not yet fifty, he knew, but they were old, liver-spotted, the skin loose over the bones. When had that happened? When had he become this?

"She was never yours," the man said. "She was never going to stay."

They pulled her through the door and it closed behind them with a sound like a tomb sealing, and Kerwin stood alone in the apartment that had never been anything but empty, that had been waiting all along for him to understand that emptiness was all he would ever deserve.

He opened his mouth to call her name, and what came out was not her name but something else that rose from his chest like bile.

You already know.

The room dissolved.

Jesus beneath the lash. His back laid open in red ribbons, the blood sheeting down to pool at his feet, and the soldiers' arms rising and falling in a rhythm that matched Kerwin's heartbeat. But his face was turned up toward something Kerwin could not see, and his lips were moving, and his eyes were bright with something that was not pain, that was not fear, that was not anything Kerwin had a name for.

He was smiling.

The lash fell. His back opened further. And still he smiled, still his lips moved, still his eyes shone with that terrible brightness, and Kerwin strained to hear what he was saying, leaned closer, closer, until he could almost make out the words—

You have always known.

The voice was everywhere. It was inside him and outside him and it knew him, knew what he had done, knew what he had failed to do, knew the thing he had buried so deep that he could not reach it even when he tried.

Kerwin opened his mouth to scream, and the room came back in pieces.

The candles resolved first, steady now and no longer pulsing, then the table beneath his hands with its wood smooth and real and solid, then the velvet on the walls turned still and unbreathing, just fabric hung for decoration and nothing more. Kerwin blinked and the room came into focus around him and he found that he was sitting in his chair with his hands flat on the tablecloth and his plate empty before him, scraped clean without a trace of sauce remaining though he had no memory of finishing what had been on it.

His mouth tasted of iron and his throat was raw as if he had been screaming, though he did not think any sound had left him at all. His hands were shaking, and he pressed them harder against the table to make them stop, but they would not stop, and so he lifted them and placed them in his lap where no one could see.

Eleanor was staring at him from across the table, her face pale with the freckles standing out against her skin, and her eyes were wide and strange in a way that told him she had been somewhere too, had seen something that had left her shaken in a way she was trying very hard not to show. Her plate was empty and her hands were in her lap, and they looked at each other for a long moment without speaking and Kerwin understood that whatever she had seen she was not going to tell him, just as he was not going to tell her, just as there were things between them now that would never be spoken aloud.

The others were watching them. Gordon had pushed his plate away and was leaning back in his chair with his hands folded over his stomach, his face flushed and satisfied like a man who had just finished a very good meal, and Mallie's eyes were bright, her lips slightly parted, a hunger in her expression that had nothing to do with food. Declan alone seemed unchanged, slouched in his seat with his arms crossed, though his jaw was tight and he was not looking at anyone, his gaze fixed on some middle distance that Kerwin suspected was not in the room at all.

"What did you see?" Mallie asked, and her voice was gentle, almost tender, the voice of a mother coaxing a secret from a child.

Kerwin opened his mouth. Nothing came out. The visions were still there, crowding at the edges of his mind—his mother's face, his father's hands, Eleanor beneath him with blood on her skin, the men dragging her away, Mary in the tomb with her mouth red to the chin—but he could not make words of them, could not shape them into anything that could be spoken in this room, at this table, to these people who were watching him with their hungry eyes.

"It takes time," Amir said quietly. He had not moved from where he stood at the head of the table, his hands folded before him, his expression serene in a way that made Kerwin want to put his fist through it. "The first vision is always the most difficult to hold. It will become clearer with practice."

12

Go On, Eat Me Then

The shop was dark when they came up through the stairwell, the shelves looming in the dimness like the ribs of some great beast and Kerwin did not look at them as he crossed to the door. The bell chimed when they stepped out onto the street, a small bright sound that belonged to some other world, some other life, and then they were outside and the rain was falling and the air smelled of exhaust fumes.

Eleanor walked beside him without speaking, her arms wrapped around herself and her shoulders hunched against the rain, and Kerwin wanted to offer her his jacket but he wasn't wearing one because he hadn't thought to bring one when Amir had appeared in his doorway and the world had tilted sideways. In the scattered puddles, both of their reflections shattered and reformed with every step and Kerwin watched his feet move one after the other and tried not to think about anything else.

The apartment was cold when they got back. He had left a window cracked in the kitchen and the rain had come in, darkening a patch of the counter near the sink and he closed it now without comment. Nothing had changed and everything had changed, and he did not know how to hold both of those things in his mind at once.

Behind him, Eleanor moved through the hallway without turning on the lights. He could hear her footsteps on the floorboards, the soft creak of the bathroom door opening and then closing and then the click of the lock sliding into place and the rush of water from the faucet. The water ran for a long time in a steady rush that did not pause or change, and he raised his hand to knock but could not bring himself to do it. He stood there in the hallway with his fist hovering an inch from the wood and did not let himself think about why she might need to wash, what she might be trying to clean off, or what she might have seen in that basement that had sent her straight to the bathroom without a word.

When she came out of the bathroom twenty minutes later with her face scrubbed pink and her hair damp at the ends, she was wearing one of his shirts. It was the tan flannel he kept at the back of the wardrobe that his mother had given him the Christmas before she died and it hung on Eleanor's small frame like a dress, the sleeves rolled up to her elbows, the hem brushing the tops of her thighs. He could see her nipples through the thin fabric, dark and peaked from the cold, and something tightened in his chest that was not desire but something closer to rage.

She had gone through his things. She had opened his wardrobe and put her hands on his clothes and chosen something to wear as if she had every right to it, as if his home were hers, as if the years he had spent alone in this apartment organizing things just how he might best tolerate them meant nothing at all. His knuckles whitened on the arm of the chair where he sat by the window, and he watched her move through the kitchen with a familiarity that made his teeth clench, opening the cupboard where he kept the glasses, filling one at the sink, drinking from it while she looked at him over the rim with those dark eyes that gave nothing away.

She was saying something. Her mouth was moving and sounds were coming out but Kerwin could not make sense of them or arrange them into words that meant anything because the visions were still crowding at the edges of his mind and the sight of her in his shirt, in his kitchen, in his life, was too much, was *unbearable* because it was exactly what he hand wanted for so long and he wanted to thrash her for this glimpse of what it could be like.

He *could* tell her to take it off...he could stand up from this chair and cross the room and tell her that she had no right, that she could not simply appear in his life and take whatever she wanted, that he was not a man to be made a fool of.

He looked up to tell her, his mouth already forming the words, and she was not there.

The kitchen was empty. The glass she had been drinking from sat on the counter, half-full, a smear of condensation pooling beneath it, but Eleanor was gone. He had not heard her leave, nor had he heard her footsteps on the floorboards or the creak of the bedroom door or any of the sounds a person makes when they move through a space and for a moment he sat very still in the chair by the window and wondered, briefly, wildly, if she had ever been there at all.

The food. It was still the food still working through his blood, still playing tricks on his mind the way it had in the basement with the candles and the velvet and the visions that had split him open and shown him things he did not want to see. He pressed his palms to his eyes and breathed and tried to remember what was real and what he knew for certain: they had eaten, they had seen things, they had climbed the stairs and walked through the rain and come back to the apartment and Eleanor had gone into the bathroom and he had stood in the hallway listening to the water run.

He stood. The chair creaked beneath him, and the sound was very loud in the silence of the room, and he stood in the middle of the kitchen and listened for her.

Nothing.

He moved through the apartment slowly, room by room, and the silence thickened around him with each step. The kitchen with its cracked linoleum curling at the edges near the stove, the faucet dripping the way it always did no matter how hard he wrenched the handle, the grease stain on the wall behind the cooker that had been there since his mother's time and that he had never been able to scrub away. He scurried through the sitting room with the sofa that sagged in the middle from years of his weight in the same spot, the water stain on the ceiling shaped like a hand reaching down, the bookshelf with its rows of paperbacks gone yellow at the spines before moving on to the bedroom with the narrow bed and the sheets that needed washing and the mattress dipped on one side from decades of sleeping alone, his mother's sewing box still on the shelf where she had left it, the lid filmed with dust he had never wiped away.

"Eleanor?"

His voice came out wavering and not like his voice at all, and the apartment swallowed it without answer. He stood in the doorway of the bedroom and listened, and he could hear something—not her voice, not her footsteps, but something else, a settling sound, a creak, perhaps?

He moved down the hallway toward the bathroom where the door remained firmly closed.

"Eleanor?"

He tried the handle. It turned but the door would not budge more than half an inch before catching on something, and he could smell steam, could even feel the damp heat of it seeping through the gap, and he thought, *her things*. She had washed at the sink because the tub was out of order, and all her things must be piled near the door, the towels and the bottles and whatever else women kept with them, the mysterious debris of female existence that he had never understood.

He pushed harder. The door did not move.

"Eleanor, are you in there?" Kerwin called.

Inside, there was the small sound of dripping water cushioned by a larger silence. He shoved his shoulder to the wood and when the door would not give, he felt something hot and panicked rising in his chest. She had left him. That was it. She had taken her things and gone out the window or down the fire escape or simply walked out while he sat in his chair by the window lost in his own useless thoughts, and now she was gone and he was alone and the bathroom door would not open because there was nothing on the other side worth finding.

Unless...

The thought came unbidden, unwanted: unless she was in there and she could not answer, unless something had happened while he sat staring at nothing. Unless the food, the visions, the things they had eaten in that basement had done something to her that they had not done to him, and she was lying on the floor of the bathroom with her face slack and her eyes open and her body cooling on the tile.

He threw himself at the door. Once, twice, and on the third try something shifted—the door swung inward and he stumbled through it and caught himself on the edge of the sink and looked around wildly, his heart slamming against his ribs.

The bathroom was empty. The mirror was fogged with steam. The sink was wet. Her things were scattered across the counter (a hairbrush with strands of dark hair caught in the bristles, a tube of something squeezed flat at the middle, a compact mirror left open to show its own fogged reflection) but Eleanor was not there.

"What are you doing?"

He spun around. She was standing in the hallway behind him, her arms crossed over her chest, his tan shirt hanging off one shoulder, and she was looking at him partly with amusement and something darker that made him feel suddenly, horribly exposed.

"I—"

He could not finish the sentence. He stood there with his hand on the sink and his chest heaving and he looked at her standing in the hallway in his shirt, alive, real, watching him with those dark eyes, and he did not know what to say.

"I thought you'd left," he managed finally, and his voice came out rough, scraped raw. I thought—"

"I was in the bedroom," she said, rubbing at the tip of her nose, "looking for something to sleep in." She tilted her head, studying him. "Kerwin, you're shaking."

He looked down at his hands. She was right. They were trembling the same way they had trembled at the table after the visions had released him, and he could not make them stop.

"Kerwin..." Her voice was softer now, the amusement gone, and she took a step toward him. "What's wrong?"

He shook his head. He did not know how to answer that. Everything was wrong. Nothing was wrong. He had eaten something terrible in a basement full of lunatics and he had seen things that could not be unseen and now he was standing in his bathroom shaking like a child while a woman half his age looked at him with pity in her eyes, and he could smell himself, could smell the sweat and the fear and the basement still clinging to his skin, and he could not bear it.

"I need a wash," he spat, and pushed past her into the hallway.

* * *

A rational man with a rational mind might have used the kitchen sink, or even the bathroom sink now that he knew Eleanor was not lying dead behind the door; a rational man might have stripped to the waist and washed himself in the warmth of his own apartment with the curtains drawn and the door locked and no one to see him but the woman who had already seen him shaking like a child in the hallway. A rational man, if he were truly desperate to be cold and miserable, might have fashioned a Judas cradle out of his washing machine's agitator before choosing to wash outside in late autumn with a garden hose.

Kerwin was not, at this moment, a rational man.

He went out the back door and down the steps into the alley where the neighbors sometimes left needles in the cracks between the paving stones and the smell of piss there rose up to meet him like an old friend. The hose was coiled against the wall where it had always been, cracked and green with age and he turned the spigot and held the nozzle over his head and let the water come.

It was cold, of course, the kind of cold that stops the breath and seizes the heart and Kerwin gasped as it hit him, keeping his eyes open and his mouth closed as he let it run down his face and his neck and soak through the shirt he had not bothered to remove. He could feel it washing away the pressure that had been building in his chest since Eleanor had appeared in his doorway and the Gastronauts had come with their velvet room and their mad gospel about a mother eating her son in a tomb.

He was cracking. He could feel it, the way you feel a bone giving way before the pain arrives, and he did not know if what lay on the other side was madness or relief or simply the absence of everything he had spent his life holding together. He had built his existence in the slim space between the things he wanted and the things he denied himself, and now that space was collapsing he had no idea who he would be when it was gone.

He turned off the water, standing there dripping in the alley with his shirt plastered to his skin and his thin hair hanging in his eyes, and when he looked up Eleanor was watching him from the window above, her arms folded on the sill, her chin resting on her hands.

"You could have used the bathroom, you know!" she called down. "The sink still works!"

He wiped the water from his face with one hand. "I know."

"So why didn't you?"

He stood there looking up at her, dripping onto the concrete, and she looked down at him, and the silence stretched until she said, "You were pounding on the door like a madman."

His cheeks went hot despite the cold. "I saw your things!" he yelled up at her. "On the counter. I didn't want to—" He stopped, not knowing how to finish.

"Didn't want to what?"

"I don't know. Disturb them."

"Disturb my things." She raised an eyebrow. "What, my bra? I needed somewhere to hang it, and the shower curtain was the only place."

"I don't have a problem with your bra." His voice came out stiff, formal, and he could feel the color rising in his face, an ugly wine-dark flush that he could not control.

"You don't?"

"No, I don't."

A curtain twitched in the window across the alley. It was Mrs. Hennessey, the nosy old bag from the apartment above the pet salon, her pale face pressed to the glass like a moon behind clouds. Kerwin saw himself suddenly as she must see him: their recluse of a neighbor, the strange man who never spoke to anyone, standing in the alley with a garden hose while a woman half his age leaned out his window in nothing but a man's shirt, the two of them shouting about undergarments like some psychiatric institute's theater production of Romeo and Juliet.

"I'm not discussing this in public," he hissed, and dropped the hose and took the stairs two at a time because it was imperative that he explain himself, vital that he keep this vaguely sexual thread of conversation alive so that he could return to it in the years to come, the interminable years stretching between now and death when he would need something to warm himself by.

Eleanor was leaning against the kitchen counter when he came through the door, arms crossed, that particular expression on her face that he was beginning to recognize as the one she wore when she was about to say something he wouldn't enjoy.

"You know," she said conversationally, "for a man who has apparently spent years avoiding human contact, you've got a real flair for public spectacle."

"I was *washing*."

"You were having some sort of episode with a garden hose!" She hadn't moved from the counter, her arms crossed, one bare foot tucked behind the opposite ankle. "The woman across the alley watched the whole thing."

"Good for her."

"She's going to *tell* people, Kerwin. And you look like a drowned rat!"

He could feel the water pooling in his shoes, the fabric of his shirt clinging to his chest in a way that made him aware of every soft place on his body. "Thank you."

"You're welcome." She pushed off from the counter and crossed to him, and before he could step back she had reached up and pushed the wet hair out of his eyes with a brisk, unsentimental hand, the way you'd adjust a crooked picture frame. "There. Now you look like a slightly drier rat."

"Your compassion is overwhelming."

A stripe of air passed between her teeth in a huff. "I'm a delivery driver, not a nurse." But even as she rebuked him, her hand lingered for a moment at his temple, her thumb brushing the skin above his ear and the touch was so light and so brief that afterward he would wonder if he had imagined it.

"Go and put some dry clothes on before you catch pneumonia and I have to explain to the ambulance crew why a grown man was screaming and hosing himself down in an alley in November."

He should have done as she said; gone to the bedroom and changed into something dry and come back and sat in his chair and let the evening proceed along whatever track it was meant to follow. But the bra was still hanging in his mind the way it was hanging on the shower curtain rod, and the fact that she had mentioned it at all, shouting it down at him from the window as though a woman's undergarments were simply another piece of weather to be reported on, had tucked itself into some seam of his brain and would not be dislodged.

"I don't have a problem with your bra," he said again, as if the conversation had not been interrupted by him fleeing up the stairs like a schoolboy caught at something shameful. "Not that I — I don't *know*, do I? I haven't really seen it."

"Good to know." She tilted her head. "I'm not wearing it now, though, so I don't know why you're still thinking about it." She jerked her chin toward the hallway, flapping her hands to shoo him out of the room. "If you want a look, it's in the bathroom."

His mouth went suddenly dry, as if he'd been stuffed through with cotton batting. He could see, now that he was looking, that she wasn't wearing one at *all* and he could map the shape of her beneath the thin flannel, the dark points of her nipples visible still through the fabric.

"And this would interest me how?" The words came out strangled, unconvincing even to his own ears.

Perhaps this was simply what she did. Perhaps she went from house to house leaving bras on shower rods like calling cards, like Mardi Gras beads flung from floats, perhaps she was the sort of woman his mother would have called *fast*. A slapper, a tart, a woman who swung loose in strange men's kitchens and thought nothing of it because she'd done it a hundred times before and would do it a hundred times again. He told himself this. He even tried to make himself believe it.

Eleanor looked at him for a long moment, and then her gaze dropped, slowly, deliberately, to the front of his soaked pants where his erection strained against the wet fabric, obvious and undeniable.

"I think," Eleanor began, tracing the dip and bow of her chapped lips with her tongue, "it would interest you very much."

He said nothing. There was nothing to say that would not make him sound like a fool or a lecher or both, and so he stood there dripping on the linoleum and watched her watch him and waited for her to laugh, to tell him she was joking, to break whatever spell had settled over this kitchen and let them both pretend this had never happened.

She did not laugh.

She reached for the top button of the flannel shirt—*his* shirt—and undid it.

"Eleanor," he said, and his voice came out strangled. "What are you doing?"

"What does it look like?" She said it simply, without guile, as though the answer were obvious and his asking the question was the strange part.

"Stop that."

"Why?"

The second button. The third. He could see the hollow of her throat now, the delicate line of her clavicle.

"Because I am telling you to stop."

"That's not a reason." The fourth button. "That's an *order*. I don't take orders from you, Kerwin."

His jaw tightened. "You're being ridiculous."

"Am I?" The fifth button. The flannel fell open and he could see the pale curve of her stomach, the shadow between her breasts. "You're the one standing there shaking."

"I'm cold."

"You're *lying*."

She shrugged her shoulders and the shirt slid down her arms and pooled at her feet, and she stood there in his kitchen in nothing but her underwear.

He did not move. He did not trust himself to move. If he moved he would touch her, and if he touched her he would not be able to stop, and if he did not stop then something horrible would happen.

"Kerwin." Her voice was soft now, the teasing gone. "Come here."

"No."

"Why not?"

"Because—" He stopped. *Because you are half my age. Because you could have anyone. Because I am a dried-up husk of a man who has forgotten how to want things without perversion, because if you let me touch you I will ruin it, the way I ruin everything.*

"Because what?"

He looked at her. She was waiting, patient as ever, and there was no mockery in her face now, no challenge as she blinked up at him through her messy fringe. Just that same calm certainty she had carried with her since she walked through his door, as though she already knew how this would end and was simply waiting for him to catch up.

"I don't—" His voice came out rough, scraped raw. "I don't know how to do this."

"Yes you do."

"I don't. I haven't—it's been—"

"I know." She took a step toward him. "I don't care."

It should have humiliated him, that she could read him so easily, that she could look at him and see the years of nothing but his own fist for company—and even that had abandoned him eventually, his body refusing to cooperate with even the most basic of urges. There had been a time, in prison, when he had been desperate enough to trade for it—favors for one of the orderlies, a man who worked in the medical wing and had access to supplies—and what Kerwin got in return was a rubber glove filled with rice and warmed in the microwave, the fingers knotted off and stuffed into a gap between his mattress and the frame so he could rut into it like an animal while the orderly watched from the doorway.

After, when Kerwin was finished and shaking and sick with himself, the man would take the glove and untie it and empty its contents of rice and piss and come and whatever else had been added to the mixture onto Kerwin's young, bare chest while he lay there and took it because that was the price and he had agreed to pay it. He had been nineteen, twenty, and so desperate for something that felt like pleasure that he would have made a deal with the devil himself for it; and perhaps he had, because in the years after, his body exacted its payment in erections that came rarely and left quickly and desire that flickered and guttered before it could catch, as though some essential thing had been burnt out of him and he had never learned how to replace it.

She was close enough now that he could smell her; her skin in the dim kitchen light had a strange translucence to it, the freckles stark against the pallor.

"You *should* care." His voice was barely a whisper. "You should run from me. You should—"

"Should I?" She reached out and touched his chest, her fingers cold against his skin where the wet shirt clung. "Is that what you want?"

No. The word rose up in him with a force that frightened him. *No, I want you to stay. I want you to never leave. I want—*

"I don't know what I want."

"Liar." She said it gently, almost fondly. Her hand moved up to his jaw, her cold fingers tracing the line of it. "You know exactly what you want. You're just afraid to take it."

He caught her wrist. The desire frothing through him was so loud that he barely felt the cool skin covering the fine bones beneath his fingers.

"I am not afraid," he said.

"Prove it."

He kissed her.

He did not mean to do it, but his body moved without his permission, his hand coming up to cup the back of her head, his mouth finding hers with a desperation that surprised him. Her lips were cool against his, and when he pulled back to look at her face her eyes were half-closed and there was a small smile playing at the corners of her mouth.

"See?" she said. "That wasn't so hard."

"Bedroom." The word came out hoarse, barely recognizable as his own voice. "Now."

She took his hand and she led him down the hallway as though she knew the way, past the bathroom where the door was open even though he was certain he had shut it in his earlier haste, and into his small bedroom with its narrow bed and its yellowed sheets.

She lay down without ceremony. She did not arrange herself or pose or do any of the things he imagined women did in these moments; she simply lay there, looking up at him, waiting.

He undressed with his back to her, his movements stiff and mechanical, shedding his wet clothes and draping them over the chair in the corner. When he turned back to her she had not moved and her eyes followed him as he crossed to the bed.

"You're sure?" he questioned.

"I'm sure."

He stood at the edge of the mattress and looked at her, and some part of him—some small, still-functioning part that had not yet been drowned by the roaring in his blood—whispered that something was wrong.

He told that part to be quiet.

She was here, and she was willing, and that the best he could hope for, surely. She had unbuttoned her shirt and led him to this room and said *I'm sure*, and if she lay so still it was because she was waiting for him, and if the smell in the room was strange it was because they had both been sick, both been through something terrible, and bodies did strange things under stress.

The smell was him, it *had* to be him. His genitals stunk like a fishmonger's stall on a Sunday boardwalk, stewing in the damp of his pants all evening and he wished now that he had thought to line up the hose, to fit the nozzle beneath his foreskin and let the pressure balloon it out, the cold water rushing in and scouring away the smegma, the dead skin, the acrid sweat that clung to him like the residue of the vomiting, that sick preemptive perspiration the body pushes through the skin when it knows what's coming.

He should apologize. He should warn her, at least, that he was not fit for this, that he had not been fit for anything in a very long time.

He could smell the bathroom, too. Whatever was leaking up there had gotten worse; the towels weren't holding it back anymore and the whole apartment had taken on that sweetish, dense quality that he associated with drains that had backed up in summer and the cans behind the shop when his father forgot to put them out. He breathed through his mouth and it didn't help.

But she was looking at him with those dark eyes, patient, waiting, and he could not bring himself to speak.

He had wanted this for so long. He had wanted *her* for so long, even if he had not let himself know it until now and she was offering herself to him, and he would be a fool to refuse, and he was tired of being a fool, tired of denying himself, tired of standing at the edge of things and watching them pass him by.

He lowered himself beside her and kissed her throat. Her skin was smooth beneath his lips, and she made a sound deep in her chest, a low exhalation that came from somewhere far inside of her. He kissed her collarbone, the hollow between her breasts, the soft swells of flesh above her sternum.

He bit down on her breast, gently at first and then harder, and she did not flinch, she only groaned, low and guttural, and when he bit her again she groaned again, the same sound at the same pitch, as though she were a machine designed to produce it. He found he did not mind. He found he *liked* it, the predictability of her response, the way she lay beneath him and took whatever he gave her without complaint or correction. He pinched the soft flesh of her inner arm until his nails left crescents and she did not pull away. He put his teeth to the skin of her throat and bit until he tasted copper and she only sighed, that same low exhale, patient as a cow waiting for the bolt. It made him want to do worse things, to see how far he could go before she stopped him because he was beginning to suspect the answer was that she would not stop him at all, that he could do anything, anything, and she would lie there and let him.

Isn't this love? The thought came unbidden. Letting someone do whatever they want to you, just because they want to?

She lay beneath him and let him take what he wanted, her body pliant and yielding, and he thought: s*he loves me. She must love me. Why else would she allow this?*

"Tell me if I'm hurting you," he said against her skin.

"You're not hurting me."

"Eleanor?"

"Mmm?"

"Look at me."

Her gaze drifted to his face, slow and unfocused. His hand moved down her body, over her stomach, between her thighs; she was slick there, wet in a way that surprised him, and when he touched her she made another of those sounds, that low guttural exhalation that must have been pleasure because her body shifted beneath him, a slow settling movement, and he heard another soft sigh, a release of air.

"Now," she said. "Please."

He positioned himself above her. She was looking up at him with those dark eyes, her face calm, almost serene, and the wanting in him was so vast and so terrible that he could not think around it.

"Please," she said, and he thought she meant for him to finish it, to push into her and take what he wanted but her hand was on his head, pushing him down, and he understood.

He had not done this in years because he had not done much of anything in years, but her hand was relentless and so he went, sliding down the length of her body, kissing her stomach, her hip, the crease where her thigh met her pelvis. The smell hit him before his mouth did, thick and ripe and strange, and for a moment he hesitated, his face hovering inches from her cunt.

It was the Gastronauts, he told himself, more specifically the food they had eaten. It had done something to both of them, had changed the way their bodies worked and the way they both smelled and tasted.

He had eaten worse things tonight than Eleanor's cunt. He hadn't even asked what they were eating, down in the basement, and this was no different, just another thing to be consumed.

He put his mouth on her.

She was slick and swollen and the taste of her coated his tongue, metallic and sweet and something that reminded him of the meals he had left too long on the counter that had started to turn, started this entire strange fugue that had settled over his apartment. He told himself he did not mind and that it was fine, good, even as he alternated between lapping at her with long flat strokes kitten-soft busses of her clit and she made that sound again, that low groan, and her hips began to move.

She bucked against his mouth in a steady pulse, up and down, up and down, and the flesh of her felt loose against his lips, softer than he expected, sliding and shifting against his tongue. He closed his eyes and focused on the task, his tongue working at her, and her thighs began to shudder.

The tremors ran through her in waves that did not crest or break, just went on and on, her body twitching against his mouth, and he gripped her hips to hold her steady and kept going because he couldn't stop now, not for anything. When he finally looked up from between the crux of her thighs he felt like something half-submerged, a gator in a bayou with its jaws locked around a piece of carrion, his chin slick with her, his lips numb and swollen, and she was staring at the ceiling with her mouth open and her eyes half-rolled back and she was still shuddering, still twitching, her hands clawed into the sheets on either side of her.

"Eleanor," he said, and his voice came out thick and strange, his pleasure turning him impossibly more taciturn. "Eleanor, are you—"

"Please," she said, and her hand found his head again, and she pushed him back down.

He did not ask again. He buried his face between her thighs, his nose pressed into the wiry tangle of her pubic hair, and sealed his lips around her clit and sucked. She ground against him and he let her, his jaw aching, his chin slick. His fingers found her opening and pushed inside, two at first and then three, and he worked them in and out of her with a relentlessness that shook the bed frame against the wall; he had become something else, something he did not recognize, a hulking slavering thing ruled entirely by the need to make her come apart beneath him.

He could hear himself grunting with the effort of it, could feel the spit running down his chin, and he did not care. He was one of those men now, the kind he had always despised, the ones who fucked like animals and thought of nothing but their own pleasure and the pleasure they could wring from a body beneath them. His fingers were buried in her to the knuckle and she was making sounds he had never heard a woman make, wet gurgling sounds that were pulled deep from her belly; he thought about nothing at all until she finally went still and then he crawled up the length of her body and positioned himself above her.

"Please," she said again, and he pushed into her.

She did not move beneath him, did not wrap her legs around him or arch her back or make any of the sounds he had imagined women made, she simply lay there, still and patient, desensitized to her own pleasure and let him take what he needed. He moved faster, harder, and the sounds he made were the only sounds in the room, his breathing and his heartbeat and the wet rhythm of their joining.

The ecstasy of it wiped everything else from his mind. He closed his eyes and lost himself in it, in the rhythm of their joining, in the wet sounds of flesh on flesh. He buried his face in the crook of her neck and breathed her in and did not let himself think about what he was doing, there was nothing but the pleasure rooting out from the base of his cock.

"Eleanor," he said, her name torn from him. *"Eleanor..."*

She did not answer. She lay beneath him with her eyes half-closed and her lips parted, and when he looked at her face he saw peace.

The pressure built at the base of his spine, a tingling heat that spread upward through his pelvis and into his gut, and he knew he was close, knew he could not hold it back much longer. He moved faster, harder, and the bed frame knocked against the wall in a rhythm that would have embarrassed him if he had been capable of anything beyond the animal need to finish what he had started. The tingling became a pulse, the pulse became a wave, and then it hit him like a blow to the back of the head, whiting out his vision, clenching every muscle in his body at once. He heard himself make a sound, a long guttural groan that seemed to come from somewhere outside himself, and then he was emptying into her endlessly, spasm after spasm, his hips jerking, his fingers digging into the meat of her thighs hard enough to pull the skin away from its bone.

He collapsed onto her chest and lay there for a long time, his breathing ragged, his heartbeat slamming against his ribs and then slowing by degrees. She did not move beneath him, did not stroke his hair or whisper his name, she simply let him rest and he was grateful for the kindness of it.

Her skin in the dim light had taken on a mottled quality with shadows pooling in the hollows of her cheeks and throat; her lips were slightly parted, the soft flesh of the lower one caught in the gap between her front teeth where it had swelled and darkened.

He touched her face.

"Eleanor, are you—"

She blinked. Her eyes opened and found his face and she smiled, slow and drowsy.

"What?" Her voice was thick with sleep. "What is it?"

He stared at her. She was warm against him now, alive, and here.

"Nothing," he said. "I thought—nothing."

"You thought what?"

He shook his head. The food. Still the food, still playing tricks. He was seeing things, feeling things that were not real.

"Go to sleep," he said. "We should sleep."

She nodded and closed her eyes, and he lay down beside her and pulled the covers over them both. She curled into him, her body warm against his side, and he stared at the ceiling and listened to the sound of her breathing.

In the bathroom, her bra hung in tatters on the shower curtain rod where he had placed it.

He did not remember putting it there. He did not remember going into the bathroom at all.

But it was late, and he was tired, and there were so many things he did not remember anymore. He closed his eyes and let himself drift, and if his dreams were strange and dark, he did not remember them when he woke.

13

Love Well, Dine Well

He did not remember getting out of bed.

This was the first thing Kerwin knew with any certainty as he stood before the open refrigerator in the blue-white dark of the kitchen, that he had not decided to come here, had not swung his legs over the side of the mattress and thought, *I'll just have a bite of something.* One moment he had been asleep, or what passed for sleep, that thick black nothing that had swallowed him after Eleanor's breathing had gone slow and even against his chest and the next he was here, one hand on the refrigerator door, the other already closing around something wrapped in brown paper, and the hunger was so immense, so total, that for a long moment he could not think at all.

The meat was cold. He registered this distantly as he tore the paper away and brought whatever was inside directly to his mouth. It was cold and dense and slick with something that might have been blood or might have been fat, he couldn't tell and didn't care because the hunger had contracted to a single bright point somewhere behind his sternum and all he could do was feed it. His teeth sank in, his jaw worked; he swallowed without chewing properly, felt the lump of it travel down his throat, and bit again before the first mouthful had even reached his stomach. The sound of his own feeding filled the kitchen but still he did not stop, he stood in the light of the refrigerator in his underwear, shaking slightly from cold or from need and he ate.

When the first package was empty (and he didn't remember finishing it, nothing except the motion of hand to mouth and the working of his jaw) he reached for another. He chose a plastic container this time, the lid coming off in his fumbling fingers, and inside was something shredded and pale that he scooped directly into his mouth without pausing to wonder what it was or where it had come from. The hunger made room for each mouthful and then demanded more. He thought, dimly, that he should stop and that this was not how people ate, that if Eleanor were to walk in right now she would see him crouched over the open refrigerator like a dog at a carcass and she would—what? Be disgusted? Afraid? Kerwin did not know, and he did not stop because above all else, he did not want to.

At some point, he couldn't have said when, couldn't have said how long he'd been standing there, the hunger began to ease. It didn't disappear; he could still feel it coiled somewhere deep in his gut, patient and vast, but the frantic edge had gone out of it. He became aware, gradually, of the ache in his jaw, the cramp in his stomach, the way his hands were trembling as they hovered over the shelf. He made himself step back and close the refrigerator door.

The kitchen went dark.

He stood there in the sudden blackness, breathing hard, and listened to the distant tick of the heater and the faint, persistent drip from somewhere in the walls that he'd been meaning to call someone about for months. His heart was pounding and when he ran his tongue over his teeth he could feel strands of meat caught between them. Slowly, like a man surfacing from deep water, he became aware of what he had done.

He opened the refrigerator again.

The light returned, and with it, the sight that had started all of this, shelves packed with food, brown paper parcels stacked three deep and plastic containers of things he didn't recognize. There were vegetables in the crisper—*when had he bought vegetables?*—and a whole joint of something in the meat drawer and butter and cream and eggs and more, so much more than he'd ever had in this refrigerator, more than he could possibly eat in a week.

He had canceled his delivery. He remembered this clearly, the woman's voice on the other end of the phone, harried and only vaguely curious about the way they'd poisoned him, (none of this was his fault, he knew, because *they* sent the food and *they* sent Eleanor...) unsurprised, too, surely, when he told her to skip all future orders. No one had come to the door, no one had knocked. Eleanor had been here with him all evening, all night, and he would have heard if someone had—

But the refrigerator was full and he had just eaten God knows how much of whatever was in it, and he didn't know where any of it had come from.

He pulled out one of the remaining parcels and turned it over in his hands. It was heavy and cold, wrapped in proper butcher's paper and tied neatly with string. There was no label or stamp that would give any indication of where it had been purchased or by whom. He set it down and reached for another and found it dressed the same way, no markings, no receipts, nothing. The plastic containers were equally anonymous; no brand names, no use-by dates, just food, sitting there, waiting for him to eat it.

Eleanor must have done this. She must have slipped out while he was sleeping—he'd slept so heavily, hadn't he? Deeper than he had in years, like falling into a well—and she'd gone out and found a butcher, one of those places that opened early for restaurants, and she'd filled bags with meat and carried them up the stairs and arranged them in his refrigerator as a surprise. A gift. A gesture of—what? Affection? Care? Thankfulness for the way he'd licked her until his jaw ached, the way he hadn't complained about how wet she was, soaking the sheets beneath them, or how loose-limbed and passive she became after, letting him arrange her however he liked? Some men would have found it off-putting, all that slickness, the way she just lay there and took it but Kerwin found he didn't mind. He'd been generous with her, hadn't he? Perhaps this was her way of being generous back.

He closed the refrigerator and the kitchen went dark again. He wiped his hands on his thighs. His palms were sticky, tacky with whatever had been on the meat, and his chin was wet, and when he touched his face his fingers came away slick.

He needed to wash and he needed to go back to bed, to lie down next to

Eleanor and close his eyes and pretend that none of this had happened. In the morning—the real morning, when the sun was up—he would ask her about the food. He might even make a joke of it. Where did all this come from, he'd say, and she'd tell him, and then he'd know, and everything would be fine.

He turned away from the refrigerator and went to wash his hands. The water in the kitchen tap ran cold and then warm and he stood there scrubbing until his skin was pink and raw, but he could still taste the meat on his tongue and feel it settling in his stomach, heavy and strange and impossibly satisfying.

He dried his hands on the dish towel and went back to bed.

Eleanor hadn't moved. She lay on her back, one arm flung above her head, the sheet pulled down to expose the pale curve of a breast, her lips slightly parted; still as a painting as he slid in beside her and pulled the duvet up to his chin. He lay there in the dark, listening to her breathe and the hunger curled in his stomach like a cat before a fire, satisfied for now but half-listening for what might come next.

* * *

The smell of coffee pulled him from the bedroom before he was fully awake. Eleanor was at the stove, barefoot, wearing one of his shirts and nothing else, humming something tuneless as she prodded at a pan.

"There you are." She glanced over her shoulder, spatula raised like a conductor's baton. "I was about to send in a search party."

Kerwin rubbed his face. The kitchen was bright with afternoon light and he was aware, suddenly, of his own body; the sourness of his breath, the stiffness in his lower back, the faint tenderness between his legs from last night from what they'd done. He didn't know how to stand, where to put his hands. Did she expect him to touch her? Kiss her good afternoon? What was the protocol when you'd spent the night with your face buried between a woman's thighs?

"What time is it?"

"Past one." She turned back to the stove, flipped something that sizzled. "I found eggs. And what I think might be bacon, though the packaging was a bit mysterious." She looked at him, the bite of her lip bubbled between her teeth. "Or should I have asked first?"

She seemed utterly unbothered. Entirely comfortable, at ease in his kitchen, in his shirt, cracking eggs into his pan like she'd done it a hundred times before.

"No, that's—" He moved toward the refrigerator without meaning to, drawn by something he couldn't name. "...that's fine."

"There's coffee on the stove. It's not very good coffee, like you said...I found your ancient jar of instant in the cupboard." She wrinkled her nose. "I didn't want to go out."

He opened the refrigerator. The shelves were still full. Fuller, maybe—had there been this many containers before? He couldn't remember.

"Eleanor."

"Mm?" She was cracking another egg into the pan, and he watched the yolk slide from the shell, watched it settle into the hot fat, the pale membrane holding it round and glossy. She cracked another one beside it—two eyes now, staring up from the pan, the whites spreading and going opaque at the edges.

"Where did all this come from?"

She looked up then, brow furrowed, and crossed to stand beside him. Her shoulder brushed his arm as she peered into the refrigerator.

"Good lord," she said. "That's a lot of meat."

"It wasn't here before."

"Before when?"

"Before you arrived. The fridge was empty—you saw it."

She reached past him and pulled out one of the brown paper parcels, turning it over in her hands. Her fingers were pale against the paper, the nails bitten short.

"No label," she said.

"No."

"And you didn't order it?"

"I canceled my delivery. You heard me."

"Hm." She set the parcel back on the shelf, her expression thoughtful rather than alarmed. "Maybe you have a secret admirer."

"Eleanor, this isn't—" He stopped, tried again. "Someone had to bring it. Someone had to come in."

"I've been here the whole time." She turned to face him, leaning her hip against the counter. "No one came to the door."

The ease of her. The absolute ease. Standing there in his shirt with her bare legs and her bitten nails and her calm, untroubled face, like nothing that had happened was worth remarking on, not the sex, not the food, not the strangeness of any of it. Maybe this was simply what she did…maybe she went from house to house, from man to man, taking what was offered and moving on when it suited her. Maybe she didn't have a mold-infested studio at all. Maybe she was some new category of person he'd never encountered before, the sort who fucked and squatted her way across the city, who showed up on doorsteps in rainstorms and made herself at home. How *dare* she! How dare she stand there looking at him like he was the strange one, like his confusion was *quaint*, like—

"Kerwin."

He blinked.

"It's probably from our friends," she said, which was ridiculous because he hadn't had a real friend since childhood. "You said Amir runs the shop downstairs…maybe it was a welcome gift. We *are* new members." She shrugged, easy, like it was obvious. "They seem like the sort of people who'd do something like that."

"Come eat," she said. Her voice was gentle. "You look half-starved." It was only then that he noticed the cut on her forehead. It had darkened overnight, the edges gone almost black, the skin around it swollen and faintly greenish like a bruise that had started to turn. She caught him looking and raised a hand to touch it, her fingers hovering just above the wound.

"Ugh," groaned Eleanor. "It's worse, isn't it? I saw it in the mirror this morning. Looks like I've gone a few rounds with someone…"

"Does it hurt?"

"Not really." She dropped her hand. "It's a little numb, actually. I must have knocked it in my sleep."

He sat down at the narrow table and watched her move around his kitchen like she belonged there, opening drawers and finding forks, pouring coffee into mugs she'd located without asking. She set a plate in front of him, two eggs, their centers still soft and trembling, watching him and slid into the chair across from his, pulling one bare foot up beneath her.

"Eat," she said, and he did. The eggs burst under his fork and ran yellow across the plate and the bacon left a slick of grease on his tongue that made him think of the things he'd done standing in the light of the refrigerator with no one watching.

"You eat like a man who's been told the food might be taken away!" Eleanor said, watching him across the table. She had her chin propped on her fist, a strip of bacon dangling from her other hand like a cigarette. "All hunched over, arms around the plate. Did you do that in prison? Guard your food?"

He stopped chewing. The directness of it, the casual way she said *prison,* as if it were a job he'd once held rather than the thing that had defined him still caught him off guard.

"You don't have to answer that," she added, wrinkling her nose. It made him want to put the entire thing in his mouth. "I'm being nosy. It's a problem of mine."

"One of many."

"Oh, there's a list, is there?" She bit the end off the bacon strip and grinned at him, and there it was, the gap between her front teeth, the crooked smile that happened to her face rather than being performed by it.

She ate with her fingers, tearing the stolen strip into pieces and licking yolk from her thumb, completely unbothered by the mystery of the food, the wound on her head or anything at all.

"I thought I might cook tonight," she said, chasing a bit of egg around her plate. "Something *good*. There's enough meat in there to feed an army."

"You don't have to do that."

"I want to." She looked up at him, and for a moment her eyes seemed flat and reflective, but then she blinked and she was Eleanor again, warm and wry and watching him fondly. "Unless you'd rather order in?"

His knife scratched across the plate at her mention of another unknown quantity knocking at his door. "No," he heard himself say. "No, that sounds nice."

She smiled at him across the table, and the cut on her forehead glistened darkly in the light.

After they finished eating, she washed the plates while he watched from the doorway, and it occurred to him that this was what people did—cooked for each other, cleaned up after each other, existed in the same space without explanation or apology. This was what normal people did, and he had never been normal, had never been capable of normalcy, but perhaps with Eleanor he could learn. Perhaps she could teach him how to be the sort of person who ate breakfast with someone and didn't spend the rest of the day organizing all the ways it could have gone wrong.

They spent the afternoon on the sofa, her feet tucked under his thigh, the weight of her small and warm and present. She had found a novel on his shelf that his mother had left behind, a romance with a broken spine and foxed pages and she read aloud from it in a voice pitched for mockery, pausing to roll her eyes at the more egregious passages. He did not listen to the words, though he watched her mouth move and felt the heat of her through his pants and thought, *I could keep this.*

The thought was new. He turned the thought over in his mind. *Keep her*. What did that even mean? She wasn't a stray cat or a library book; she was a person with a life somewhere else, a job, presumably friends and family and all the other apparatus of a normal existence and she would leave eventually.

But she hadn't left *yet,* and the longer she stayed, the more the idea took root. Maybe she didn't have to leave, maybe the roads were still flooded... maybe her van was ruined and she couldn't go back to work and the terrible studio she'd mentioned was uninhabitable and she needed somewhere to stay for a while, just until she sorted things out. He could offer that, couldn't he? A place to stay? It was the least he could do, really, after what they'd done together, after the way she'd let him touch her.

"You're not listening," Eleanor said, closing the book on her finger.

"I am."

"What did I just read?"

He considered lying. "Something about a duke."

"There hasn't been a duke for thirty pages." She shifted, resettled, her foot pressing harder against his thigh. "Where did you go?"

He shook his head. "Nowhere."

"Don't sulk," she said. "I'm not criticizing. I'm just saying—" She opened the book again, found her place. "Also, the duke is dead. He's been dead since chapter six. You'd know that if you'd been listening."

Then she stopped. The book lowered an inch. She was watching him the way she'd been watching him all afternoon, he realized, sideways, through the veil of her own performance and whatever she was about to say had been sitting in her mouth for a while now, waiting for its moment.

"I was thinking, actually," she said, and paused to twirl a lock of dark hair around one finger, "about the basement..."

Here it comes, he thought. The ask. She'd let him put his mouth on her and now she wanted something in return and he was already calculating what he'd be willing to give, how much of himself he could carve off and hand over before there was nothing left—

"When's the next meeting? The Gastronauts, I mean. When do we go back?"

He blinked. That wasn't what he'd expected.

"What?"

"The *Gastronauts.*" She said the name without hesitation, as if it were perfectly ordinary, as if they hadn't spent an evening in a candlelit basement eating meat they couldn't identify and listening to a man read from an apocryphal gospel about a woman eating God. "When do we go back?"

He hadn't thought about the Gastronauts since—when? Since they'd come home, since they'd stumbled up the stairs and he'd pressed her against the wall and kissed her and she'd let him, since everything that had happened after. The basement and the ritual and the strange communion of it all seemed to belong to a different life, a different Kerwin, one who had still been hungry in ways he hadn't understood.

"I don't know," he said. "I don't know when the next one is."

"But you want to go."

Did he? He thought about it. The velvet walls and the silver domes and the fountain, though he still wasn't certain what had been in it, Amir's measured voice reading about Mary in the tomb, about the body of God, about swallowing what you loved so that it could never leave you. He had wanted it then—the ritual, the permission, the sense that he was part of something larger than himself...

But now he had Eleanor.

Now he had the meat in the refrigerator, anonymous and abundant, refilling itself through some mechanism he didn't understand and didn't particularly want to examine. Now he had her body beneath him, above him, opened to him in ways he hadn't known bodies could open and now, most importantly, he had the taste of her on his tongue—and he let himself linger on it, on the memory of his face between her thighs, of the slickness and the salt and the low sounds she made when he worked his tongue against her—and what could the Gastronauts offer him that he didn't already have?

They had given him permission. That was what the meeting had really been about, wasn't it? Now that he had it, he didn't need the people who had granted it; he had the source, right here in his apartment.

"I don't think so," he said slowly. "Not right now."

"No?"

"I have everything I need here," he said simply, surprised by his own truthfulness.

"That's sweet," she said. Her voice was not as animated as he would have liked, but the words themselves were warm, and he chose to believe her words instead of his own.

"I was thinking..." he said slowly, "...that you don't have to rush off."

She raised an eyebrow. "Rush off where?"

"Wherever. Your... home, your job. I just mean—" He stopped, aware that he was making a mess of this. "The roads might still be bad."

"The storm ended yesterday."

"Did it?"

She laughed, that crooked-toothed thing that did something complicated to his chest. "Kerwin, it's *Tuesday*. The storm ended Sunday night."

Was it Tuesday.? He'd lost track. Time had gone strange on him, folding in on itself like a napkin badly creased, and he couldn't quite reconstruct the sequence of events that had led from Saturday night to this moment on the sofa with her feet warm against his leg.

"Right," he said. "Still."

"Still what?"

"Still. You could stay, if you wanted to." He couldn't look at her as he said it, keeping his eyes fixed on a point somewhere past her shoulder where the paint was peeling. "There's plenty of food now. And I'm not—" He swallowed. "I'm not using the spare room."

The spare room. As if he expected her to sleep down the hall like a lodger, like someone who hadn't spent the previous night with his face between her thighs and his fingers digging bruises into her hips. But he couldn't assume, could he? He couldn't presume that because she'd let him touch her once she'd want him touching her again but she must know, surely, what staying in his bed would mean—she'd felt the way he'd set himself upon her, the greed of it, the years of nothing finally breaking open into something ravenous and clumsy. If she stayed in his bed she would not be spared his attentions. He would want her again. He would want her constantly. And perhaps that was more than she'd bargained for when she'd unbuttoned her shirt and led him down the hallway; perhaps she'd only meant it as a kindness, a temporary thing, and now here he was offering her a room of her own like some proprietor, giving her an out she hadn't asked for because he couldn't bear to hear her say she didn't want him that way again.

The silence stretched between them, elastic and strange and his heart was doing something unpleasant behind his ribs, a rapid stuttering beat that made him feel faintly sick.

Then Eleanor set the book aside and swung her legs down from the sofa, pivoting until she was facing him properly. Her expression was difficult to read—something careful and considering that made him feel like a specimen under glass.

"Kerwin," she said. "What exactly are you asking?"

He didn't know. That was the honest answer, the one he couldn't quite bring himself to give. He wanted her to stay. He wanted to introduce her to people—what people? He didn't know anyone, but the fantasy persisted regardless. *This is Eleanor, she lives with me now.* He wanted to go to the Gastronaut meetings with her, sit beside her in Amir's basement while the candles burned low and the fountain dripped its endless patter. He wanted to feed her. He wanted to be fed.

"I'm asking you to stay," he said. The words came out smaller than he'd intended, thin and reedy, a child's voice from an old man's mouth. "For a while," he shrugged. "Or as long as you like."

She was quiet for a long moment, her thumb tracing the edge of the book's cover. "I have a job," she said, "or I did…I'm meant to be driving my routes, you know…"

"You could call them."

"And say what? Sorry, I've moved in with a man I met four days ago, please hold my position indefinitely?"

The words landed harder than she'd perhaps intended. He felt his face do something—close off, probably, seal itself shut the way she'd described earlier—and he turned toward the window so she wouldn't have to watch it happen.

"Forget it," he said, the tips of his ears steaming pink. "It was a stupid idea."

"I didn't say that."

"You didn't have to!"

"My apartment has mold…" she said slowly, considering…"Black mold, you know, in the bathroom and the landlord won't do anything about it. I've been coughing for months."

He turned back to look at her.

"The van is probably towed by now," she continued, as if working through a problem aloud. "And I don't—" She stopped, chewed her lip. "I don't actually have anywhere I need to be other than work, and I've probably already been fired. I've been acting like I have something to go back to, but I don't. Not really."

She stopped. The thread she'd been picking at had come loose in her fingers, a long pale strand that she wound around her knuckle and then unwound again.

"Eleanor—"

"I don't really talk to anyone," she said abruptly. "Have I told you that? My dad sends emails sometimes…but he doesn't know what to say so he just forwards articles about gut health and I delete them without reading them." She looked at him, and there was something raw in her face now, undefended. "I don't have anywhere to *go*, Kerwin, not really. That's what I'm trying to tell you. So if you're offering me somewhere to stay, you should know what you're getting. It doesn't have to be some big thing. You're just—" She shrugged, a quick little motion. "—giving me a room."

He crossed to the sofa. She watched him come and didn't flinch when he sat down beside her.

"I'm not offering you a room," he said.

"No?"

"No." He turned her hand over in his, traced the lines there, the bitten edges of her nails. "I'm offering you—" He stopped, not knowing how to finish the sentence without sounding like a fool or a lunatic.

"Something else?" she said, and there was something in her voice he couldn't quite place, something almost sad, as if she understood something about this offer that he didn't.

"Yes," he said. "If you want it."

She looked at him for a long moment, her dark eyes unreadable.

"All right," she said.

He blinked. "All right?"

Eleanor reached out and took his hand. *"All right."*

She smiled at him and he wanted to pin the wings of this moment while it was still alive, to press it flat under glass and keep it on a shelf where he could look at it whenever he needed proof that something good had happened to him once. "I'll stay. For now."

For now. It was a provisional answer, hedged and careful, but it was enough. He turned his hand in hers so that their palms were pressed together.

"We could get your things," he said. "From your home. We could—"

"Later." She squeezed his hand once, briefly, and then let go. "There's no rush."

There wasn't. There was all the time in the world, stretching out before them and so Kerwin leaned back against the sofa cushions and felt something in his chest loosen, some tension he hadn't known he was carrying finally beginning to ease. She was *staying*. She had said she would stay.

Outside, the afternoon light was beginning to thicken toward evening, the shadows lengthening across the floor. He didn't remember the hours passing, couldn't have said what they'd done between breakfast and this moment, but it didn't matter. Time had always been slippery for him, prone to stretching and compressing in ways that didn't quite match the clock on the wall.

Eleanor picked up her book again and found her place, and he let his head fall back against the cushion and listened to her voice rise and fall, the words blurring into pleasant nonsense at the edges of his consciousness. He must have drifted off at some point because when he opened his eyes again the room was dark, the only light the pale glow from the kitchen where she'd left the stove light on, and Eleanor was standing at the window with her back to him, looking out at something he couldn't see.

"What time is it?" His voice came out thick, crusted with sleep.

"Late." She didn't turn around. "Past midnight, I think."

Midnight. He'd slept through the entire evening, the entire dinner she'd promised to cook. He sat up, his back protesting, his neck stiff from the awkward angle he'd been lying in.

"You should have woken me."

"You needed the sleep." Now she did turn, and in the dim light from the kitchen her face looked wrong somehow—the shadows falling in unfamiliar places, the cut on her forehead a dark slash that swallowed the light. "You haven't been sleeping well, have you? Even before, I mean...before I came."

He hadn't. The insomnia had started in prison, where he learned to sleep like a dog with one ear cocked because the sounds of other men breathing and shifting and weeping in the dark kept him skimming just below the surface of true rest. Forty men to a wing, and every one of them afraid of something—the ones who cried out in their sleep, the ones who paced until the screws told them to stop, the ones who lay perfectly still and silent in a way that was somehow worse than all the rest. Kerwin had learned to track them by sound, to map the night by its disturbances and the habit had never left him.

Even now, years later, in a home where the only sounds were the building settling into its bones, he lay awake for hours with his eyes open in the dark, listening for footsteps that never came, for the scrape of a key in a lock, for the particular quality of silence that meant someone was standing just outside your door deciding whether to come in. He often drifted off just before dawn, if he drifted off at all, and woke with the sun already hot through the curtains and his mouth tasting of something stale and sour. He'd forgotten what proper sleep felt like, really, and had begun to suspect, in the small hours when the suspicions came easiest that even as a child he'd been this way. Waiting, always waiting, for the next bad thing to arrive.

"I sleep fine," was what he said instead.

Eleanor made a small sound in the back of her throat and then she was moving toward the kitchen, her bare feet silent on the floor.

"I made soup," she said over her shoulder. "It's probably cold now, but I can heat it up if you're hungry."

He *was* hungry. He was always hungry now, it seemed. He followed her into the kitchen and watched her move around the small space, taking a pot from the stove and setting it on the burner, turning the flame up beneath it. The soup inside was thick and dark, chunks of something floating in it that he couldn't quite identify.

"What kind?"

"Does it matter?"

It didn't matter, not really. He sat down at the narrow table and watched her stir, watched the contents of the pot turn slowly, and after a while she ladled some into a bowl and set it in front of him with a spoon.

"Eat," she said, and sat down across from him.

He ate. The soup was rich and savory, the meat tender enough to fall apart on his tongue, and he couldn't have named what it was if someone had paid him. Beef, maybe. Or pork.

Eleanor watched him from across the table, her chin propped on her hand. She wasn't eating, she hadn't even picked up her spoon. She was just watching.

"Aren't you hungry?"

"Not tonight. I had something earlier."

"When?"

"While you were sleeping."

He couldn't remember hearing her move around, couldn't remember anything between closing his eyes on the sofa and opening them in the dark; but then he *had* been sleeping deeply, which was a rare enough occurrence that he refused to prod at the conditions surrounding it. Too deeply, maybe, he'd admit to only himself, the kind of sleep that swallowed whole hours and left you feeling drugged and disoriented when you surfaced.

He finished the soup and scraped the bowl clean with his spoon, and the hunger in his belly eased but didn't disappear entirely. It was always there now, that hunger, like a second heartbeat. He wondered if this was what addiction felt like, this constant low-grade need, this awareness that something was missing even when you'd just had your fill.

Eleanor had gotten up at some point while he was eating, had moved to stand by the sink with her arms wrapped around herself. The light was behind her now, and he couldn't see her face properly, just the dark outline of her body, the suggestion of features.

"Are you all right?"

"I'm tired," she said. "Just tired. I think I'll go to bed."

"I'll come with you."

She didn't answer, just turned and walked out of the kitchen, and he sat there for a moment longer, the empty bowl in front of him, the spoon still in his hand. Something was off. He could feel it, a wrongness in the air like the smell before a storm, but he couldn't name it, couldn't locate it, and after a while he gave up trying and rinsed the bowl in the sink and went to find her.

She was already in bed when he got there, curled on her side with her back to the door, the blanket pulled up to her chin. He slid in beside her and reached for her, his hand finding the curve of her hip like a longtime lover.

"Mmm," she hummed softly.

"Goodnight," he said into the back of her neck, into the dark mess of her hair.

She didn't answer, but she was here. She had *said* she would stay.

14

You Don't Know Me, And I Don't Know You (Until I Do)

In the following days, Kerwin Merle made a great many things.

He made soup on the third day, and then again on the fourth, and by the fifth he had stopped counting and simply kept the pot going, adding things as they ran low—water, stock, whatever meat was nearest to hand in the refrigerator—so that it became less a meal he was preparing than a condition he was maintaining. He made eggs that he'd found loose in the back of the fridge, oddly sized and without a box, their yolks dark and gelatinous, almost brown, with a richness that coated his tongue; he fried meat in the heavy pan his mother had left behind, slicing it from brown-paper parcels without looking too closely at what he was cutting. The meat was always cold when he started and he could never quite get the chill out of the center, but he ate it anyway, and the pink juice ran down his wrist and he wiped it on his pants and cut another piece.

He had not left the apartment. The knowledge sat on a shelf in his mind, present but unexamined, and each day it remained it became easier to leave it alone. The stairs were right there, of course, the door to the shop was right there, he simply didn't use them. There was food in the refrigerator and Eleanor was in the apartment and these two facts between them eliminated any reason he could think of to go outside. The funny thing, he thought to himself, was that the apartment had never felt small to him before Eleanor; only empty, a fishbowl with one fish circling the same four walls but now it had the quality of something self-sustaining, a sealed glass terrarium he'd seen once in a secondhand shop window, green and damp and living off its own breath. Everything he needed was in here. Everything that *mattered* was in here. The ordinary world with its ordinary demands could press itself against the glass all it liked.

Eleanor was still here, which was perhaps the most important thing. She sat on the sofa with the book she'd been reading, though he hadn't heard her turn a page in some time. She stood in the kitchen doorway and watched him cook, she lay beside him at night, on her side, facing away, the duvet pulled up. She was here, and this was the thing he held on to, the fixed point around which everything else arranged itself. Eleanor was here and she had said she would stay.

Although she *was* quieter, maybe, or maybe he was just talking less, which amounted to the same thing—he had begun to worry that she was tiring of him. This was not a new fear, it was the oldest one he had, older than prison, older than the shop, the quiet certainty that proximity to him was something people endured rather than chose and it expressed itself the way it always had: he began to make himself smaller and kept his habits out of her sight. He clipped his nails in the laundry closet with the door shut and the kitchen faucet running, he ate his largest meals when she was sleeping, or when she'd gone still on the sofa in that way she had now, surely regretting the way she'd run from her problems into a recluse's crumbling hovel, her eyes open and fixed on some middle distance he couldn't follow her into. He avoided the bathroom when she was nearby, though this had less to do with her and more to do with the smell, which had thickened despite the towels he'd stuffed against the base of the door and the air freshener he'd balanced on the cistern.

His horrible fucking apartment and his horrible fucking landlord—

But that was a stupid thought, he'd say in the next breath, soothing himself, because people didn't argue all the time, people who lived together didn't spend every conversation scoring points off each other and if Eleanor had settled into something less combative, then that was just what happened. It was comfort, it was ease. He'd never lived with anyone and had no way of knowing what the normal rate of attrition was for the small frictions that made a person distinct, whether it was days or weeks before the edges wore down and two people began to move through the same space without resistance like water finding its level.

In the end, it was the vomiting that broke the routine.

He heard it before he saw it, a wet, convulsive sound from the bathroom followed by a silence that was worse than the sound and then it came again, a retching so deep and so sustained that it pulled from somewhere below the gut. He stood in the hallway and listened and did not go in because the bathroom had become a place he avoided by unspoken agreement, the smell in there having crossed some unpleasant threshold the day prior.

Still, the retching went on.

He pushed the door open. Eleanor was on her knees in front of the toilet, one hand braced against the rim, her hair hanging in lank ropes around her face. The bowl was dark with something that wasn't food; it was too dark, too thick, with a greenish-black sheen that reminded him of the water that had pooled in the basement of the shop after a pipe had burst when he was a boy. Eleanor's shoulders heaved and another string of it came up, ropy and viscous, and it hit the water with a sound he would remember for a very long time.

"Eleanor." He said her name from the doorway because he could not bring himself to step onto the tiles. "Eleanor, what—"

She didn't look up. Her body convulsed again, a spasm that started in her back and rolled through her like something being wrung out. More of the dark fluid came, the smell of it joining the smell that was already in the bathroom to become something new, the mix of it bad enough to pull him across the threshold.

He knelt beside her on the tiles that were damp and slightly tacky and pulled her hair back from her face and held it at the nape of her neck and she retched again, dry this time, her body heaving against nothing, and he could feel the bones of her spine through the shirt she was wearing (*his* shirt) and the skin beneath the fabric was clammy and loose.

When it stopped, she sat back on her heels and wiped her mouth with the back of her hand. Her face was the color of tallow, a yellowish gray, and the cut on her temple had opened again and the skin around it was the soft, bruised purple of a plum left too long in a bowl.

"I'm calling a doctor," he said.

"No."

"Eleanor—"

"No." Her voice was certain, the most animate she'd sounded in days and she looked at him with an expression that was almost fierce. "*No* doctors."

"You need—"

"I said *no*."

He knew why he couldn't call a doctor. If a doctor came to this apartment, a doctor would see the weight she'd lost and the bruises he'd left on her arms and her thighs, and the doctor would not see a woman who'd been sick. The doctor would see a woman who'd been kept, and then there would be questions—how long has she been here, has she been eating, has she been conscious the entire time, has she left the apartment...and what could he say? That she'd come in from a storm and stayed? That she'd *chosen* this? That it was for spiritual purposes? That she'd pushed *him* to choose this, too?

Please. They'd think him mad, or worse, they'd think him one of those men, the kind he'd read about in the papers that other inmates left on the tables in the common areas, the ones who kept women in cellars and attics and locked rooms, who dressed them and fed them and talked to them and loved them after their own fashion and never seemed to understand what they'd done. He'd sat in his cell and read those stories about the kind of men who wished to bury themselves inside of a woman's armpit and die with the distant disgust of a man who believed himself fundamentally different from the people described, and now here he was, unable to call a doctor because a doctor would see what he saw and draw the conclusions he was refusing to draw.

"At least eat something," he said, because this was the one domain where he still felt competent. "Let me make you some soup."

The change in her was immediate. She'd been slumped against the bathtub with her eyes half-closed, passive, emptied out, and now something came into her face that he hadn't seen in days—a sharpness, as though a light had been turned on in a room he'd thought was vacant.

No." She pushed herself up from the floor, her arms trembling with the effort. "Not that soup, Kerwin! I don't want that soup."

"It's just soup, Eleanor. You need to eat. You haven't—"

"I won't eat it, I *won't*, it's disgusting, the whole apartment smells of it, can't you smell it? Can't you—" She broke off and retched again, a dry heave that bent her double, and when she straightened her eyes were streaming and her lips were wet and she was shaking.

"I don't know what you're talking about."

"That soup," she said. "I can't—Kerwin, *please*. I can't eat that."

"Then what? What do you want? Tell me what you want and I'll make it."

She was quiet for a long time. Her breathing had steadied but she was still trembling, a fine continuous vibration that he could see in her hands and in the tendons of her neck and in the wet clumps of hair that hung on either side of her face. She looked up at him and something in her expression shifted, the fierceness draining away and leaving behind it something softer.

"I need to go back," she said.

"Back where?"

"Downstairs. To Amir's. The—" She swallowed and he could see the effort it cost her, the muscles of her throat working around nothing. "The Gastronauts…I need another meeting, Kerwin, I need to eat *properly,* the way they do it. The way *we* did it. It helped, it made me feel—I was better, after. You remember. I was better…"

He stared at her. She had been better, hadn't she? After the meal in the basement she'd been warm and present and she'd teased him, she'd kissed his cheek, she'd unbuttoned his shirt in the kitchen and looked at him with those dark eyes and said *prove it.* That had been the good Eleanor, the real Eleanor, the one he wanted back.

"I think you're too weak for that," he said. "I think you need rest, not—"

"Rest isn't helping. Nothing you're doing is helping." The words landed like a slap and he flinched. "I'm sorry," she said, immediately, and her voice went soft again. "I'm sorry, I didn't mean—but Kerwin, *please*. I can feel it. Whatever they gave us, whatever that food was, it did something, it *changed* something and I need more of it. I need—" She stopped and looked at the floor and then back at him and her eyes were wet. "Please."

"Eleanor."

"Please. For me."

He didn't say yes, but he didn't say no either, and she must have taken his silence for what it was, the sound of a man whose last objection has been overruled by the only person whose opinion mattered to him because something in her face relaxed, and she reached up from where she sat on the bathroom floor and took his hand.

"Come here," she said.

"You're ill. You just—you were just sick, Eleanor, you can't—"

"Come here."

She tugged his hand and he let himself be pulled down, sinking to his knees on the damp tiles beside her, and she kissed him. Her lips were sour and he could taste the bile on them, the residue of whatever she'd brought up, and beneath it something that he recognized from the nights he'd spent with his face between her thighs, that copper-sweet thickness that had become, for him, indistinguishable from the taste of wanting her.

"Eleanor, we shouldn't—"

"Shh." Her hand was at his belt. Her fingers were clumsy and cold and she fumbled with the buckle and he should have stopped her, taken her hands and held them and said *not now, not here, not like this*, but he was already hard, had been hard since she'd said his name with that fierceness, and when her fingers closed around him through the fabric of his pants all of his objections tumbled out of him. She pulled him toward the sitting room, half-crawling, half-stumbling, and they made it as far as the sofa where she pushed him down and climbed on top of him, her knees on either side of his hips, and he could feel how thin she'd gotten, the bones of her pelvis grinding against his through the fabric. She pulled the shirt over her head and he saw her body and something in him lurched, some last outpost because her ribs were showing and her skin had a waxy translucence to it and the bruises he'd left on her hadn't faded at all, they had, in fact, darkened and spread as though they were feeding on whatever was beneath them.

She put her mouth on his throat and he stopped thinking.

Her hand worked between them, pulling at his pants until he was free, and she lowered herself onto him without preamble and the sound she made was the same low guttural exhalation he knew from the first time but he didn't care because the feel of her around him shocked him; that she could be so cold everywhere else and so hot here, clenching around him in slow, rhythmic pulses.

She rode him with her hands braced on his shoulders, her head tipped back, her mouth open, and he gripped her hips hard enough to feel the bones shift under his thumbs. The motion was steady and relentless and he could hear himself making stupid helpless sounds beneath her and she was so thin above him, the flesh drawn tight across her ribs like a starving animal, and he should have been horrified but he wasn't, he was just grateful that she was here, that she still wanted this, that whatever was happening to her body hadn't taken this last, functional thing from them.

He was close when it happened.

She made a sound that wasn't her usual groans of pleasure or impending orgasm, a wet, gurgling hiccup that started in her stomach and climbed her throat—and then the first hot rush of it hit his chest. It was some dark fluid, the same greenish-black from the bathroom that splashed across his sternum, his neck, before pooling in the hollow of his collarbone. The smell of it was immense, the stink of the bathroom and the drains and the apartment concentrated to a single awful point and her body convulsed above him, her stomach clenching, and more of it came, running down his chest in thick rivulets, and she was still moving on him, her hips still grinding in that steady mechanical pulse, and he was still inside her, and the terrible thing, the thing he would never be able to explain to anyone, the thing that would live in him forever like a stone swallowed whole—

He came.

He came so hard that his vision whited out and his hips snapped up off the sofa and he was pulling her down onto him, into the mess, the hot dark fluid between their bodies making everything slick as the orgasm tore through him in wave after wave while she retched and rode him. The sounds of his pleasure and her sickness filled the room until they were indistinguishable from each other.

When it was over she collapsed against his chest and lay still. The fluid cooled between them, tacky and dark, and his heart slammed against his ribs and his stomach turned slowly, once, like a dog circling before it beds down, and then settled. He lay beneath her and breathed through his mouth and stared at the ceiling and waited for the horror to arrive.

It did not.

What appeared to him instead was a calm so total it felt chemical, as though whatever had just happened had flushed something toxic from his system and left behind only her weight on his chest, her hair in his face, the slow fade of his erection inside her and the wet cooling mess between them that he would clean up in a moment, in a minute, as soon as he could bring himself to move.

"I need to wash," he said.

She didn't answer. She might have been sleeping.

He eased her off of him and laid her on the sofa, pulling the blanket over her before padding softly to the kitchen and standing at the sink. He turned the sink on and let the water run over his hands and his forearms and did not look at what was swirling down the drain. He stripped his shirt over his head and dropped it on the floor and wiped his chest and stomach with the dish towel and dropped that on the floor too. He stood there in his pants, bare-chested, and breathed, and the apartment was very quiet around him.

He needed more than the sink.

The hose was where he'd left it, coiled against the wall in the alley behind the shop and when he stepped outside the cold hit him like a cannonball to the chest and the light was far too bright. The water came out icy and he stood there in the alley in his pants and nothing else and let it run over his head and his chest and his stomach, gasping at the cold, his teeth clenched and his hands shaking, scrubbing at his skin with his fingernails until it was pink and raw and the water at his feet ran clear.

A kid was sitting on the low wall by the bins, smoking a roll-up and Kerwin knew him immediately—Declan, Gordon's boy, the sullen teenager who'd slouched at the far end of the table picking at his napkin with bitten fingernails while his father leaned forward and talked too much and too eagerly.

"Declan," Kerwin said.

The kid looked at him— or through him, rather, the way one might look at a piece of street furniture or a stain on the pavement, something to register and dismiss in the same glance; just a teenager looking at a half-naked, wet stranger who had said his name and finding nothing in the encounter that warranted a response.

Kerwin smiled at him. It was an unnatural thing, a smile from Kerwin, and he could feel it sitting wrong on his face, the muscles pulling in directions they weren't used to.

Declan took a drag of his cigarette and turned away, exhaling a thin plume of smoke into the cold air, and Kerwin stood there with the hose dripping in his hand and the smile dying on his face and felt something open up beneath him.

He dropped the hose and went into the shop.

"Amir," called Kerwin.

The man behind the counter looked up from his newspaper. "Can I help you?"

Kerwin stood there, water dripping from his hair onto his bare shoulders and running down his chest in thin streams and pooling on the mat beneath his feet.

"It's *me*," he said, leaning across the counter with his arms crossed over his bare chest. He was shivering badly now, the water from the hose drying cold on his skin, gooseflesh spreading up his sides, aware suddenly and completely of how he must look dripping in a convenience shop at whatever hour this was, his feet bare, his ribs showing more than they should have given how much he'd been eating—"It's Kerwin," he whispered. "From upstairs." "

Amir's expression did not change. It remained pleasant, faintly quizzical, the expression of a man who is trying to place a face and cannot.

"I'm sorry," Amir said slowly. "Do we know each other?"

The ground did not open beneath him; the walls did not close in. Nothing as dramatic as that. What happened was smaller and worse, a tiny, almost imperceptible shift in the way the world was arranged as though someone had picked up the room and set it back down a quarter inch to the left, and everything was where it had been and nothing was where it had been.

"The Gastronauts," said Kerwin, his voice sounding far away and tinny, as though it were coming through a bad phone connection. "The meeting in your basement. You—we ate together, you read from the—"

Amir shook his head slowly. "I think you may have the wrong shop, brother," he said, not unkindly. "There's nothing like that here."

Kerwin opened his mouth and closed it. He looked at Amir's face and searched it for some some crack in the polite facade that would let him in but there was nothing but a shopkeeper looking at a stranger standing in his shop and wondering, reasonably, whether to be concerned.

"Sorry," Kerwin heard himself say. "Sorry. My mistake."

He turned and walked out. The bell above the door chimed behind him, a small bright sound, and the cold hit him again and he stood in the alley with the water drying on his skin and the kid had gone and the wall was empty and the hose lay coiled where he'd dropped it and the world was exactly as it had been five minutes ago except that a piece of it had been removed and in its place was nothing at all.

He went upstairs.

Eleanor was on the sofa where he'd left her, the blanket pulled up, her eyes closed. The stain on the sofa cushion where the fluid had soaked through was already drying and going dark at the edges. He stood in the doorway and looked at her and waited for the world to snap back into place.

He sat down in the chair by the window and put his head in his hands.

The knock came hours later, or what felt like hours—it might have been twenty minutes. Time had stopped working properly; it came in clumps and gaps, thick and then thin, and he'd been sitting in the chair watching the light change on the wall opposite and not thinking about anything at all.

Three knocks, steady and evenly spaced, not the knock of someone selling something or checking a meter.

He opened the door.

Amir stood in the hallway. Not the Amir from the shop, the polite stranger with the newspaper, or not *only* him, this Amir was wearing a dark sweater with a small carry-bag in his hands and his face held an expression that Kerwin recognized with such desperate relief that his knees nearly buckled. Mild reproach. The look of a friend who has been embarrassed on your behalf and has come to sort it out.

"Kerwin," Amir said, and squeezed his arm above the elbow the way as if to steady him against a stumble. "May I come in?"

"You—" Kerwin's voice came out cracked, his hand still gripping the doorframe. "You didn't know me. In the shop, you—"

"Of course I know you." Amir stepped past him into the sitting room without waiting to be invited, the way he had the first time. He set the paper bag on the kitchen counter and turned to face Kerwin with his hands in his pockets and that same expression, fond and slightly disappointed, nothing more than a teacher who has caught a promising student cheating on a minor test.

"Kerwin, you know we can't speak of this outside. We *talked* about this. The society is private. It *has* to be. You can't just walk into the shop and start asking about meetings in front of—" He sighed and rubbed the bridge of his nose beneath his glasses. "You frightened Yasmin. She thought you were having some kind of episode."

"But you looked at me like you'd never seen me before!"

"What was I supposed to do? You came in half-naked, dripping wet, raving about—" He lowered his voice, cupped a hand beside his mouth as if the empty shop might be listening. "—about what we do downstairs. In front of customers, Kerwin! What would you have had me say?"

It made sense. Of course it made sense. The Gastronauts were a secret society—hadn't Amir said that from the beginning? Discretion was the foundation. You didn't talk about it outside, and you certainly didn't acknowledge each other in the street or in the shop or anywhere that wasn't the basement with the velvet walls and the silver domes and the candlelight. The kid on the wall hadn't been ignoring him; the kid had been following the rules. Amir hadn't been pretending not to know him; Amir had been protecting them both.

The relief was so vast and so physical that Kerwin had to put a hand on the wall to steady himself. He laughed—a strange, barking sound that didn't belong to him and Amir's face softened.

"How is she?" Amir asked.

Kerwin did not wonder how Amir knew Eleanor was ill. It seemed right that he should know, that a man who had spent years conducting rituals in a candlelit basement and served meat that made you see things would know things that ordinary people didn't. The oracles at Delphi had been no different, had they, priestesses drunk on fumes rising through the rock, babbling truths to strangers who'd traveled for weeks to hear them? What were those fumes, really, but the earth's own fermentation, and what was the wine they drank but grapes gone rotten, and hadn't pilgrims come from across the ancient world bearing gifts for the privilege of a few words from a woman who'd poisoned herself into wisdom? Amir had his own fumes, his own small temple beneath a convenience shop and if fifteen years of that communion had given him the ability to ask after a woman's health without being told she was unwell, then perhaps that was simply what happened when you ate your way through the veil often enough. Perhaps one day Kerwin would have that air about him too, that quiet authority, and strangers would knock on his door bearing brown-paper parcels and asking for his counsel.

"She's not well," Kerwin managed, his voice catching on something in his throat. "She's been sick...and she's not eating."

Amir nodded slowly, as though this confirmed something he'd already suspected. "She needs another meeting," he said. "We'll arrange something soon."

"She said the same thing. She said—"

"Eleanor is a smart woman." Amir glanced toward the sitting room where Eleanor lay beneath her blanket, and then back to Kerwin. He straightened, tugging at the cuffs of his pressed shirt the way Kerwin had seen him do in the basement before a reading. "Take care of her until then. Can you do that?"

"Yes," Kerwin said. His throat was tight and his eyes were stinging and he was grateful that Amir was already turning toward the door because he did not want this man, this *good* man, to see him cry.

"Good." Amir squeezed his shoulder and then he was gone, pulling the door shut behind him, his footsteps receding down the hallway and then the stairs.

He opened the bag. Inside were two cuts of meat, wrapped in brown paper and tied with string, identical to the parcels in his refrigerator.

He put them away without looking at them before going to the sofa and kneeling beside Eleanor to touch her face.

"Amir was here," he crooned. "He says there'll be another meeting. *Soon*."

She opened her eyes and looked at him, and for a moment she looked like Eleanor again, the real one, the one who'd stolen bacon from his plate and told him he wasn't as invisible as he thought.

"Good," she said.

He pulled the blanket up to her chin and went to the kitchen and stirred the soup.

15

Dinner For Two,

Kerwin shaved on the morning of the meeting, but not in the bathroom because he hadn't been in the bathroom in days, even going so far as to piss in the kitchen sink and bird bathe at the faucet to avoid it. He told himself this was a temporary arrangement, a practical response to the plumbing situation that would sort itself out eventually and so he neatened himself up instead in the laundry closet where he'd angled his mother's compact against a shelf of detergent bottles until it caught enough light from the hallway to show him his own face. The razor was dull and it dragged at his skin enough that he had to press a washcloth to his jaw afterward to catch the small red blossoms seeping through the cloth.

He studied himself in the compact's small round mirror and was startled, briefly, by the face that looked back. He'd lost weight. The bones of his cheeks stood out beneath the thinned skin and the hollows under his eyes had deepened into something more than the purple smudges of a few sleepless nights; actual cavities, as though pieces of him had been scooped away. His neck had gone ropy, his collarbones jutted and he looked, he thought, like a man who had been ill for a long time and was only now seeing the damage, though he did not *feel* ill. He felt fine. He felt, if anything, too awake, too alert, his senses running high and hot the way they did when he'd gone without food for too long, everything condensing to a single point.

He had not gone without food, though, which was the oddest bit of it all. He'd been eating constantly and still the weight fell off him, his pants hanging loose at the waist and the shirts he put on swimming at the shoulders. It didn't make sense, or it made a kind of sense that he wasn't interested in examining and so he turned from the mirror and rinsed the razor and dressed with more care than he'd taken in a very long time.

He chose the shirt he'd worn to his aunt's funeral, years before he was sent away. It was the only good shirt he owned, white cotton gone slightly yellow at the collar and he ironed it on the kitchen table with the iron his mother had kept beneath the sink, pressing the creases flat and running the point along the seams the way she'd taught him when he was fourteen. The iron hissed and the starch smell rose and for a moment he was standing in this kitchen some thirty-odd years ago, his mother at his elbow correcting his technique, her hand closing over his on the handle to show him the angle, the pressure, the long smooth stroke from shoulder to cuff. He blinked and she was gone and the kitchen was as it was with the soup on the stove, the smell in the walls and the weak light coming in through the window above the sink.

He buttoned the shirt and tucked it in and looked at himself and thought, *I look like a man going somewhere.* It was such a novel thought that he stood with it for a moment, turning it over. When was the last time he'd been going somewhere? Not the bus, not the circuit of watching and waiting that had constituted his life before Eleanor, but *somewhere*, a place where people would see him and he would be seen and it would matter how he looked. He couldn't remember. Perhaps never; perhaps this was the very first time.

He polished his shoes with the edge of a dish towel. He combed his hair, what was left of it, with water and his fingers. He stood in the hallway and checked himself in the long mirror that his mother had hung there decades ago, the one whose glass had gone dark and spotty at the edges so that his reflection came back to him mottled and incomplete, a strange man seen through strange fog. He straightened his collar, he smoothed the front of the shirt and he did these things with the solemn concentration of a man preparing for a ceremony, which, he supposed, was exactly what he was doing.

Eleanor, bless her, was on the sofa.

She had been on the sofa for two days now, or what he thought was two days (time had gone strange again, folding and pleating, and he'd stopped trying to track it by anything other than the light in the window and the level of soup in the pot). She lay on her side beneath the blanket he'd tucked around her with her knees drawn up and her hair spread dark against the cushion and had not spoken since the morning Amir had come.

But today was different because there was somewhere to go and something to do and so Kerwin moved around the apartment with a purpose he hadn't felt since the first days of her illness, when he'd still believed that soup and blankets and vitamins could fix whatever was wrong. He filled a glass of water and brought it to her and set it on the floor by the sofa, within reach. He knelt beside her and touched her hair, smoothing it away from her face and tucking it behind her ear the way he'd seen men do in films.

"Tonight," he murmured, his voice quiet but steady. "Amir said soon and I think he meant tonight. I can feel it. Can you feel it?"

She didn't answer, but her eyes were open, and he took this as confirmation.

"You'll feel better after, you said so yourself…you were better after the last time, remember? You were yourself again. You'll eat properly and you'll feel better and then we'll — we'll carry on. We'll be all right."

He knew he was talking too much because Eleanor would have told him so, the old Eleanor, the one who cut him off mid-sentence and told him where he'd gone wrong but this Eleanor only lay there and blinked and her eyes caught the dull glow from the lamp and held it without reflecting it back.

He straightened the blanket and went to the kitchen, coming back with a ladle of soup in a bowl and brought it to her and set it beside the water.

"Just in case…" He touched the rim of the bowl, adjusted its position on the floor, a fussy, pointless gesture. "In case you're hungry before we go."

She wouldn't touch it. He'd known for days that whatever he put in front of her would sit there cooling and untouched until he took it away and ate it himself, but the act of preparing it and bringing it to her was a ritual of his own and he was not ready to give it up. He was not ready to give up any of the small domestic performances that proved, each time he carried them out, that there was someone in his home to carry them out for.

He sat in the chair by the window and waited for dark.

He timed the dust swirling across the floor with his own breathing and thought about the basement, about the fountain with its three tiers of hammered brass, and about Amir's voice reading about the body of God given willingly and consumed in love. He thought about Eleanor sitting beside him at the long table, animated and present and *alive*, her knee touching his beneath the cloth, her hand reaching for his in the dark. He thought about the food and the warmth that had spread through him afterward and the visions that had cracked him open and shown him things he could not explain. He thought: *this will fix her, this will bring her back. This is what she needs and I am going to give it to her because that is what you do when you love someone, you give them what they need even if it frightens you and, most importantly, even if you do not understand it.*

Outside, the streetlights came on.

He stood, crossing to the sofa and kneeling beside her once more.

"It's time," he said as took her hand. Her fingers did not close around his own but he held them anyway. "Can you stand?"

She could not stand, or could not stand alone. He got his arm beneath her shoulders and lifted her to sitting and then to her feet, and she leaned against him, her weight barely there, and he could feel the bones of her through the shirt she was wearing, and the smell of her was the smell of the apartment, the smell of the bathroom, the smell of everything and he breathed through his mouth and held her up.

"I've got you." His arm tightened around her waist. "We're just going downstairs. Easy now, I've got you…"

The stairwell was dark and cold and so he went first, one hand on the loose banister and the other arm around Eleanor's waist, and she came down behind him one step at a time, her hand on his shoulder, her weight shifting with each stair.

At the bottom, the door to the shop was closed. He tried the handle and it opened smoothly, just as he expected, and they entered without pause so as to not to offend the waiting party.

They were already seated; Gordon at his usual place, his hands folded on the table, his face ruddy and expectant with Declan beside him, slouched, picking at the edge of his napkin. Mallie sat across from them with her hair pinned up and her back straight and that thin smile she wore like a brooch. Their faces turned toward the door as Kerwin and Eleanor came through, and the expressions on them were warm and welcoming and this alone was enough to bring the sting of tears to his eyes.

"There you are," Mallie murmured, rising to help with Eleanor, her hands finding the girl's arm with careful attention. "There you are, darling. Come sit down." She settled Eleanor into the chair between herself and Kerwin, who adjusted the blanket around her shoulders and tucked a strand of hair behind her ear automatically.

Amir emerged from behind the curtain at the far end of the room. He was wearing the same dark suit from the first meeting and he carried the book in both hands, that dark, mottled thing with its soft, almost fleshy cover and translucent pages. He set it on the table and looked at Kerwin and then at Eleanor and nodded once.

"Before we eat, we remember *why* we eat."

The candles guttered, the fountain dripped, and Amir opened the book.

"We have heard how Mary came unto the tomb and found her Lord," Amir began, his voice settling into the measured, almost liturgical rhythm that made the words feel older than the room. "We have heard how she took him unto herself, that corruption should not claim him. We have heard how she ate of his flesh and drank of his blood and crawled forth from the tomb with the body of God within her."

"But it is not told what Mary saw when the flesh of her son began its work within her; it is not told what visions came upon her as she lay upon the hillside with the dawn breaking and his blood still wet upon her mouth."

Amir paused. His eyes moved over the table, over each of their faces in turn, and came to rest on Eleanor.

"Hear now the visions of Mary," he continued, "which were hidden, for the world was not ready to receive them."

He read:

1 *And when Mary had eaten, and the flesh of her son was within her, the LORD opened her eyes and she saw things which no woman had seen before.*

2 *And she saw first the tomb as it had been, the body upon the slab, the linen stained with blood and gall. And she saw herself kneeling there, and the sharp stone in her hand, and the sound of her own weeping as she cut.*

3 *And she cried out, LORD, why dost thou show me this? For I know what I have done!*

4 *But the vision would not release her.*

5 *And she saw the flesh as she had torn it, the ragged edges of the wounds where her teeth had been, and the exposed bone beneath, white and gleaming, and the dark hollows of the body where the organs had been taken.*

6 *And she saw that what lay upon the slab was not the Son of God transfigured but a body, broken and consumed, the body of a man killed by other men, the body of her child whom she had nursed and bathed and held in her arms when he cried in the night.*

7 *And the vision showed her the desecration the world would see if it should look upon this thing.*

8 *And Mary wept, and said, LORD, is this what I am? Am I no better than the beasts of the field that devour their young?*

9 *And the LORD said, Thou art what thou hast always been. Thou art a mother who would not let her son be taken from her.*

10 *And Mary said, But I have destroyed him! I have eaten his face that I loved, his hands that blessed the sick, his eyes that wept Lazarus back from the dead! How is this love? How is this anything but the most terrible sin?*

11 *And the LORD said, It is both. It is love and it is sin and it is the way of all flesh that loveth beyond the bounds of what flesh can bear.*

12 *And Mary saw then a terrible thing, she saw other women and men also, in times yet to come, who would do as she had done. She saw them in their kitchens and their cellars, in their hovels and their locked rooms, and she saw that they did not eat in faith but in hunger, and they did not weep as she had wept, and the ones they consumed had not given themselves willingly.*

13 *And she said, LORD, what is the difference between me and these?*

14 *And the LORD was silent.*

15 *And Mary understood, in that silence, that there was no difference, or that the difference was so small as to be invisible to God, who seeth all things and judgeth not as men judge.*

16 *And this was the most terrible vision of all, that what she had done could not be separated from what others would do in darkness without love, without faith, without the blessing of a son who had said, Take, eat, this is my body.*

17 *And Mary carried this knowledge within her for the rest of her days, and she told no one, for who would believe that the mother of God had seen herself reflected in the faces of monsters?*

18 *Blessed are they who hunger, for they shall be filled; but cursed are they who cannot tell their hunger from their love.*

Amir closed the book and set on the sideboard. He folded his hands before him and the room was silent.

Kerwin looked at Eleanor.

She was sitting very still in her chair, the blanket around her shoulders, her hands flat on the table on either side of her plate. She had not reacted to the reading; she had not wept, had not flinched, had not turned to look at him with those dark eyes the way she had at the first meeting. Instead, she sat as she had sat on the sofa for days, present and absent at the same time, her face turned toward the silver dome in front of her but her eyes fixed on some point ahead.

Amir closed the book and set it aside. He did not return to his seat; instead he moved around the table, pausing behind each chair, and from somewhere—his pocket, perhaps, or a fold of his jacket—he produced a stack of large linen napkins, the kind that came folded into swans at restaurants Kerwin had never been able to afford.

"Tonight is different," said Amir, laying a napkin beside Gordon's plate, then Mallie's, then Declan's. "Tonight we eat in the *old* way." He paused behind Eleanor's chair and looked at her for a long moment, his expression unreadable, and then he set a napkin beside her plate and moved on.

"The ortolan...You know of it?"

Kerwin shook his head. Amir laid the last napkin beside Kerwin's plate, smoothing it flat with his palm.

"It is a songbird; very small, no bigger than your thumb. The French used to catch them in nets and keep them in the dark, force-feeding them until they were fat with millet and figs." He returned to his place at the head of the table but did not sit. "When the bird was ready, they drowned it in Armagnac and then they roasted it whole. They ate it bones and all, the entire thing, in one bite."

He mimed it as he spoke, his thumb and forefinger pinched around nothing, his head tipped back as he dropped some invisible thing into his open mouth. Gordon hooked a finger into his cheek and pulled it loose with a wet pop, and his laugh came out like a bark, sudden and pleased with itself. Mallie's chuckle was softer, almost fond as Declan snorted, dragging his sleeve across his nose.

Kerwin watched them laugh; Gordon with his head thrown back, the wet red cave of his mouth gaping open, Mallie dabbing at her eyes with the heel of her hand, Declan grinning sideways at nothing. He had spent years watching these people from his window: Gordon on the 8:42, Mallie with her gray dog at quarter past, Declan slouching past in his school uniform with his collar undone and his tie stuffed in his pocket. He had pressed his face to the glass and ached to be part of whatever ordinary thing they had that he did not, and now here he was, sitting at their table in his one good shirt and the only thing he wanted now was for them to disappear. He wanted them to shrink back down to the size of figures seen from a window, distant and safe and unable to look back; he wanted back the days bleeding into each other unmarked and above all, he wanted Eleanor on the sofa and no one else to see what he had made of his life.

His collar was damp. He could feel the slow crawl of the sweat at his hairline down the back of his neck, and he didn't know why—the basement wasn't warm, if anything there was a chill coming off the concrete beneath the velvet—but his body had clearly settled something that his mind hadn't caught up to yet. Beside him Eleanor made a sound, low and wet, something that started in her chest and didn't quite make it out of her throat and he reached for her hand under the table and held it and her fingers were cold and did not close around his.

The laughter ran out. Gordon was still grinning, his shoulders shaking with the last of it, and Mallie had her hand pressed to her chest.

Amir was smiling too. He let the moment stretch and then he said, still smiling, "You think it's funny?"

Gordon nodded, wiping his eye. "It is a little, isn't it? The whole thing… drowning a bird in brandy—"

"What about the bird?" Amir's smile hadn't changed but something behind it had. "Does the bird think it's funny?"

Gordon's hand stopped moving.

"Imagine you are the bird." Amir leaned forward, his palms flat on the table, his voice dropping to something barely above a murmur. "You are small, you weigh less than an ounce. You have spent your whole life in the hedgerows of southern France, eating seeds and insects, singing because that is what you were made to do and then one day a net falls over you and hands close around your body and you are lifted out of the world you knew and put into a box."

The candles flickered at his pause. When he spoke again his voice had not risen but it filled the room anyway, finding every corner.

"The box is dark, *completely* dark; you cannot see your own wings. You call out and no one answers, or perhaps other birds in other boxes respond in kind but you cannot reach them and they cannot reach you and then a hand comes into the dark and it brings food. Figs, millet, certainly more than you have ever seen…and you eat because you are afraid and because there is nothing else to do and then the hand goes away and you are alone again in the dark."

Kerwin could feel his heart in his throat, in his wrists, in the soft place behind his knees.

"Days pass. You cannot tell how many." Amir tilted his head, studying Gordon's face, now as still as a carving. "The hand keeps coming and you keep eating and your body begins to change. Your liver swells, presses against your lungs and you find it harder to breathe but still you eat, because the food keeps coming and you have forgotten that there was ever other than this constant gorge. You have forgotten the hedgerows, you have forgotten the sky. Before long, you have forgotten that you ever had wings at all."

Mallie's smile was gone. Declan had stopped slouching.

"And then one day the hand comes and it does not bring food." Amir's eyes moved to Kerwin and rested there, patient and unblinking. "It closes around you and lifts you out of the box and the light hits your eyes for the first time in weeks and you cannot see, you are blind with it, and before you can understand what is happening your head is pushed down into Armagnac. It fills your beak and your throat and your lungs and you drown in it, slowly, your whole body saturated with brandy, and the last thing you feel is the burn of it in your chest and you do not know why this is happening to you. You die confused. You die, as most will, wondering what you did wrong."

The room was very quiet.

"And then—" Amir straightened, brushing something invisible from his sleeve, his tone shifting to something almost conversational. "Someone puts you in the oven and when you come out you are golden and glistening and you are placed on a plate in front of a man who has paid a great deal of money for the privilege of eating you. He is hungry, as hungry as you were in the hedgerow and so he picks you up by the beak and he puts your whole body in his mouth and he bites down and your bones crack between his teeth and your fat bursts across his tongue and he chews you—the organs, the heart, the liver that killed you, all of it—and he swallows."

He reached for his napkin.

"But he covers his head while he does it." He lifted the napkin from the table and held it up, letting it unfold. "Like this."

Amir draped the napkin over his head and the white linen fell to his shoulders. He stood there for a moment, faceless, a shape where a man had been.

"Some say it was to trap the aroma..." His voice came muffled through the cloth. "And some say it was to hide their shame from God, that they were embarrassed to be seen doing something so decadent and so needlessly excessive." He pulled the napkin away and his face emerged, calm and half-smiling. "But *I* think it was something else...I think they understood that certain truths have to be taken in darkness. There are things the body knows before the mind is ready to receive them, and if you try to see too clearly, too soon—" He folded the napkin in half, then in half again. "—you will not be able to swallow it."

He set the napkin down and looked at Eleanor. She had not moved through any of it, not the laughter, not the story of the bird, not the demonstration with the cloth.

"Our sister is unwell," Amir continued, "and she has given so much to be here tonight, more than any of us can know...except perhaps *you,* Kerwin. You know, don't you? You've been with her, you've seen what the rest of us have only glimpsed." His head tilted, just slightly, a small inquiring motion. "Tell me. What has she given?"

"—Never mind," Amir said softly, after Kerwin had been silent too long. "You don't have to say it, not yet." He turned back to the others, and his voice shifted again, settling into its liturgical register. "What we offer her in return is this: a meal taken in darkness and a truth revealed slowly, as much as she can bear, and then a little more."

"We cover our heads, but not for the reason the French did. Mary did not cover her eyes in the tomb, she saw *everything*. She watched her own hands do what they did, and she did not look away." He paused. "But we are not Mary, we have not been given what she was given. We are only people trying to follow where she went, and most of us are not strong enough to see clearly, not yet. The napkin is a kindness."

Amir sat and the chair creaked beneath him.

"When I tell you, you will cover your heads and you will eat what is beneath the dome. You will not look at each other and you will trust your *mouth* to tell you what your *eyes* are not ready to see." He reached for his silver dome and his fingers rested on the handle. "This is the final communion. After tonight, you will understand everything."

Kerwin looked at Eleanor. The cut on her temple had gone black at the edges and the skin around it had a greenish tint that the candlelight could not soften.

"Now cover your heads."

Around the table, napkins rose and fell. Gordon's head disappeared beneath white linen, then Mallie's, then Declan's. Kerwin lifted his own napkin and the cloth smelled of starch and something that he recognized from the soup he had been making for days.

He draped it over his head. The world went white, then dim, the candlelight filtering through the weave in a soft glow that erased the edges of the table.

"Now," Amir said, his voice distant, muffled, coming from somewhere outside the tent of cloth. "We eat!"

The domes came off together in that same coordinated motion from before and Kerwin looked down at his plate. The cubes were the same cubes from before, gray-pink and glistening, arranged in their neat pyramid but something about them looked different tonight, though he couldn't say what. The color, maybe, or the way the light caught the fat. He thought of the bird in the dark, its liver swelling, its lungs compressed, and he put his fork down and picked it up again and told himself to stop being ridiculous.

The first cube was on his tongue before he could think about it. It was rich and dense and dissolved with extraordinary softness, and so he chewed and swallowed and reached for another. Around him he could hear the others eating—Gordon's wet, appreciative sounds, the delicate clink of Mallie's fork against her plate, Declan chewing with his mouth open the way teenagers do—they came muffled through the cloth, intimate and strange, and Kerwin ate another cube and another and the warmth began to spread through him, loosening the thing that had been clenched in his chest for weeks.

He lifted the edge of the napkin. He knew he shouldn't, that Amir had said not to look but Eleanor was beside him and he needed to see her to know that this was working and that he hadn't carried her down the stairs for nothing.

Her napkin was still draped over her head but her hands were flat on the table on either side of her plate, exactly where they had been when they sat down. Her fork lay parallel to her knife and the pyramid of cubes sat untouched, gleaming, not a piece out of place.

"Eleanor." His voice came out a hiss, muffled by his own cloth. "Eat. *Please.* This is what you wanted."

She didn't move. Beneath the napkin her face was a white shape, featureless and still.

"Eleanor."

Nothing. The others ate on around them, their sounds filling the room and still Eleanor did not eat.

He reached over and lifted the edge of her napkin.

"Eleanor!"

She was looking at him. Her eyes were open and fixed on his face with a directness he had not seen in weeks, an attention so focused and so steady that it felt like a hand pressed to the center of his chest, holding him in place.

"Eat," he whispered, pleading. His throat had gone tight. "Eleanor, *please.* This is why we came. This will make you better. You said so yourself, you said—"

Eleanor looked at him and did not eat.

Desperate, he ate another piece and the warmth came the way it had the first time, spreading outward from his stomach through his chest and into his limbs, loosening something locked inside of him. The meat dissolved on his tongue with that same extraordinary richness, and he closed his eyes and let the feeling take him because this was what he'd come for, this was what Eleanor needed and if she wouldn't eat then he would eat enough for both of them.

The visions themselves started gently. He saw his home as it had been before Eleanor, seen from above as if he were floating near the ceiling; he saw himself as a figure so reduced by routine that he barely disturbed the air and the loneliness of it hit him with a force that made his jaw clench around the food in his mouth. He had been nothing but a man-shaped absence that the world flowed around without registering, and he knew then that the vision wanted him to understand what he had been before she came.

Then he saw the night of the storm: rain hammering the windows and the buzzer going and Eleanor on his doorstep with her delivery bag and her soaked jacket and that look on her face, half-drowned, half-defiant, and he felt the whole thing again—the shock of another person in his space, the animal terror and the animal want so tangled together he couldn't tell which was which. He saw himself stepping back to let her in, he saw the towel he'd fetched from the bathroom, he saw her standing in his hallway dripping onto the same floorboards his mother had polished every Saturday morning when he was a boy.

But then the vision kept going, past the parts he knew and into something else entirely.

He saw the hallway, he saw Eleanor, and he saw himself, and something was happening between them that he couldn't — the vision was trying to show him *something*, he knew, but his mind kept sliding off of it, lubed fingers on a smooth cliff's edge. There was a specific sound that his body knew, and every time the vision brought him close to it his mind flinched away and showed him something else instead: the kitchen, the soup, his father standing behind the counter with that look on his face that meant Kerwin had done something wrong again.

Kerwin opened his eyes to find that the basement was the same. Gordon was still eating, Mallie was still eating, Declan was still eating but something had shifted in the quality of the light or the air or the way the fabric hung on the walls...

He looked at the velvet on the nearest wall where a fold had fallen and where it gaped he could see bare concrete behind it, drab and pitted and streaked with damp. He looked away and when he looked back, the fold had fallen properly and the velvet was seamless again, hanging in its heavy folds, and he thought, *I imagined it. I'm tired. The food does this, Amir said the food does this, it opens you up and shows you things and some of the things aren't real...*

He tried to pick up his fork, but the room kept slipping. There were things he might not have noticed if he hadn't been looking, a candle that guttered and, in the instant before the flame recovered, became something that was not a candle at all but instead a bare overhead bulb. Mallie murmured something appreciative and the words she used were Eleanor's words, a phrase she'd used weeks ago lifted whole from a conversation he'd had with her on the sofa.

"Kerwin."

It was Eleanor's voice speaking, and it was not the mechanical *I'm all right* or the whispered *please* of late, this was her real voice, the one that had cataloged his empty cupboards and told him he wasn't invisible, the one that had argued with him and teased him and called him out on every lie he'd told himself since the day she walked through his door.

He turned to look at her. She was sitting upright in her chair, and the blanket had fallen from her shoulders, and her eyes were clear and fixed on him with an expression he had never seen on her face before.

"Kerwin," she said again. "Look at your plate."

He looked down.

The cubes of meat on his plate were the same cubes of meat he'd been eating for weeks—the same gray-pink, the same glistening texture, the same faint sweet smell beneath the richness. They were the meat from the brown-paper parcels in his refrigerator, they were the meat from the soup that had been simmering on his stove for days; they were the meat he sliced and fried in his mother's heavy pan, the meat whose chill he could never quite cook out of the center and the same meat whose pink juice ran down his wrist.

"Look at it." Her hand closed over his wrist, her fingers cold and firm, pressing the bones together until he winced.

The room was very quiet and the others had stopped eating and the velvet on the walls was gone and the candles were gone and the fountain was gone and he was sitting at a table in a bare concrete basement under a fluorescent light that buzzed and flickered and cast everything in the same flat, unforgiving white.

There was no Gordon. There was no Mallie. There was no Declan. There was no Amir with his book and his suit and his reading glasses pushed up into his hair.

There was Kerwin, and there was his plate, and there was Eleanor sitting beside him in the chair where he had placed her, the blanket pooled at her feet, her head tilted at an angle that was not quite right, her eyes open and looking at him and not looking at him because, he knew exactly then, that Eleanor's eyes had not looked at anything for a very long time.

"You *know*," she said, or he heard her say, or he needed to hear her say one last time in that voice he would have followed anywhere. "You've always known, Kerwin. You just wouldn't let yourself see it."

The fluorescent light buzzed. The concrete walls were bare and damp and the plate in front of him held what it had always held.

Kerwin put down his fork. It made a small sound against the plate, a clink, nothing, the most ordinary sound in the world, and then his hands were in his lap and his mouth was full of something he could not swallow and could not spit out and the fluorescent light buzzed above him in the empty basement and he understood, with the whole of his body and all at once, the way one understand a fall the instant their foot leaves the edge that there was no one in the room with him and there had not been anyone in the room with him for a very long time. The meat on his plate and the meat in his stomach and the meat in the soup on the stove and the meat in the brown-paper parcels in his refrigerator was Eleanor, had always been Eleanor, and that he had known this, had known it the way he knew his own name, and had eaten her anyway.

The sound that came out of him was not a sound he had ever made before. It came from somewhere below his stomach, below his diaphragm, from whatever was left at the very bottom of a man when everything above it had been stripped away and it filled the basement the way the smell had filled the apartment; completely, leaving no room for anything else.

16

For One

He did not know how long he sat there. The fluorescent light buzzed above him and the concrete walls were bare and the plate was in front of him and at some point he had put his hands over his face, his fingers pressing into his eye sockets until he saw colors that weren't there, and at some other point he had taken his hands away and looked at the room again and the room had not changed. It was still the basement as it had always been, before the velvet and the candles and the fountain, the bare concrete utility space where his father had stored crates of stock and his mother had mopped up floodwater on her knees.

The table in front of him was the kitchen table. He did not remember carrying it down the stairs but he must have done because here it was, and on it was his plate and his fork and the brown-paper parcels and the kitchen knife he used to slice the meat, and beside it was the chair where Eleanor sat, exactly where he had placed her.

He looked at her. There was nothing else left to do, no vision to flinch toward, no Amir to explain, no gospel to frame what was in front of him as anything other than what it was. The fluorescent light did not flatter and did not forgive; it showed him everything.

Her head was tilted to the left at an angle that a living neck would not have held, resting against the back of the chair in a way that exposed the underside of her jaw. The skin there had gone dark, a deep mottled purple-black, and he understood now, with the flat, useless clarity of a man reading an instruction manual after the machine has already broken, that this was where the blood had settled. *Lividity.* He had read that word once in one of the papers the inmates left on one of the common room tables, and it had meant nothing to him then to learn that the blood sinks to the lowest point and stays there, but now, he knew—the lowest point of Eleanor's body, for however long she had been sitting in this chair had been the underside of her jaw and the backs of her arms and her hands where they rested in her lap, which were the same dark, saturated color, swollen and taut.

The cut on her temple had not been a cut for a very long time. The skin around it had receded, pulled back like the edges of a cloth burned through and what was visible beneath was bone, pale-white and slick in the fluorescent light. This same cut he had told himself was healing slowly, that some cuts took their time and he had believed this because he had needed to believe it the way he had needed to believe everything else.

Her eyes were open; they had been open for weeks and he had looked into them and seen Eleanor looking back, animated with pity and absence and patience and love, and what was in them now was nothing.

Her mouth was open. He could see her teeth. He could see, between her teeth, the dark swollen shape of her tongue where it had pushed forward against the gap he'd noticed the first night, the one she'd been self-conscious about and the tongue was black and distended and did not fit in her mouth anymore.

The shirt she was wearing had ridden up on one side and he could see the skin of her stomach—which was taut and discolored and swollen—stretched shiny over whatever was happening beneath it and there were marks on her that he had made. The bruises on her arms, on her thighs, on her hips where he had gripped her…he had left these marks during sex. He had gripped her hard enough to feel the bones shift under his thumbs and she had not flinched and now he knew why she had not flinched and the knowledge was in his hands, in his fingers, in the muscle memory of holding her hips while he pushed into her, and he could not get it out.

The smell of the apartment and the bathroom and the soup…he had been breathing it for weeks and sleeping in it and eating beside it and it was her, it was Eleanor, it was the smell of Eleanor's body breaking itself down into the things that bodies become when there is no longer a person inside to hold everything together.

He turned away from her and vomited onto the concrete floor, a thin acidic stream that was mostly bile and meat and the taste of it coming back up was the taste of what he'd been eating, and what he'd been eating was on his plate, and what was on his plate was —

He vomited again, harder, his body folding over itself, his hands braced on his knees, and the sound of it echoed off the bare walls in a way that the basement with its velvet drapes would never have allowed; and this too was real, the echo, the concrete, the buzzing light. None of the other things had been real, not the candles, not the silver domes, not Amir, not Gordon, not Mallie, not Declan, none of them had ever been in this room, none of them had ever sat at this table. The only person who had sat at this table was him, him and the thing in the chair that he had loved and fucked and fed and eaten.

He wiped his mouth with the back of his hand. He stood up. The chair scraped against the concrete and the sound was very loud and Eleanor did not react to the sound because Eleanor did not react to anything.

"I'm sorry," he said, and then again, louder, his voice cracking open on the second word so that it came out instead as a sound an animal makes, "I'm sorry, I'm sorry, Eleanor, I'm sorry, I'm so sorry," and he could not stop saying it, could not stop the words coming out of him in a wet, hitching rush that shook his whole body, his hands gripping the edge of the table, his forehead nearly touching the surface, saying it to her, to the room, to the concrete walls that sent it back to him unchanged.

She did not answer, and it was clear to him then that she had *never* answered. Every word she had spoken to him since the night of the storm — every argument, every endearment, every *please, Kerwin*, every *come here*, every *I'm all right* — had been him. All of it, him. The voice he'd heard from the next room, the questions he'd answered, the shape of her presence that he'd moved around and cooked for and slept beside and talked to and made love to…all of it had been Kerwin Merle, alone in his dingy home, talking to himself, touching himself, feeding himself the body of a woman he had killed.

He climbed the stairs without holding the banister. His hand hung at his side and his feet found each step and at the top he went through the dark shop and up the second flight and through the door to the apartment and closed it behind him.

He stood in the doorway and looked at it as if he had never seen it before, or as if he were seeing it for the first time through someone else's eyes, a doctor's eyes, a policeman's eyes, the eyes of any person from the ordinary world who might walk through this door and see what was here.

He made it as far as the hallway before his legs gave out. He caught himself on the wall with one hand and slid down it until he was sitting on the floor with his back against the plaster and his knees drawn up and his mouth still leaking a thin string of bile that dripped onto the front of the white shirt he had ironed that morning, the funeral shirt, and he sat there and shook. The shaking was not something he was doing, it was something that was happening to him, a full-body tremor that started in his hands and spread through his arms and into his chest and his jaw so that his teeth chattered and his breath came in short, hitching gasps that was some middle sound between retching and sobs.

He crawled to the kitchen. He did not stand up and walk there, he crawled, his hands and knees on the linoleum and when he reached the doorway he pulled himself up on the counter and stood there swaying with the taste of vomit coating his teeth and the tears running down his face and into the stubble on his jaw and he looked at the room and the room looked back at him and it was just a kitchen, his kitchen, his mother's kitchen, and on the stove was the soup.

He had been making this soup for weeks. He had stood at this counter and diced the meat into careful cubes the way his mother had taught him, had trimmed the fat and the sinew and the parts that didn't look right and dropped them into the stockpot to render down, had added water and salt and the dried herbs from the cupboard and he had stirred it and tasted it and adjusted the seasoning and let it simmer and the care he had taken with it, the attention to flavor and texture and temperature was perhaps the most obscene thing of all because he had made it *well.* He had made it the way you make food for someone you love and the meat he had been dicing and trimming and seasoning was Eleanor. The cubes in the pot were Eleanor. The fat he had skimmed from the surface and discarded was Eleanor. The stock that had thickened and darkened over days of simmering was Eleanor rendered to liquid, and every bowl he had ladled out, every spoonful he had eaten standing at the counter, every bowl he had brought to her and set on the floor beside the sofa with *just in case, in case you're hungry* — he had been feeding Eleanor to Eleanor, and when she didn't eat it he had scraped her portion onto his plate and eaten it himself.

The sitting room was three steps from the kitchen doorway and he made it in five, his shoulder catching the frame, his hand finding the wall and then the back of the sofa where he held on and breathed until the room stopped tilting. The sofa with its dip, the stain on the cushion. He pressed his thumb to the stain and it crackled under the pressure, stiff and dark, and he was thinking about the sex, about the weight of her in his lap and the way her head had fallen back and the sound she'd made, or the sound he'd *made* her make, or the sound he'd imagined she was making. He was thinking about the first night, the *real* first night, when she had been alive and asleep on this sofa and he had lain in his bed and touched himself with the furious, self-lacerating shame of a man who knew exactly what he was, working himself in short vicious pulls with his jaw clenched and his eyes squeezed shut; the fantasy had been her thighs and her gap tooth and the slick flesh of her cunt that he'd imagined tasting, and he had come with a groan loud enough that she'd knocked on his door to ask if he was all right.

He was hard, now, standing in this room with the stain under his thumb and the blanket at his feet and the knowledge of what he'd done in every corner and he was harder than he'd been that first night, harder than he'd been in her lap with the vomit on his chest, and the shame of it was so enormous, so total, that it ceased to function as shame at all. It just sat there, hot and stupid, while his cock throbbed against his palm.

He put his hand on himself through his pants. He did not decide to do this, his hand went there of its own accord the way it had done that first time, wicked, traitorous thing, and he pressed against himself and his breath hitched and he thought of her on this sofa, on the floor, in his bed, against the wall, every position and every surface. He slipped into the memory of the way her body had been under his hands (cold and unresisting and *his*) and he worked himself through the fabric with a rough, grinding urgency; his body would not stop wanting her, not even now, not even knowing what she was, what he'd done, what the stain on the cushion actually was, and when he came it was brief and ugly and silent, a single hot spasm that left him hunched over with his hand wet inside his pants and nothing, nothing, nothing was different about the room or the apartment or himself except that now he knew he was capable of this too.

He stood there with his hand on himself and his head bowed and then something broke.

It started as a sound, low and thick in his chest, and then it was in his throat and then it was coming out of his mouth it was rage, white and blind and screaming, and he was pulling books from shelves and hurling them at the wall, he was sweeping the cups and the plates from the counter and they shattered on the floor in a bright spray of ceramic and he kicked through the pieces and felt them crunch under his shoes and he grabbed the chair by the window, and swung it against the wall hard enough to crack the plaster and he swung it again and again until one of the legs snapped off and he stood there holding the broken thing and screaming, actually screaming, a sound that had words in it now—*she did this!* She came into his home with that gap between her teeth that he'd wanted to roll his foreskin down against and feel the hard ridge of enamel on the tender underside of him, and she'd opened his cupboards and she'd looked at him and she'd *seen* him and what right did she have? What fucking right, to come into his home and make him want things and make him need her there so badly that when she stopped being there he couldn't let her go, had to keep her, had to find a way—and this was her fault, wasn't it? She'd been killing him since the moment she sat at his table and he had wanted to put his hands around her throat then and he wanted it now and he had done it, hadn't he, he'd done it on the night of the storm, he had—

He stopped.

Kerwin stood in the middle of the kitchen, breathing hard, the chair leg in his hand. Broken crockery was everywhere, white shards in the puddle of soup that had slopped from the pot when he'd knocked the counter. His knuckles were bleeding where they'd caught on something, the wall or the shelf or his own teeth, he couldn't tell. The rage had passed through him the way the vomiting had, a purge, and what it left behind was the same thing the vomiting had left behind, just him, standing in a room, with less inside of him than before.

He put down the chair leg. He looked at the mess on the floor and the mess on himself and the blood on his knuckles and he thought, very clearly, *none of this was her fault.* None of this was *ever* her fault. She came to deliver his food and she stayed because of the storm and they ate something that made them sick and she put her hand on his back while he was vomiting and he — the memory came in pieces, fragments with gaps between them like a film with frames cut out...Her hand on his back was warm, he remembered, and then there was the shock of contact. His body reared away from it because no one had touched him in years and the reflex was faster than thought, and his hand had found the ceramic soap dish on the edge of the tub and he had swung it the way an animal startles, the way a man who has not been touched in years flinches from the thing he wants most, and there had been a sound, and then there was no sound at all. Then, terribly, finally, there was Eleanor on the bathroom floor with the cut on her temple and the blood in her hair and his hand still gripping the dish.

It had been an *accident.* It had been the most terrible accident a body could commit. She had touched him because he was sick and he had killed her because he had forgotten what it felt like to be touched. That was all.

He lurched into the hallway with one hand on the wall, his hip catching the small table where his mother had kept the phone and sent it skidding across the floor. He stood outside the bathroom door with its towel stuffed against the base and he put his hand on the wood. The towel was damp and discolored, saturated with something that had been seeping under the door for weeks and the smell here was the worst because, he knew now, that it was the place where it had all started, the epicentre that he had spent weeks building towel-dams and airing rooms and buying air fresheners to contain.

He did not open the door precisely because he knew what was behind the door; he had always known what was behind the door. The not-knowing had been an elaborate and sustained performance and now the performance was over and the audience had left and there was just a man standing in a hallway with his hand on a bathroom door and the knowledge of what he had done sitting in him like a meal that would not digest.

He went to the kitchen and turned off the stove, letting the flame out with a soft pop. The soup sat there in the pot, and he looked at it, *really* looked at it for what felt like the first time. The surface was a slick, yellowish film, greasy and opaque, with small bubbles of fat trapped beneath it that caught the light like blisters. Where the ladle rested against the rim, the film had broken, and he could see what was underneath — a murky, brownish liquid, thick as gravy, with pale threads of something fibrous suspended in it that he had told himself was onion, or celery, or gristle from cheap cuts, but which clung to the ladle in long, translucent strands that did not look like any vegetable he had ever cooked with. There were small, soft pieces in it that had broken down over days of simmering into something that no longer held its shape and among them, here and there, harder pieces that had not broken down, that resisted the spoon when he stirred, little knots of white that he now understood were cartilage, or tendon, or the connective tissue that holds a body together at its joints. The smell coming off it was sweet and thick and cloying and so he put the lid on the pot, standing at the counter with his hands flat on the surface and his head bowed and he breathed, in and out, in and out; the apartment silent around him in a way it had not been in days, the absence of the ambient noise of a shared fantasy life.

He stood there and felt the tiredness come down on him like a physical weight, and it was so sudden and so total that his knees buckled and he had to grip the edge of the counter to stay upright. He was *so* tired. He was tired in a way that sleep would not fix, tired in the bones, in the meat of him, in whatever was left under the skin that was still technically functioning and he pulled at the skin beneath his eyes with his wet fingers and felt how loose it was, how thin, and he thought— *if I kept pulling it would come away, all of it.* He could peel it off in strips the way one might peel wallpaper from a damp wall, he could pull the whole face off and the neck and the chest and stand here in the kitchen as nothing but the red wet thing underneath, and wouldn't that be simpler? Wouldn't that be more honest, to look like what he was instead of standing here in his mother's kitchen in his soiled shirt pretending to be a man?

The fantasy wrung him out and left him standing there empty, a dishrag twisted dry. He staggered to the chair by the window.

Kerwin Merle had sat here before Eleanor and he would sit here after Eleanor and the nothing that his life had been before she came through the door was a different kind of nothing than the nothing that was here now. The first nothing had been an absence, a life unlived, a man unseen, a set of empty rooms with one person rattling around inside of them like a single coin in a coffer. This nothing, however, had weight and texture and smell and it would sit in this chair with him for whatever came next and he understood, in the plain way that he now understood everything, that there was no assembly large enough to contain it, certainly no gospel, no ritual, no secret society, no theology of the consumed body and the transfigured flesh. There was only a man in a room with what he had done before.

The light moved across the wall. The afternoon passed. He did not move.

He thought about his mother, who had scrubbed the basement stairs until her hands cracked and bled. He thought about his father, who had stood behind the counter of the shop and sold things to people and spoken to them and been a part of the ordinary world in a way that Kerwin had never managed. He thought about prison, the cell, the cot, the narrow routine of it, how the walls had been so close he could touch both sides at once and how that had felt like safety, because the smaller the world got the less there was in it that could hurt you. He thought about Eleanor standing on his doorstep in the rain with her delivery bag and her gap-toothed smile and the way she had walked into his home and opened his cupboards and seen him, actually seen him, for the first time since his mother died.

He thought about the hallway. The vision in the basement had tried to show him and his mind had flinched away, but now the fragments were there, laid out like pieces of a broken plate: the food poisoning, the vomiting, her hand on his back, warm and steady, the first kind touch he'd felt in years and the horror that answered it. Everything after that—the sex, the tenderness, the Gastronauts, the soup, all of it—had been the edifice he'd built over the top of that single, unsurvivable fact that she had touched him gently and he had killed her for it.

* * *

In the days after, the light moved across the wall and Kerwin Merle did not move with it.

He had been watching the slow progression of the afternoon sun through the gap in the curtains, tracking left to right across the wallpaper his mother had chosen; cream, with a pattern of small brown diamonds that he had counted years ago during a bout of flu that kept him in this chair for three days. There were sixty-four diamonds on the visible portion of the west wall. He had been wrong then; he had counted sixty-two and felt certain, and later recounted and found the two he'd missed, both half-hidden by the edge of the curtain. He'd felt a small, stupid satisfaction at the correction. Sixty-four, an even number. A number you could halve and halve again and arrive at one.

The light touched the forty-third diamond and moved on.

He could smell the soup through the kitchen doorway, the stockpot on the stove sending its smell out into the apartment layered on top of the other smell that he had spent weeks explaining as damp, as the pipes, as the leak. The two smells braided together in the air and he breathed them in with every breath and the inside of his mouth flooded, warm and involuntary, a rush of spit that coated his tongue and the backs of his teeth. His throat clicked over his swallow and his stomach answered, he could feel it working—a low churning he could hear if he held his breath, its walls touching and releasing, touching and releasing.

He gripped the arms of the chair. The wood was smooth and cool and his mother had polished it on Saturdays with the same cloth she used on the dining table, and the dining table was in the basement, and Eleanor was at the dining table, and the soup was on the stove, and he could not eat it.

He knew what it was. His hands had done this, they had had cut her and cooked her and stirred the pot and lifted the spoon to his mouth and tasted and adjusted the salt; they rested on the arms of the chair and they looked like hands. He had used these hands to hold the knife, he had used them to hold her hips while he fucked her. He closed his hand, opened it again.

The forty-seventh diamond.

Eleanor's voice said something from the other room and he turned his head toward it before he understood that the other room was empty. It had been empty for—how long? He did not know. The days had started slipping. He tried to count back from the ortolan towel, but the towel hadn't been real, and Amir hadn't been real, and the counting snagged on this and would not continue. There had been a storm, that he *knew*. She had blown in in the beginning of it and then there had been the sickness, and the bathroom, and his hand finding the soap dish, and after that there had been everything else, and he could not put the everything else into order because the order required him to know which parts he had built out of nothing. The building had been so thorough, so careful, so complete that the demolition was taking longer than he had expected.

She said something again but he did not turn his head this time. He sat very still and listened and there was nothing there, just the tick of the pipes contracting in the walls. She was not in the other room because she was in the basement in the chair with her head tilted to the left and the lividity under her jaw and the black tongue and the bone through her temple and she was not talking to him because she had not talked to him since the storm. Every word she had spoken since had been Kerwin Merle talking to himself in an empty apartment, and the voice he could hear now was his own voice still trying to do it, still reaching for her, the machine winding down but not yet stopped.

He wiped his mouth on his sleeve and leaned back in the chair and the light was on the fifty-second diamond, or the fifty-third. He had lost count. He started again from the curtain edge.

One.

Two.

Three.

***

The second day was different from the first because on the second day he pissed himself.

He thought it woke him, though he was not sure he had been sleeping; it was possible he had simply stopped being present for a while and then started again, the way a television with a bad connection drops its signal and returns. A heat spread across the tops of his thighs with a slow heavy warmth and he registered it from a great distance and then registered it from very close and looked down and his pants were darkening, the fabric turning black in a widening stain that spread from his crotch down the inside of both legs. He watched it happen; it did not feel like something he was doing, or rather it felt like something the chair was doing, or the pants, or the apartment itself—the whole place finally expressing what it had been holding for weeks. The trickle reached his left knee and ran over it and down his calf and he heard it hit the floor in a thin irregular pattering until the pattering stopped and the piss cooled against his skin.

Sometime later, an hour, three hours—the light had moved but he had stopped counting the diamonds—he became aware of a different warmth beneath him, lower, set in the seat of the chair. This was thinner, looser, and more liquid; there was a cramping that preceded it but by the time it arrived it had no force left. It seeped into the fabric of the cushion and he smelled it and the smell was fecal but also not quite, something richer and stranger beneath the ordinary stink, a sweetness that he recognized. The last thing his body had processed was the soup and he last thing his body would *ever* process was her, so he sat in it.

His cock stirred. He felt it thicken against his thigh, sluggish and half-hearted, and he did not look down at it and did not touch it. It lay there in the wet folds of his trousers with its dull hydraulics misfiring and he stared at the wall and counted the diamonds again: forty-seven, forty-eight. It softened and the counting continued.

The light left the wall. The room went dark and he sat in the dark and the dark was the same temperature as the rest of him, and it was then that he heard it coming up through the floorboards, faint but steady—a wet, busy sound with a rhythm to it, the click of teeth meeting through something soft, and a pulling, a thick pulling like fabric being torn slowly, and he knew immediately what it was. He had sat at the kitchen table and made that sound himself with a bowl and a spoon, chewing and swallowing, chewing and swallowing. They were eating Eleanor. They worked steadily and they took their time and once there was a thin squeal which must have been two of them at the same piece of her, a scrabble of claws on concrete and then the squeal stopped and one of them had won and the eating resumed its tempo as he lay in his chair with his hands on the armrests and listened.

He could not do this. He had eaten her and fucked her dead body and built a secret society out of strangers' faces and sat in his own waste counting diamonds on his mother's wallpaper and all of that, apparently, had been within the range of what Kerwin Merle was willing to do or to have done to him, but this—lying in the dark and listening to rats eat Eleanor Fletcher through the floor—this was the the final boundary in a life that had turned out to have almost none.

He stood and the room pitched sideways and bright specks swarmed his vision and he gripped the chair arm and waited, doubled over, his heart stuttering, fast then slow then very fast, and when the specks cleared and the room came back he understood that this was the last of it, the last standing up, whatever the body stores for the end burning off in him now, and when it was gone he would sit down and not get up.

He went down the hall with one hand on the wall, the wallpaper cool and slightly tacky under his palm, past the bathroom door and its stuffed towel, past the brown drag mark on the baseboard that he still could not look at, down the back stairs and at the street door he pressed himself flat to the wall and edged past the glass with the blinds drawn and the orange bleed of the streetlights through the edges. He had always been careful, that was the damning thing, worse than the eating and the fucking and the soap dish—some sober, operational part of him had been running beneath the delusion the whole time, drawing the curtains and stuffing the towels and timing his movements to the hours when the street was empty, managing the concealment while the rest of him dressed up in a suit and ate bones under a napkin. It had worked because he lived where he lived, this strip of stained street where everybody kept their own disasters behind their own doors and you did not phone the authorities about a *smell*.

Down the basement stairs he went, and on the fifth his bare foot came down on something small and wet and scored on its surface with tiny parallel grooves. He stepped over it and went down into the fluorescent light where Eleanor was waiting for him in the chair with her head tilted to the left and her mouth pulled wide, the gap between her teeth fully exposed now that the skin had drawn back from them. Through the gap the black mass of her tongue pressed forward, cracked at its edges, and below the hem of her skirt the rats had opened her legs in ragged patches and worked into what was underneath, and three of them were still there at the base of the chair, sleek, unhurried, one with something pinkish clamped in its teeth. They looked up at him with their dark, wet eyes. He stamped his foot on the concrete and two of them bolted and the third studied him a moment longer before flowing into the gap behind the a stack of boxes with a boneless, liquid ease.

He crossed the room and put his arms under her and she came away from the chair with a wet, sucking sound and she was lighter than he expected, so much of her gone, but the fluid that had pooled inside her shifted when he moved her, a slow thick settling he could feel against his forearms. Her head fell against his chest and her hair stuck to the front of the white shirt, wet and matted; her shirt rode up as he turned for the stairs and the skin of her stomach gave where his hand gripped it and what came through was warm against his forearm for a moment and then cool. The smell of it was the inside of her, the sealed center, and he gagged and nearly went down and held on and started climbing.

Her head bumped his collarbone as the fluid left a dark trail on the stairs behind him, step to step. At the shop door he pressed his face to the glass and the street was empty save for the streetlights and a cat on the opposite wall watching him with flat green eyes. He went through the shop and up the second flight with his thighs burning and his arms shaking and her body sliding in his grip because his forearms were slick with what had come out of her, and when he hitched her higher his hand slipped because the fat beneath her skin had liquefied and the skin moved over the tissue underneath, loose and heavy and untethered. He gripped harder and felt his fingers sink into the softened tissue of her flank and held on. He made it to the landing, through the door and down the hall into the sitting room.

He laid her on the sofa, the same sofa where she had slept the first night with the blanket pulled up to her chin and her shoes still on because she did not know him yet which, as it turned out, had been the correct instinct. He had given her the blanket from his own bed and gone to his room and closed the door and lain on his back and pressed the heels of his hands into his eyes and known that he was going to touch himself and that it would be to the thought of her, and he had, and she had knocked on his door afterward to ask if he was all right.

Her shoes were still on. Between the shoes and the hem of her skirt her legs were what the rats had left of them. Above the hem was the swollen, torn, leaking ruin of her torso and her hips jutted above the waistband of her skirt.

On each hip there was still a small mound of flesh, soft and intact—the last of the padding that had been there when she was alive. He had held her by those hips. He had gripped them and pulled her toward him on this sofa, in this room, and felt the bones shift under his thumbs while he fucked her, and the bones had shifted because there was nothing holding them in place, because the ligaments and the muscles that hold a living body together had already begun their work of letting go, and he had felt them shift and had not wondered *why*.

He had been hard since the stairs, or since he'd lifted her out of the chair, perhaps, since the weight of her had settled against his chest and her hair had stuck to his neck. He looked at the two soft mounds and thought: *she is right here, on the sofa where she slept the first night, and I am dying, and she is here.*

He was already damned. He understood this clearly, the way he now understood everything, flatly, and without appeal. He had killed her with a soap dish, he had fucked her while she sat in his lap and did not breathe. He had built a church around the eating and a love story around the fucking and the whole elaborate edifice had been a machine for not knowing, and now he knew, and it made no difference, really, because the wanting had outlasted the knowing. It had outlasted everything. A condemned man gets a meal and a cigarette and a woman he has killed is lying on his sofa with her hips exposed and this is what he has instead of a cigarette. One more thing that cannot damn him further, surely.

He undid his trousers. His hands shook and the button gave him trouble and he stood there fumbling with it, his breath coming fast and shallow, and when he freed himself he was so hard it ached, straining against the soiled fabric of his pants, and the ache was the same ache he had felt that first night behind his bedroom door, the same furious want, and he had hated himself for it then and he hated himself for it now.

He pressed the two mounds of flesh together above her pubic bone. They met with a soft, dense resistance. He squeezed them into a seam and pushed the head of his cock into the gap and the flesh was cold in a way that should have killed the erection instantly, cold in a way that said *dead*, that said *this is not a woman*. He pushed further and the tissue compressed around him; the friction was wrong, too soft, too loose, his cock sliding through the channel he had made without enough purchase, and he adjusted his grip and pressed the mounds tighter together and thrust and this time there was some thick drag of dead flesh against the underside of his shaft, and his breath hitched and he thrust again.

He kept his face turned away from hers. He could see the arm of the sofa and the wall behind it and the edge of the curtain and the window beyond, and he looked at the window while he fucked the gap between her hips, and outside the window the street was coming light and somewhere out there people were waking up and making coffee and turning on the radio and none of them knew that this was happening.

The sounds he made were low and cracked. They came out of him without his permission, guttural, wretched, the sounds of a man in the last of something and he thrust again and again, short, grinding strokes, his thumbs digging into the meat of her hips so hard that the tissue deformed around them, and he could feel the bone beneath, ridges under the thinning pad of flesh. When he came it was a thin, weak spasm, barely anything, a contraction he felt in his abdomen and his knees more than in his cock and what came out of him was little more than a smear. It landed on the cold skin between her hips where his hands had pressed the flesh together.

He pulled away. Her skin held the shape of his grip—two dents in the meat of her hips, thumbprints in dead tissue, and between them the wet shine of his cum on her skin already going dull as it cooled. He looked at what he had left on her. This last deposit, this final mark on her body that no one would see and no one would know about unless they found the two of them here and even then they might not understand what the marks on her hips meant.

He hoped they would not understand.

He hoped they would.

His legs went next. They folded under him and he caught himself on the edge of the sofa and slid down it to the floor and crawled from there to the chair. He pulled himself into it the way a man pulls himself into a lifeboat, hands first, then the dead weight of the rest of him and the cushion was wet and stiff beneath him with days of his own waste, and Eleanor was on his hands, the fluids from inside her dried in the creases of his fingers and under his nails, and the come was cooling on the inside of his thigh where it had smeared when he pulled his pants up, and he was not going to stand again.

His bowels emptied one last time and his cock lay against his thigh and did not stir. It was done. It had finally spent the last of what it had on the gap between her hips and it was done, and this struck him as funny, that his cock—which had driven him to the frenzy of self-loathing that had defined every moment since—had outlasted his kidneys and his bowels and his dignity and most of his mind, and had finally, at the end, with nothing left to spend, gone quiet. The last soldier off the field. He would have laughed if he were a different man.

Eleanor was on the sofa, which was what he had wanted, really; to have her here and to not be alone. She would not leave because she would never leave. He had what he wanted and the having was this—this room, this smell, this chair, Eleanor on the sofa with his come drying between her hips. The soup on the stove with its skin of yellow fat, and between them the whole impossible history of what he had done to her laid out on the floor and the stairs and his skin and his hands.

Outside, the woman with the gray dog walked past on the pavement below. She turned the corner at the end of the street and she was gone, and she would walk this route tomorrow and the morning after that, and Kerwin Merle would not be in the window, and she would not notice because she had never noticed. None of them had. Not Amir behind his counter, or Gordon, or Declan, or Mallie. He had stolen their faces and dressed them in dark suits with his mind and sat them at his table and fed them her body and made them tell him he was chosen, that he was clean, that he *belonged,* and they had never known he was alive.

They would find him eventually because someone would smell it—the neighbors or the mailman, and they would come through the door and find him in the chair and Eleanor on the sofa and the soup on the stove and the trail of her on the stairs, and there would be an article, naturally. He could see the headline and the photograph they would pull from the court records, the one taken when he was a teenager, gaunt and terrified in the dock, and the article would say that Kerwin Merle, aged forty-seven, convicted of the murder of his father Raymond Merle, had been found dead in his apartment alongside the remains of Eleanor Fletcher, twenty-three, a delivery driver for the Daily Bread meals service, and the article would use the word "cannibal" and the word "monster" and it would draw a line from his father's death to Eleanor's and the line would be clean and straight and obvious: a man who had killed before had killed again, a man with violence at the root of him. They would not know that he had not killed his father. They would not know that he had sat in a courtroom and listened to the verdict and understood, with a calm that frightened him more than the sentence, that it did not matter whether he had done it, that the world had looked at Kerwin Merle and seen someone capable of it, and that was enough.

They would not know that Eleanor's death had been an accident, they would not know about the storm, or the coffee, or the sound of her voice asking him if he was all right through his bedroom door. They would write their story and their story would be wrong just as the Gastronauts had been a story and *that* story had been wrong. The love, the communion, the gospel, the meals shared at the candlelit table—all of it had been a story Kerwin Merle told himself so that he could go on living in a room with what he had done, and that story had been wrong, too. The only thing that had been true was the thing underneath all of them, the thing the stories were built to cover, the thing in the chair and the thing on the sofa and the thing in the pot on the stove, which is death.

The light moved across the wall. It reached the diamonds and moved on through them, one by one, and he did not count them this time. Eleanor was on the sofa and Kerwin was in the chair and the soup was on the stove and none of it had ever been anything else.

www.ingramcontent.com/pod-product-compliance
Lightning Source LLC
LaVergne TN
LVHW100525110826
845146LV00002B/784

* 9 7 9 8 9 9 5 4 7 5 8 1 1 *